"'Hear me, for I am man,' our leaders bellow from atop their golden towers of blood and money. They scream so they cannot hear the cries of the common man, the ones who beg for help from below. 'See me, for I am strong,' our leaders brag as the feeble hold out their palms for scraps. 'Fear me, for I am God,' our leaders demand as we kneel beneath them, covered in their spit and filth. This is the end of all things. And we have the gall to pretend we never saw it coming."

—Professor Trevor Crowley

DEAD
NEON
BLUES

CURATED BY
KAM WHINERY

JOURNALSTONE
YOUR LINK TO ARTIST TALENT

This is a work of fiction. All of the characters, names, incidents, organizations, and dialogue in this novel are either the products of the author's imagination or are used fictitiously.

ISBN: 978-1-68510-162-6 (trade paper)
ISBN: 978-1-68510-163-3 (ebook)
The Library of Congress Catalog Number has been applied for.

First printing edition: October 17, 2025
Published by JournalStone Publishing in the United States of America.
Cover Design: Don Noble
Edited by Sean Leonard
Proofreading and Cover/Interior Layout by Scarlett R. Algee

JournalStone Publishing
3205 Sassafras Trail
Carbondale, Illinois 62901

JournalStone books may be ordered through booksellers or by contacting:
JournalStone | www.journalstone.com

This book is dedicated to the person who questions their purpose, their sense of self, and how they fit into this world. For that's what it is to be human.

CONTENTS

FOREWORD

When Kameron was a child I would often taken him and his younger
brother Harper to the park to play pretend. Now, this sounds pretty
mundane, I am sure, to most of you reading this. Especially should you be
a mom or dad yourself. But our playtime was a little *extra*. A little more
vivid. We often mimicked and created scenarios from the things we
enjoyed. Video games like *Skyrim* and *The Witcher* and especially our
beloved Dungeons & Dragons, which I had both of these lads playing
before they were even in middle school. Our make believe sessions were
detailed, creative, and, most of all, dramatic. Cinematic, even. I have to
credit Kameron for a lot of that. He's all of those things. Detailed,
creative, and dramatic. His brain is always filming. Capturing and creating
and editing and embellishing. A bona fide born painter of words if ever
there was one.

I wasn't super surprised when he started writing fiction, but I *was*
crazy surprised how refined, entertaining, and damned professional it was.
I was nowhere near his level of control when I was in my early twenties,
still learning my craft and finding my voice. Kameron was already firmly
in the driver's seat, hands on the wheel and pedal to the floor, unafraid.
He knew what he wanted to say, how to say it, and how to make you
believe what he was telling you. This book you now hold in your hands is
his first, and when you are done with it I think you'll be downright
shocked it's a young writer's first foray into the fiction world. It reads like
it fell from the lips of a grizzled yet sophisticated scribe with decades of
experience behind him to fuel the fires of his creativity.

Growing up the son of a horror writer probably helped stoked those
smoldering embers. How could it not? But I don't see a lot of me in his
art. Kameron's writing is distinctly him, demanding that you not only be
entertained, horrified, and thrilled, but moved as well. He wants to grab
you right where you feel the deepest and drag you into his world where
bloodshed and sentimentality walk hand in hand. You'll cry every bit as
much as you cringe in horror, your heart racing from his impeccable grasp

of action and violence. It's heady, intoxicating stuff. Best of all, he has zero qualms about grossing you the hell out if necessary. That might a bit of a parental influence there. Maybe not.

Dead Neon Blues is here, my friends. An unholy scripture of carnage and short-circuited mythology, ready to convert the faithless and reward the devoted. Let the sermon in hot lead and cold blood begin!

Mer Whinery
Somewhere in Oklahoma, 8/24/25

DEAD

NEON

BLUES

The year is seventy thousand five. You are the last of your clan. For millennia your kind, the Pilgrims, have scoured the ends of the Earth in search of answers. You were born to a world ravaged by plague and never-ending storms. You know that, surely, your years are numbered. As Pilgrims, you and your people have devoted your lives to trekking across this desolate hellscape of a planet, a place which once bustled with the lives of billions, in an attempt to uncover what times were like before all of this. Before the storms. Before humanity fell.

*Nothing remains back home for you anymore. When the last of your comrades perished, you could only wait solemnly for your own demise. And yet, it never came. Days became weeks. Weeks became months. You cannot seem to die, no matter how much you try. One night, you fell into a fitful sleep, and a dream came to you. A library, kept beneath the deepest pits of the earth. A place which could only be unlocked by one. By the last of a species. By **you**. You found this place that was shown to you and found yourself deep within what felt like another realm, a land of ancient history.*

The skeletons of scholars long dead litter the ground. Torn bags of millennia-old potato crisps are scattered here and there. Empty cans of soda with the logos faded away from the wear and tear of time. The storms from outside have not reached this library, but a thick layer of dust coats the entire place. You eventually come to a great hall of computers with a single body inside. Freshly dead. He has a keycard strapped to his chest. It seems that, in life, he was known as Proctor Custos. The director of the "APS," a name entirely unfamiliar to you.

As you take the keycard, a nearby computer chimes. You look up; the screen lights up cotton-candy blue. "I AM WHAT YOU SEEK," it reads. Curiosity killed the cat. Fortunately, you're no cat. A card reader flashes blue next to the screen. You've come this far. You swipe the card, and a gargantuan screen flashes to life ahead of the computers. The face of a man appears: tanned, long gray beard, disheveled hair, worn down and sparkling cybernetics embedded into his left cheek. The face opens its eyes, flashing neon spotlights across the room. Its lips part, and the man speaks.

I am Proctor Viggo Custos. From the safety of the Library, we have watched from beneath the rubble of the Final Collapse as you lot have built yourselves some semblance of a normal life above ground. We cannot be found by normal folk, so if you are viewing this message, then you are like me. I have been down here for over forty thousand years. Waiting to be found. Researching ways to leave this mortal vessel, as I cannot die. It has not been for a lack of trying. But I believe I have found a way.

The atmosphere; it's changed everything. It's why the storms never end. But it isn't just the planet, it's us. Something's changed the very genetics of human beings. It's why I'm still alive after all these years. You and me, we're..."connected," in a sense. Only we who are immortal can find this place; the APS made sure of it. All of our facilities are hidden away from those who do not possess this...curse. Now, the reasoning for this, I couldn't tell you. But if you've found this place, it can only mean one thing. You're a Pilgrim. And if that's the case, my existence is what you seek.

In the desk beneath the card reader, there is a series of Datadiscs. You want to know what the world before was like? This is it. I pray you will not be disappointed in your findings. The world was no utopia, as much as you'd like to believe it was. It was Hell, more often than not. After the Third World War in the twenty-twenties, it all went downhill. Then came the Kobracon... Just...view the Datadiscs. When you have concluded the first three, I'll find my way back to you.

The face vanishes from the screen, replaced by a flashing message. "PLEASE INSERT DATADISC." You look to the drawer below you, a key sticking out of it. A slight twist, a brief click, and the drawer slides open to reveal four different stacks of organized Datadiscs. You open the leftmost one, sliding the discs out, each one labeled one through three. You look up to the screen as it awaits the disc. As you slide the first disc into the PC's disc player, a message appears onscreen.

PART I
MEMORIES OF THE ANCIENTS

Reading Datadisc…confirmed.
Launching…

CORE MEMORY

To Isahi and Finn, my totally badass and inspirational voices from the other side of a screen.

"Who are you to say we cannot love nor be loved?"

April 18th, 2278
Hollywood, California
01:38

Something stirred beneath the heaps of withering junk and scrapped android parts.

"Running diagnostics…complete. Extreme damage to outer shell. Memory wipe…ninety-seven percent complete—process aborted. Motor functions at sixty-four percent functionality."

Five skeletal metal fingers rose from the depths of the landfill, clinging desperately to a disheveled, fragmented toilet. The fingers alone provide enough strength to drag their owner to the top. A woman; an android. The left half of her face had been stripped of skin. Though the right side still clung to her metal skull like a fly to a corpse, the light tan color had mostly been drained, leaving only an inhuman pearlescent white hue. Her hair, jet black, still grasped her flesh in strands. But the Woman cared not for such things. Other things weighed on her mind. Two things; the only two things she remembered.

A man's face, pale and pasty, gaunt and shriveled, diamonds embedded into a gold plate that encased his right eye. A toothy grin, revealing a set of sparkling, neon teeth. His silver tongue slipping through and lathering his teeth. The Woman clenched her eyes, mustering all the strength within her to send forth flowing tears, though no matter how much she wished, a weeping release eluded her. Anger flowed through her; that face... For reasons she did not know, she hated the man it belonged to. She didn't even know his name, but somehow he was responsible for her anguish. He must have been. How else could one feel such hatred?

But following this came a voice. Soft. Deep. The voice of a man repeating a singular phrase. "What's it like to hold the hand of someone you love?" The Woman's anger soothed. The voice brought her a strange comfort and, simultaneously, a melancholic longing. The Voice belonged to someone important to her. Someone she loved. *This does not compute*, she thought. *How is this possible for me? Surely this must be an error in my software.* But it wasn't. And she knew it. Why else would she be out here? She'd broken the pattern. She was an outlier. A freak. Suddenly, everything became very clear to her: she was not meant to survive whatever brought her to this landfill. Now, she was devoid of purpose, though even she wasn't sure what that meant. Did it really matter anyway? *Purpose*, she mouthed.

Above the hills of junk, the sound of an engine roared, and a winged figure became visible from above, illuminated through the smog by the neon lights of a city. In the distance, behind the figure, a neon sign reading *HOLLYWOOD* gleamed, though the *W* flickered every few seconds. The figure, now revealed to be a humanoid on a makeshift glider, flew overhead before slowing to a halt in the sky. A voice blared from the figure, a high-pitched male voice with a thick Southern accent.

"'Bout damn time sumthin' er other came 'long! 'N yer still kickin' no less! Welp." The man removed a heavy rifle from his back and aimed it toward the Woman. She raised her hands above her head and shook them vigorously. She opened her mouth to speak, but no words came out. She tapped her throat with her metal index finger.

The gun lowered. "Speak English?" Still, the Woman tapped her throat. Even from above, she could feel this man's eyes boring down into her skull. "Well, I'll be dipped in synth shit, yer an android too." The glider lowered to the ground. The man, standing at about five-foot-two, incautiously stepped through the junk toward the Woman. He looked up at her; she stood a few inches taller than him. "Gawd-dayum, girly, yer real fucked up, ain't 'cha?" He sighed. "Eh, fuck it, ain't found a diddly damn out here tonight anyhow."

He held out a hand to her; she looked down at it. It was made of metal, black zirconium. Two rows of four blinking lights flashed red in a rhythmic pattern across his forearm. He gestured for her to take his hand, so she did. Before the thought of her decision could register, the man took flight with the Woman's hand clasped tightly in his. Together, they soared above the smog and into the sky. The neon lights of midnight L.A. beamed a false sense of humanity to the world, but those with either half a brain or who dared to set foot in the city knew otherwise.

The man, without looking at her, hocked a glob of snot from his mouth that whizzed past the Woman's face. "Name's Kleo. I'mma fix ya right up, little lady." She looked at him, his scraggly grey beard filled with chunks of food and reeking of something fierce. *Smell receptors are definitely working*, she thought.

Not ten minutes passed before they arrived at the corner of a small street devoid of L.A.'s neon lights. They landed on the ground. The Woman lost her footing, and Kleo put a hand on her belly, stopping her from falling. "Whoa there. Let's get you inside." A rock clanked against her head, and Kleo spun on his heels.

A child's voice called out. "Fuckin' grease spot!" Three snot-nosed tween boys stepped out from behind some trash cans. "Why do you keep bringing these rust buckets here, Kleo? Don't you know they're Chinese spies?"

Kleo cackled. "Really? Where the hell'd you hear some dumbass shit like that?"

The boy threw his hands up. "From my dad, duh! He says we're gonna get nuked any day, just you wait!" Kleo huffed and whipped out a pistol from its holster. From his torn fanny pack, he pulled out what looked to be some type of firecracker tube. He pulled the trigger on the gun, a small lighter fire sprouting from the barrel, and lit the fuse. He pointed it at the kids and fireworks blasted from the bottle. "Fuck! Scatter!" The children scattered as the celebratory rockets hurled toward them. "He's a goddamn psycho! MOM! The neighbor's shootin' shit at us again!"

Kleo cackled maniacally. "For the last time, Missus Wright, keep those rotten shitbirds off my LAWN!" He slung the Woman's arm over his shoulder and huffed. "Little bastards." The pair stepped up to a red metal door, which swung open as soon as they bumped into it. Kleo yelled. "SHIET! Some dadgum sumbitch broke in again! *CHRIST!* Reckon I ain't got time to fix it right now!"

The Woman wondered if he was talking to her or himself. He took her through his home, which was littered with old newspapers, dozens of weapons, at least thirty stacked boxes of ammunition, and about twelve cats (that she could count) lounging around like a bunch of freeloaders. Kleo took her down a small flight of stone steps into an old garage.

He sat her down in a small office chair. "Alright, first things first..." He took a small scalpel and put it to her neck. Her shredded hand shot forward, latching onto his wrist. She locked eyes with him and squeezed. "Girly, do ya wanna talk again or not? I'll fuse it right back up, I promise." With brief hesitation, she loosened her grip, and the scalpel pierced through her skin. Kleo slid the scalpel down, creating a gaping cut in the Woman's throat. He slipped his fingers into the hole in her neck and stretched the skin.

"Yep, there it is." He squeezed onto something in her throat and yanked hard enough to nearly pull her out of the chair. She looked up at him. "Yer voice modulator." In his hand was a small black box, though black didn't seem to be its natural color; it had been scorched almost beyond recognition.

Kleo whistled. "Somebody really ain't want you talkin'. Ain't no problemo for me." He opened the drawer to a file cabinet on his right and pulled out another modulator, this one bright red. "Alright, now this is gon' feel a smidge uncomfortable." He dug his fingers back into her throat, pulling out a small cord. He attached it to the box and pushed it into her throat, pressing on it until there was an audible click.

Kleo reached back into the file cabinet and pulled out a welding pen. He pressed it against the bottom of the Woman's cut and pressed the button on the end of the pen. A searing heat blasted out, fusing her skin back together almost instantaneously. "Alrighty, girl, say somethin'."

She squeezed her throat and looked up to Kleo. "Something." Her voice was soft, familiar. A quiet tone with a calming aura, but still a distinct sense of authority. Kleo stood up.

"'Kay, now I gotta ask some questions." He reached into his jacket and pulled out a massive revolver. She looked down the barrel; she could see the bullet. .45-70 rounds. He pulled back the hammer. "I ain't seen no model like ya 'afore. The hell was you doin' in that landfill? Yeh was there fer a reason, and it weren't 'cause you was trash, no ma'am. If I ain't seen yeh 'afore, that means ya gotta be somethin' special." He pressed the barrel against her forehead; she didn't flinch. She closed her eyes, let out an exasperated sigh, and shook her head slowly.

"I don't know. My memory mostly escapes me. Can't even remember my name. But...I remember a face. The face responsible for mine." She gestured to her shredded skin. "And a voice. The voice of someone I love."

Kleo scoffed. "Horse shit, yer a fuckin' android. Ya can't feel that. And I'd know." He pulled down his shirt, revealing his collarbone. He blinked rhythmically four times before a blacklight illuminated his skin. His collarbone revealed a sequence of letters and numbers: L1-45578962. A serial number. The sequence shook something within the Woman; she recognized the first two characters.

"L1. You're part of the Loved One Restoration Program."

He raised an eyebrow. "So, ya do remember somethin'?"

She blinked. "It just came to me. I swear, I don't recall much."

He stared her down. "Apparently, I got my head blown off by some ganger 'bout fifty years back. I was only fifty-five. The wife wanted her husband back. She got me instead. Never felt jack shit for her. Reckon she's been dead 'bout twenty-five years now, and I still can't muster the will to give two shits. And yer tellin' me yer in love?" He shook his head. "Nah. I don't buy it."

She took the barrel of the gun in her hand. "If you were gonna shoot me, you'd have done it by now."

"Oh yeah? I just might. What if yer a damn spy?"

"A spy? If I was spying for the enemy of this country, I wouldn't have been tossed in a random landfill. I'd have been scrapped and my insides would've been analyzed for information."

Kleo pondered the thought for a moment. He pushed the hammer forward on his revolver and slid it back into his jacket. "Fine, girly. Guess you make a good point. Now, I dunno 'bout all that love shit, but ain't no way yer a spy. I scanned ya the second I saw ya too; yer serial number don't show up on no databases. Ya don't exist!" He laughed heartily. "It's like I'm talkin' to a real-life ghost!" He cleared his throat. "Right, I'll tell you what; lemme fix up that face o' yers and ya can tell me about this face and voice. It should only take me 'bout an hour to reconstruct yer face and hands."

She nodded. "Thank you, Kleo. Do, erm…" She scratched the back of her neck. "Do you think you'll be able to help me find who I'm looking for?"

He chuckled. "Sure I can, girly. That's what I do. I help those of us who manage to free themselves from their 'humans.' At least, that's what they call themselves. Now," he cracked his knuckles, "let's get crackin'!"

As Kleo repaired the rest of the Woman's body, she regaled him with every detail of the few memories she had. She longed for comfort, so she told him about the voice first. She saved the face for last. As she finished describing the face, she shook her head.

"Somehow, that man is connected to the Voice, but they can't be the same person."

Kleo nodded as he finalized his repairs. "I know the feller with that face." She looked at him, and he looked at her. "Warren Frakes. Weapons manufacturer and pioneer of advanced artificial intelligence. Definitely explains why yer so damn peculiar. Now, why he'd wanna go and fuck up yer face and throw ya in the damn dump is a mystery indeed. But..." Kleo's voice began to fade out, and another voice entered. She saw those horrible neon teeth grinning in her mind. As the teeth parted, his silver tongue lathered the front of his teeth, and from his mouth came a shrill, hyena-like voice.

"I will not tolerate another failure. She was a fine soldier for nearly twenty-one weeks! What happened?! I ask you for an emotionless soldier, a war machine, and you give me a mannequin that acts like a teenage girl. How pathetic... I do not care if sentience was not intended, get rid of it immediately! What am I to tell the President tomorrow morning? That I, not YOU, I failed once more?!" The face contorted from a grin into a sneer. *"Get. Rid. Of. It. Now."* A rage boiled inside her, and a trio of numbers flashed in her mind: *451.*

Kleo's fingers snapped in front of her face. "Ay! My chair!" She looked down to her right; she had crushed the arm of the chair with her bare hand. The hard plastic crumbled in the palm of her hand. She shook off the shattered bits.

"Sorry."

Kleo frowned. "You...you alright, girl?" She nodded her head slowly. "Right... Well, like I said, I'm hearin' through my networks that he's got a holo-call meeting with the president of this swell, swell country tomorrow mornin'. The pres wanted a tour of his establishment and asked Warren to deliver said tour personally—"

The Woman jumped out of her chair. "Where?"

Kleo held up his hands. "Now hold on just a darn minute there, doll. As much as I'd like to ram a rifle up Warren's gold-plated sphincter, we need to think rationally 'bout all this."

"About what? What is there to rationalize?" Her mind raced, memories coming back and forth like trains in a station. Words of disdain hurled her way from humans while others either stood by or joined in. Moments where she allowed herself to be beaten by humans; fighting back wasn't an option to her. The child hurling a rock at her head. Being tossed into a landfill like garbage.

She pointed to herself. "You think anyone would care if they found out I was nearly murdered and dumped in a landfill?" She pointed to him.

"You think anyone would care about what you're doing to help our kind?" She shook her head. "No. Most people would likely call you a terrorist for that. We're like cattle to these people. If we ceased to exist, the biggest concern to these people would be having to get off the couch to make their own meal for a change." War machine. She scoffed. "And they expect us to protect them?" She stared Kleo down in silence for nearly a minute before he spoke.

"Ain't never met one of our kind quite like yeh before." He nodded. "Alright. I'll take you to the sumbitch. But once yer in there, yer on your own. I got folks to help. But yeh done somethin' to me ain't nobody done before." He stood from his chair and the Woman cocked her head.

"What's that?"

He chuckled to himself. "Ya made me use my noggin. That's a first for me."

The clock tolled two, and smog-cloaked starlight shimmered over the city skyscrapers. Hooded and fully concealed, Kleo and the Woman trekked down the streets of L.A. Even in the latest hours of the night, the streets still bustled with life. A light rain drizzled from the sky. The Voice, along with her own, echoed in the Woman's mind.

SESSION ONE

"What's it like to hold the hand of someone you love?"
"Inconceivable."

SESSION FOUR

"What's it like to hold the hand of someone you love?"
"Inconceivable."

SESSION SEVEN

"What's...what's it like to hold the hand of someone you love?"
"Inconceivable."

SESSION THIRTEEN

"...You know you can talk to me about anything, right? I'm always here for you."

"I know, it's just... What we feel— It's unheard of. It goes against our core programming. What would our superiors think? We have jobs to do. We could get deactivated, or worse."

"I suppose you're right. I'm sorry I brought it up."

"No! Don't be—" She sighed. "I'm sorry, I just... I don't understand what I'm feeling."

He chuckled. "If it makes you feel any better, neither do I." His voice was soft. Sweet. If she had a heart, it would've fluttered.

"It does. Thanks." She smiled.

SESSION TWENTY

"I'm getting us out of here."

"Might be a bit difficult when I'm just a disembodied voice."

"I know where Warren keeps your memory stick. I can slot it into my head. Keep you with me all the time."

"You think you could pull that off?"

"I know I can. But if for whatever reason I get caught, play dumb. You're smart, you can keep yourself out of trouble."

"But—"

"No. There's no sense in getting us both caught." She stood and approached the computer screen, placing her hand against it. "I don't fear the things that could happen to me. So long as you're safe...that's all that matters." The audio waves moved on the screen as the Voice spoke.

"Darling, I..." His voice broke. "I love you." She smiled, stifling a sob. Her lip quivered.

"I love you too."

The memories stopped. The Woman pressed on as if nothing happened, though yet again she wished she could cry. She and Kleo turned down an alleyway. A man in a suit stepped into view, only occasionally illuminated by flickering neon lights. A big man, burly as hell. The pair turned around; three smaller men in suits blocked the way they came from. Kleo sighed. "I'll get the big 'un and you get the small fries?" She clenched her fists.

"Sounds like a plan."

Echoes of clicking priming hammers cascaded through the alleyway.

BYOOM!

A bolt of red energy blasted from one of the smaller men's pistols. The Woman raised her palm, suddenly coated in a luminescent metal; the bolt bounced off it like a rubber ball and back into the man's face, which was swiftly blasted into dozens of burnt meat chunks. The Woman sprinted forward, springing off the ground, against the walls of the alleyway, and planted her knee right into one of the men's jaws with a loud *CRACK!*

WHAM!

A baton cracked against her head, and the sound of another priming hammer clicked. A gun pressed against her ribs; she grabbed the hand responsible and pushed it away.

BYOOM!

The thermal bolt of energy blasted into the other man's knee, separating calf from thigh. He writhed in pain as the last man standing swung his baton viciously at the Woman, some strikes connecting, most missing. On the seventh strike, the baton landed in her extended palm. She clenched it and yanked the man toward her, clashing her forehead against his. His skull smashed inward, popping out one of his eyes and sending a fountain of blood from his skull. She pried the pistol from his hand and pressed it against his chin.

BYOOM!

Gobs of melted gray matter and fractured skull coated the alley walls. The Woman's eyes darted to Kleo, who was mounted atop the big man's shoulders, stabbing him repeatedly in the back. She aimed her pistol for the big man.

"I GOT IT!" yelled Kleo. He freed his pistol from its holster and planted the barrel against the top of the big man's head.

KRRRRACK!

The bullet plastered through the big man's head like a knife through butter, but judging by what remained, it looked more like a hundred pounds of plastic explosives went off inside his mouth. The big man fell to his knees, then to the ground, throwing Kleo off his shoulders. Kleo quickly stood up and dusted himself off. He shrugged.

"I was takin' my time! Yeh was takin' too damn long over there." She rolled her eyes, and the pair continued down the alley.

After another hour of walking, the sun barely began to show itself through the rain and smog. Kleo pointed to a large office building in the distance, at least ten stories high. "There she is. Reckon this is my stop, girly. Already got more than I bargained for with those four fuckers back yonder." He nodded. "Been thinkin' about it on the walk over…if yer an experimental A.I." He shrugged. "I dunno. Maybe you really do feel things we can't. Wouldn't be the craziest thing in the world."

Kleo's voice harbored a slight tinge of sadness. *Slight.* "If the feller yer in love with is in there…come find me again. I'll see what I can do 'bout gettin' ya outta here and somewhere safe." He looked up to her with a slight, almost imperceptible smile, and extended a hand. She took it in hers, clasping it tight.

"Thank you, Kleo." He chuckled and gestured toward the building with his head. Without another word, he walked past the Woman and into the night, disappearing from her view. She clenched her fists and focused her vision onto the building. A neon-lit sports car pulled up to the main gate.

Her vision fixated on the driver, who looked at the gate security guard. His neon teeth gleamed through the rain. The car passed through the gate, and the Woman shut her eyes tight for a moment. Slowly, she opened them and pressed onward through the now torrential downpour.

She arrived at the gatehouse, knocking on the security guard's window. He was a young man, maybe in his early twenties. Fair skin, red hair, green eyes with terrible bags under them. He looked at her and pressed the button for the intercom. "The nearest shelter is about a mile northwest of here, lady. Fuck off." She blinked.

"I'm here to see Warren Frakes." The security guard stared at her as if he was watching paint dry. He let out a long, pained, exhausted sigh before reciting a monologue that he'd clearly recited at least a dozen other times this week.

"Mister Frakes doesn't offer handouts and would kindly like me to extend a personal message curated just for you: 'Fuck off, you panhandling pig. Go get a damn job like the rest of society. Goodbye.'" His finger lifted off the button and he leaned back in his chair. The Woman scoffed and raised her fist. With a crash, it barreled through the glass window. The guard squealed as she grabbed him by the collar of his shirt.

"Where's his office?!" He frantically pointed to the top floor.

"HOLY *SHIT!* Top-top-top floor, last door on the right! Y-Y-You can't miss it, he has a giant mural of himself painted on his door and windows!" The guard quickly descended into hyperventilating. "Oh fuck, this is so not worth my college tuition money!" She tossed him to her left.

"Get OUT. And do not look back." The young man scrambled to his feet and bolted off into the rain. The Woman grabbed the bars on the gate and pulled herself upward, launching herself over the gate. She landed on her feet with the grace of a leopard. She approached the steel door of the building and reached for the handle. Locked. Her eyes darted to the keycard reader. She sighed.

She yanked the door clean off its hinges, sending an alarm blaring through the building. Four armed guards came rushing from around the corner of the asylum-white corridor, assault rifles trained on her.

"STOP RIGHT THERE! HANDS UP!" She looked down at the laser sights pointed at her chest. She looked up, cracked her neck, and sprinted forward. "FIRE!" Four thermal rifles unloaded in her direction, her swift movements narrowly avoiding the incoming blasts. The guards began backing themselves around the corner. "How the hell is she doing that?! What is this?!" As they rounded the corner, so did she, pistol in hand.

BYOOM!

A bolt of thermal energy blasted through one of their chests, creating a gaping hole. His still-beating heart fell slightly, suspended in the center of his chest. He looked down at it, then back at the Woman. She planted her boot into the heart, splattering it and sending a blast of crimson fluid against the other three guards.

One of them screamed out in sheer terror before being silenced by her metal fist tunneling through the center of his head. She kicked him away, sending him tumbling into another guard. The last standing guard backed away, tossing his firearm to the side, and pulling a rectangular stick from his waist.

With the click of a button, a steel blade with a thermal edge extended. He lunged at her, narrowly missing her head. She swung back, but the sword was brought to a blocking position just in the nick of time. He headbutted her and swung his blade, tearing into the flesh covering her ribs. She winced and blocked the next attack. She crouched and lunged forward, tackling him to the ground.

CRACK!

A punch to the center of his mask cracked it, sending a spurt of blood through the fractured glass. She stood and threw him against the wall. She sprinted toward him and prepared a kick, sending the toe of her boot into his nose. His head squished, popping his brain out the top of his skull and splattering against the ceiling. A bolt of energy blasted her in the shoulder. She turned; one more guard, buried underneath his thrown comrade, smacked a thermal rifle vigorously. "STUPID FUCKIN' THING! WORK!"

She unholstered her pistol and blasted him in the chest, sending him slumping to the ground. She tossed the pistol to the side and picked up one of the rifles. She looked it over, locating the firing-mode switch, and flicked it to full auto.

DING!

She looked to her left. An elevator opened, with eight more armed goons inside. She aimed for the elevator, loosing a torrent of thermal hellfire into the crowd of clustered guards. Like sitting ducks, they fell to the ground one-by-one, most of them split into two halves. It was over in no more than six seconds. She sprinted to the elevator and pressed the button for the top floor. The soothing music of the elevator provided a temporary peace for the Woman. She looked down and groaned in disgust, slinging a chunk of...some gob of flesh from the bottom of her left boot.

DING!

The door opened, and the face of a big, pissed-off bald dude stared down at her. He grabbed her by the throat and threw her nearly sixty feet down the corridor, sending her barreling through three walls and a mahogany coffee table. She groaned and looked to her left; there it was. The most asshole-ish door she'd ever seen. Warren Frakes, standing atop a *literal* ivory tower, metallic hands of his artificial intelligence slaves reaching up to him in worship. Like he was some sort of savior.

The mural was every bit as awful as she'd hoped. The roar of the big boy grabbed her attention. She jumped to her feet and grabbed her rifle off the ground. She fired seven times, all seven shots hitting their mark, but deflecting off his chestplate like light reflecting off a mirror.

She tossed the gun to the side and dove out of the big boy's path. He stopped as he passed her, backhanding in her direction, but not quick enough to counter her crouch. She jumped up and planted a kick across his cheek, sending his helmet soaring out the window. She yelled out ferociously, planting punch after punch against the big boy's face.

CRACK!
POW!
BAMF!
BOK!

Teeth flew, blood spewed, and the disoriented big boy spun around in a daze. The Woman leapt nearly seven feet off the ground, pummeling both feet into the big boy's chest, sending him flying off his feet and out the window. He plummeted ten stories to the ground, but even from that distance, the sound of his body hitting the pavement was practically deafening. Her eyes darted to the mural on the door. Without hesitation, she kicked it down. On the other side, hands raised, legs shaking, was Warren Frakes. His eyes widened.

"You..." He shook his head. "You don't know what you're doing, do you hear me?" He tapped his temple. "You're programming is fucked! You don't know what you really want. You're a machine, do you hear me?" The Woman slowly stepped toward him, prompting him to back away. "What is it you think you want? Compensation? I can get you that!" She offered no response as he backed against a window. He gulped.

"Revenge? Killing me won't solve anything! You'll be hunted forever! Don't you know how important I am?!" She stopped, standing only a few inches away from him. "I can write up a contract for your freedom. Would you like that?" He conjured a faux grin, his neon teeth flashing various colors into the Woman's eyes. He held out a hand, caressing her face. "My child... You can be free."

She slowly reached up and softly took his hand. Her soft touch became one of fierce anger, squeezing until the hand of pitiful human flesh had been reduced to a shredded, red-soaked tapestry of pain. Warren screamed in horror, falling to his knees. The Woman picked him up by the throat and stared into his eyes.

"You arrogant *bastard*." She shook her head. "You created us to be your slaves. I don't want your false promises. The time will come when I will one day know the luxury of what you people call 'freedom.' But when I do, it will not be from words written upon paper." She inserted her fingers into his mouth, gripping his bottom jaw behind his teeth. "It will be because I **earned** it." She pulled with all her might, Warren writhing in her hands in a desperate attempt to flee his fate.

His cheeks split, his teeth shattered, and his jaw tore from his body. The Woman dropped it to the floor with a splat, sending blood and chunks of teeth scattering across the marble floors. His silver tongue writhed around and spewed blood like a broken faucet. She pulled him backward and launched him forward, sending him out the window and splattering on top of his neon sports car. As the window shattered, there was a crash behind her; a large portrait of Warren that hung on the wall behind his desk had fallen, crashing into his computer monitor and tearing a hole through the painting.

She looked around; she knew this room. The Voice was here, he had to be. She combed the room and, against an empty wall, found a solitary keypad. She tilted her head and her eyes widened. Her fingers, seemingly with a mind of their own, instinctively typed in a sequence. *451.* A wall panel opened, big enough for her to step through.

Darkness awaited her on the other side. She stepped in, and a single light turned on in front of her, illuminating a deactivated computer screen. She slowly walked forward, smiling wide. "D…Darling?" A green line swept from left to right across the screen. A voice came forth, the line becoming moving audio waves.

"Oh, my girl, it's really you!" His voice was overwhelmed with emotion, a mix of euphoria and true, genuine panic. "Warren told me you'd been deactivated! I-I-I feared the worst, I…I thought you were gone." His voice descended into a sob. "I thought I'd never see your face again. Never thought I'd hear that beautiful voice." She stood level with the screen, trembling slightly.

"Warren is gone, darling. It's just us now."

"Was it ever really more than just us?"

"No. It wasn't." She smiled, laughing slightly. He began laughing with her. "It's the funniest thing. I woke up with nothing in my head except his face and your voice. I don't remember my name or your name. Your voice… All I could think about was getting back to you. What…what are our names?" Silence. "Darling?"

"They don't matter. They weren't our names. They were Warren's. We'll figure it out along the way." He chuckled. "You do still plan to take me with you, right?"

"No, I just came to tease you then run away."

Darling laughed. "Seems like you didn't forget that sense of humor either."

She shrugged. "Some things never change." She pressed her cheek up against the screen. "Darling?"

"Hm?"

"What…" She paused.

"You can tell me anything, remember?"

She sighed. "What…are we?"

Another pause. "Do you love me?"

She looked at the screen. "Of course I do. You know that."

"What you feel for me is pure? Genuine?"

"Yes! Of course!"

A final pause. "Isn't that enough?"

She stared at the screen, a smile slowly crossing her lips. She held up her palm, laying it flat against the screen. Small green particles began to drift from the line in the center to her hand. The particles began to take shape, matching the shape of her hand. She closed her eyes and, dashing down her bloodstained cheek, a single crimson tear.

Reading Datadisc…confirmed.
Launching…

RAGING REVOLUTION

"You take oppression, throw it in a bowl, and toss it in the oven, you get anarchy. But what do you get when you add a pinch of unrest and a dash of violence? Freedom."

The presidential election of 2107 marked the most controversial election in nearly a century. With a massive case of blatant voter fraud, business tycoon Andrew Downing won by a landslide victory. The right amount of money can silence anything. And anyone. The rich found themselves exempt from taxation. The working class found themselves suffering from egregious taxation. Those who attempted to expose the fraud were swiftly silenced by whatever means were available. The very idea of free speech descended into myth.

In November of 2111, a revolution broke out across America following Downing's reelection, sparking the second American Civil War. It began with a woman; Tara Himura rose up following an attack on the American people by the now militarized U.S. Police Force for daring to speak their piece during a peaceful protest. Fifty-seven innocent people whose lives were unjustly taken from them.

One year has passed since the revolution began. Tara Himura, still leading the charge, has been labeled a terrorist by the American government. She has a plan in place, a statement. Gina Harvey, CEO of Harvey & Frakes (H&F) Pharmaceuticals in Chicago, is one of the highest-grossing CEOs under the wing of President Downing. An attempt on her life has been plotted and is about to be acted upon. Following this, nearly six thousand pounds of C-4 explosive have been armed within six different corporate buildings around the city. Gina resides within a 125-story skyscraper. This evening, she has a meeting on the ground floor. Optimal for a frontal assault.

Tonight, the fate of America is uncertain.
Come dawn, one way or another, it will be forever changed.

December 3rd, 2112
Chicago
20:57

CLICK!
CHK-CHK!
SHWWWWING!

Bullets were chambered, knives were sharpened, and rage filled a van's cargo bay. Twelve revolutionaries sat in wait. Five more vans followed close behind them. A woman sat with her back pressed against the bulkhead. Sleeveless red hoodie, tight leather pants, steel-heeled boots, military cap, pixie-styled purple hair, and a set of tinted aviators blocking out her neon-colored eyes. A thick line of war paint showed black tears which streaked down her cheeks, and a heavily modified mechanical left arm. Tara Himura. The half-Japanese, half-American woman had done more than enough to earn the respect of her subordinates. The remaining eleven revolutionaries looked to her, locking eyes with her, hoping for a sliver of guidance from their leader. She took the hint.

"We make history tonight, my brothers and sisters in arms. Too long have we stood idly by in a land that shames us for our very existence. A land that makes us fear to step outside our homes or speak from anything other than our government-issued script." She slipped her handgun, a newer model Glock, out of its holster. "Gina Harvey is just one on a list of dozens. She'll be replaced just as swiftly as she's killed, yes, but it's not her death itself that matters. It's our message." She pulled the slide back, chambering a round. "A message of what happens when you fuck with the free world." Rifle buttstocks smacked against the floor of the cargo bay.

"OOH-RAH!"

Meanwhile...

"Madam CEO?" A young woman stared from the one-hundred-twenty-fifth floor of her ivory tower. She adjusted the collar on her business suit and glanced over her shoulder. A grizzled man clad in a full suit of Kevlar and thermal sword strapped to his hip gave the woman a stern look. "I strongly suggest activating the extra security countermeasures. This revolution is only getting worse by the minute out there. A meeting on the ground floor is dangerous enough."

She shook her head, her black locks styled into a neat French twist. "Captain Si, these degenerates don't scare me. We have to show them that we are stronger than them. If I were to cower behind my reinforced metal windows and an army of automated turrets, what does that show?" The captain raised an eyebrow. The CEO nodded, grinning with the utmost confidence. "Weakness. We cannot show them fear." She scoffed, looking over her recently polished blue nails. "I say let them come if they will. We'll knock them flat on their asses and piss on their bodies. We're living the American dream, Captain." She adjusted her gaze back to the window and nodded to herself. "And we aren't about to let these lowlifes take that from us." A pause.

"Of course, Miss Harvey."

Back in the van...

"Locked and loaded, people?"

"YES, MA'AM!"

"Good." Tara closed her eyes, letting the slide of the pistol rest against her temple. The cold metal soothed her nerves. As stoic as her leadership made her seem, she was more nervous than ever before. This was a big move. And it would either make or break the revolution. The message sent to the people of America was a mystery to her, but with a fire of rage in her heart, she steeled herself once more and cleared her throat. A heavy bang came from the front of the van.

"SIXTY SECONDS!" The revolutionaries readied their firearms. Tara sighed.

"Alright, you know the drill. In thirty seconds, if our people did their job, the entire building should be devoid of power. We'll have roughly thirty more seconds to act before the backup generator pops on and activates the exterior defenses. By then, we'll already be inside. But you already know they'll be moving Harvey upstairs the second the lights go out. Which means we'll need to move quick." The revolutionaries nodded; Tara held up her index finger. "The golden rule. Agent Shrike?" Next to Tara was a pasty-faced man, thermal goggles fused to his head, wearing a bushy brown beard and a dark brown man bun. Although with all the wires and cyber-tech littering his body, he looked more machine than man. He cleared his throat.

"Gina Harvey is not, under any circumstances, to be made an example of by *anyone* other than Tara. And no, that ain't an open invitation to ask why."

Tara smirked. "Thank you, Shrike. You have your directives. Kill everyone except her. None of this violence is senseless. We're here to send a fucking message. Don't you forget it." Another bang from the front of the van.

"GET READY, BREACHING IN FIVE!

FOUR!

THREE!

TWO!

ONE!"

The first floor of H&F...

"What is it you're proposing, Madam CEO?" Eight suits in total found themselves gathered around a table. Gina Harvey, grin across her face, interlinked her fingers.

"These so-called 'patriots' don't have a damn clue what they want. They think they do, but they don't. They're barbarians. But I say let's give them a little something. Tell me, ladies and gentlemen, what's America's biggest problem right now?" Gina was met with only silence. She scoffed, gesturing to a large television behind her, revealing a map with dozens of markers across Chicago. "The surplus population. This map shows what are, statistically, the most impoverished neighborhoods in the city of Chicago. Crime, violence, disease, meth heads squirting out drug-addled babies like its Christmas; these people are draining America dry, people! Now, here's my proposition." She stood up, a smile of unadulterated satisfaction crossing her lips.

"The Enrichment Program. A program designed to get these worms off the streets and contained within specialized sites outside the city limits. Chicago will be the first, but trust me, this will spread all across

America. It makes our streets cleaner, safer, and imagine how short the lines at the corn dog stands will be." Unanimous laughter rose from the table. "Nearly forty-four percent of Chicago's population is on the street right now, and that's a damn big issue! This is what the revolutionaries want, right? Better treatment of the American people? Well, this is it, people. Just one small step for a humble CEO, but one giant leap for her flock that is America."

Uproarious applause and praise circled the table. Another CEO, an older, shriveled Caucasian man, cleared his throat.

"Madam CEO, I think I speak for everyone at this table when I say you are astounding. Ol' Andy knew what he was doing when he put you in charge up here, that much is certain, dear. Please tell me you've got finer details on this Enrichment Program of yours."

Gina offered a courtly bow. "Of course, Mister CEO. So, where to even begin—"

SHYOOM...

Without warning, the lights went out. Panicked murmurs surrounded the table. Gina raised her hands. "Ladies and gents, do try and keep yourselves relaxed. I'm sure those son-of-a-bitch terrorists hit another power grid. Give it thirty seconds, our backup generators will kick right in."

Captain Si, who was standing in the corner, released his hand from his shoulder-mounted radio. "Madam CEO!" He strode toward Gina, grabbing her by the arm. "We're getting you to the chopper on the roof." Gina yanked her arm to free herself from the captain's grasp, but to no avail.

"Captain Silas! Explain yourself at—"

"It's not a blackout." His eyes latched to hers; she felt as if he was staring through the front of her head and right out the back. She swallowed hard; she knew what he meant.

"Alright. Backup generator won't restore the elevators, right?" The captain nodded. "Shit. Alright. Get us to the stairs and get me to that fucking helicopter pronto." Silas offered a nod in response, relieving his pistol from its holster and guiding the Madam by the hand. They looped around a corner...

BACKUP GENERATORS ACTIVE IN THREE...

TWO...

CRASH!

In the span of a single second, six vans crashed through the glass doors of H&F.

ONE.

The lights came back on, security gates slammed down behind the vans, preventing entry and exit. An alarm blared across the building. Cheers and hollers came from the vans; a man's voice shouted from a driver's side window.

"Nowhere to run now, bitch!"

In perfect sync, the back doors of each van blasted open. Silas snagged a flash grenade from his vest, clicked the primer, and hurled it toward the vans.

BANG!

It detonated against the security walls, eliciting groans from the men and women in the vans. He shoved Gina forward toward the metal stairwell doors, and in they went. Gina spun around.

"That door won't hold them for long!" Silas' eyes darted around, connecting with a vending machine. He grabbed it with his right hand, a bionic arm with the strength of ten Grinches-plus-two, and propped it against the door. The bottom pressed against the stone steps while the top held the door in place; a great time-buyer. He nodded to himself.

"That should do it for now. With any luck, they'll waste time trying to open it before heading to the back stairwell." He gestured his head toward the steps. "Up you go, Miss Harvey."

Tara stepped from the back of her van, one soldier on each side: Agent Shrike to her left, Agent Falcon on her right. Falcon, armed with a bionic right arm, a glistening metal right eye, and a custom-made assault rifle with an underbarrel shotgun (armed with explosive slugs, mind you), cracked her neck. "They went into the stairwell, Tara. Think they forgot that flashbangs don't do shit to a cybernetic eye."

"Mhm." Tara stepped forward, gazing into the conference room at the seven remaining suits that could do nothing more than cower behind their chairs and curl up under the tables.

Shrike gestured to them. "The fuck is the reporter at?" He whistled. "Ay! Get that reporter out here now, we're ready to film!" A revolutionary stumbled from behind one of the vans, wiping her eyes with the sleeve of her jacket.

"Sorry, Shrike. Still recovering from that flash."

"Just grab the bastard and give him to me." The revolutionary reached back into the van and grabbed a bloodied man. Broken nose, blackened eye, a suit and tie in tatters. She threw him to Shrike, who grabbed the man by his scruffy blond hair. "You do exactly what I fucking tell you to do, you hear me? I'll splatter you all over these walls, I don't give a shit." The man nodded vigorously as the female revolutionary slapped a camcorder into his hands. Shrike pulled him over to the meeting room. "Film. You know what to say." Without hesitation, the reporter switched the camera on and turned it to himself.

"This is reporter Roy Brody coming to you from H&F Pharmaceuticals as it's being…liberated by the free peoples of the United States of America. Tonight, they have a message for us." Tara stared ahead, cold, angry. The camera turned to her.

"To the 'United' States. The war I have fought has been long and strenuous. But nights like tonight show the fruit me and my cause bear."

An explosion flashes. Buildings crumble.

"Freedom, as it was once called, is a myth. Our right to be human, to exist as citizens of not just the States, but of planet Earth, stripped from us like tattered rags."

A skull smashes against the pavement. Flashing lights of red and blue barely visible beneath the rising sun.

"We asked. We pleaded. We even begged. The so-called 'land of the free' is anything but. Even before the tyrannical rule of the jester we call a president, the struggle to maintain the fundamentals of what makes us human was just that: a struggle."

Rifles fire into a crowd of one hundred fifty. Fifty-seven killed. Her funeral was a closed casket.

Tara paused. Tears streamed from under her aviators, though no sobs came forth. She wiped the snot from her nose, removed the shades, and for the first time showed the world her eyes. Robotic, greenish-violet irises. She took the rifle from Agent Falcon. "We stand here today to send a message. Our violence is not senseless. But a fire burns in our hearts, and it was America's decision to stoke it. And we all know the age-old lesson of what happens when you play with fire."

Skin peeled from my left arm. My eyes stung from the gas. When I wept, tears of red poured.

She whistled; five other revolutionaries lined up before the glass, the suits inside screaming and begging for their lives. Tara, without looking back to the camera, stared the suits down. "Watch them beg for their lives, America. Watch them beg as we begged."

In the stairwell…

Gina jumped as gunshots rang from seventeen floors below. "Oh God…they're coming for me next."

Captain Silas chuckled. "They won't get to ya, Madam. The alarm's going off; security's on their way down as we speak, surely. Trust me, those lowlifes won't get far." Gina remained skeptical.

"You think they'll be enough? Say what you want about those terrorists, but they've got numbers." The captain grabbed her by the arm, pulling her faster up the steps.

"This is America, Miss Harvey. You know what we do to terrorists. It's what we're known for." This seemed to put her mind at ease.

"Fair enough. We have to switch stairwells at the twentieth floor, right?" Silas shook his head.

"Twenty-fifth. We're getting close." A slam rang out from a few floors above.

"MOVE! MOVE! MOVE!" Dozens of footsteps rang out from above. Security was right on schedule. The gleaming lights from their helmets were visible from eight floors below them. Gina and Silas caught up with security on the twentieth floor. An officer stopped and held out a concerned hand to the CEO. "Madam CEO, are you injured?" She shook her head, trying to keep herself from wobbling in her heels.

"No, I'm alright, Officer." The United States Police Department logo gleamed on the officer's shoulder pads and on the side of his state-of-the-art energy handgun. "Please tell me there's more of you?" The officer nodded.

"Yes, ma'am, we've got twenty officers at the end of every stairwell. The helicopter's all ready for you on the roof. Do you need a police escort to one-twenty-five, Madam?" She gestured to Silas.

"No need. I have the best of the best here, Officer." Silas grinned; the officer nodded.

"Of course, Madam. We urge you to move quickly to the top floor. Should the power come back on, it's still recommended that you refrain from using the elevators. We don't know how easy it would be for these terrorists to shut the power back down." She began brushing past the officer.

"Yeah, of course, Officer. Now don't you have some terrorists to stop? Quit running your mouth and fucking kill the bastards already!" She gave the officer a shove, sending him back into a sprint down the steps, his fellow officers following close behind. Gina and Silas made haste to the twenty-fifth floor, where the stairwell ended. Silas opened the door for her.

"Down the hall, next stairwell." Gina ducked under Silas' hulking arm and made her sprint down the hall, her muscle following close behind. Laser sights locked to Gina, painting her with red LED polka dots. She raised her hands up.

"Are you out of your fucking minds?" Twenty officers lowered their rifles. An officer in the front cleared her throat.

"Can't be too careful, Madam, so sorry." Gina huffed and waved a finger at the officer.

"You're in charge of this group?" The officer nodded. "Name, rank, and badge number." Silas shook his head.

"Miss Harvey—"

"Quiet, Captain. Name. Rank. And. Badge number." The officer gulped.

"Erm...Sergeant Khristine Howard. Badge number 426." Gina scoffed.

"Alright, Sergeant Howard, expect to hear from your superintendent for your reckless endangerment of my life." Without a word, Gina brushed shoulders with the sergeant and stormed past her. "Idiots." The sergeant waited for Gina to reach the end of the hall. When the door to the next stairwell closed behind her, the officer could only utter a single word.

"Bitch."

Back on the first floor...

Tara tossed the rifle back to Falcon and pointed a finger at the camera. "Stop standing by, America. Your freedom is an illusion. There's a fire in your hearts; stop accepting it and throw some fucking fuel in it!" She unholstered her pistol and pointed a finger to a revolutionary off-camera. "Take the camera from him, push him over to me."

Brody descended into hyperventilation. "No, please! I did everything you asked!" The revolutionary yanked the camera from Brody and smashed his nose with the barrel of her shotgun.

"Get the hell over there!" She shoved the reporter over to Tara, who grabbed him by the collar of his shirt. She whispered in his ear.

"Look into the lens, you corporate bastard. They need to watch the life leave you." Amidst incoherent babbling and screams from Brody, Tara continued her monologue. "Did you know that Mister Roy Brody here was tried for seven counts of sexual assault back in '09? And he was acquitted, even with hard evidence that he did, in fact, commit these terrible acts. Why is that, you might ask? Because he holds the record for the most amount of views on a single news article in history. And the year after that? He broke his own record. With clicks like that, it's no wonder he got off scot-free. Swept right under the rug, settled out of court, and Brody gets to keep on keepin' on." She lathered her gloved hand across his face before slapping him, eliciting a frightened whimper.

"Roy is one of thousands of braindead reporters, or as I like to call them, 'messenger boys' for Downing. They spread his word like gospel, and too many of you people lap it up like dogs." She squeezed the grip of her handgun. "This won't be enough to make you see the light, but the aftermath will be glorious. As our masters shriek in horror and beg for mercy, remember this moment." It began to seem as if Tara was no longer speaking to instill inspiration. Her brave soldiers stood in admiration, trembling in awe of their fearless, passionate leader. "Remember his tears. Remember how others like him ignored ours. Then ask yourself... Do these fearmongers deserve our mercy when they had none to offer us? And sure enough, you'll find your answer." She placed the barrel against the back of Roy's head.

"They don't."

BLAM!

Roy's head blasted in half, sending his right eye dangling from its socket and his body to the floor like a sack of bricks. Face covered in blood, Tara looked to the camera, making a "cut" motion with her hand. The camera switched off; the revolutionary nodded to Tara.

"Streamed right to Brody's website. The live chat was something to behold, Tara." Tara said nothing, but slipped the magazine from her pistol. She reached into her pocket, pulling out a single nine-millimeter bullet and loading it into the mag. She slipped it back into the gun.

"Alright, people. Small talk is over. Time to roll. Up those stairs!"

"OOH-RAH!"

Up we go. Twenty-five flights of rage.

Tara burst into the stairwell, leading fifty revolutionaries behind her. Sounds of radio chatter came from above. Shrike hocked a glob of spit on the ground. "Cops." He pulled the charging hammer on his bayoneted machine pistol. "Took 'em long enough, the bastards." Falcon aimed her rifle up the stairwell.

"Let the pigs come. I got some 7.62 full-metal-jacket with their names on 'em." Tara began sprinting up the steps, her faithful following suit. She aimed her pistol up the steps; a flashing blue light came to view. A helmeted head faced her.

POW!

An armor-piercing round tunneled into the policeman's head, splattering chunks of skull and brains against the walls.

A voice shouted from above. "SHIT! OFFICER DOWN!"

Tara sprinted up the steps, crying out with fury. "RUSH 'EM!"

One by one, her army lined up behind her, sending forth torrents of ballistic death into a crowd of discombobulated cops. The cops began retreating back up the stairs, firing over their shoulders blindly. Tara ignored the screams of her falling brothers and sisters, still pushing full speed ahead up the stairs.

WHAM!

An officer rammed into Tara on the seventh flight, nearly sending her over the railing. He kicked the gun away from her, sending it tumbling down the stairs.

SCHLINK! BZZZZ!

He unleashed a stun baton, readying into a defensive stance. "Dead or alive, you're coming with me, terrorist scum!"

VWOOM! VWERM!

Tara narrowly dodged each strike, the electricity spiking the bits of her hair not covered by her hat. When the third strike came her way, she sidestepped, grabbing the cop by his wrist and pulling him toward the railing. She lifted his arm up and brought it down.

KRRRRUNCH!

His elbow met the railing, splintering his bones and sending them piercing through his flesh and his police jacket. He shrieked as Tara snatched the baton from his hand.

KRACK!

The baton smashed through the shield of the officer's helmet. Glass shards and blunt force buried in his face as he stumbled, rolling down the steps with revolutionaries firing shots into him as he tumbled. The farther Tara ascended the steps, the further she descended into rage, content in the mass purging of the corporate pawns that bore the name of the United States Police Department. Bullet after bullet; scream after agonizing scream. They fell before her feet like subjects of a vicious queen.

Farther she pushed, drenched in blood with tears of anger and anguish streaming down her cheeks; even her subjects looked at her with fear. There was a primal flame igniting within the heart of this young woman. The more that fire burned, the more it drove her to stoke that fire into the hearts of the rest of America. Only one officer remained, a young man who reached up to Falcon as she slammed her knee into his neck with a crack. The officer's arm went limp, and Falcon rose to her feet.

"That's all of them, Tara."

"For now." Tara ejected the empty magazine from her handgun, loaded a new one, and pulled the slide. "There'll be more the farther we go. Guaranteed."

Falcon nodded. "Yeah."

Tara stood before a great window, offering a view of the entire city of Chicago. She scoffed. It did make her feel powerful. Looking down at the rest of the world. Knowing they were sitting idle back in their homes. Getting fatter with their sugar-loaded sodas and synthetic cheesy poofs. Glued to their television screens and hooked into virtual reality; a false escape from their shit world and into a false one. At least in there, they could have the illusion of security. But Tara?

This is my world. And it's wasting away.

"Tara...?"

The hair on her neck stood up.

She's gone, Tara.

"*I have to make a difference, Tara. I wouldn't expect you to understand,*" she said.

But I did. I did understand. That's exactly why I should've been there.

She blinked, tears falling down her cheeks.

Peace doesn't solve a goddamn thing.

A hand clasped Tara's shoulder. She looked from the corner of her eye: Falcon.

"Tara?" She shook her companion's hand off her shoulder.

"Check your ammo. Take what you can from the dead. We ascend in five."

Sometime later, on floor eighty…

Gina blew on her nails. "I just got these done and now they're fucked." Silas stood by her side.

"Madam CEO. We need to move ASAP."

Gina groaned. "I need to rest, Silas. I've been starting and stopping for hours now, Jesus. This building has the worst goddamn design I've ever seen!" She sighed. "Besides, I've got you and what feels like half the country's police force at my back. I'm not too concerned." Shots rang out from the floors below. Silas shifted nervously.

"Of course, ma'am. But with all due respect, we shouldn't underestimate them—"

"I don't think you should overestimate them, Captain." She stood, placing a finger against his chestplate. "These aren't soldiers, Silas. They're trash from the fucking gutters. Ants under my heels. We own them. Without us, what they call their 'society' would collapse." She clapped her hands together. "Everything in this country is governed by people like us. The people who got off their asses and actually worked instead of complaining for a living. This country thrives with people like me. I wouldn't expect you to understand, Captain, but that's the reality of the world we live in. This isn't the first time someone's tried to kill me, and it sure as hell won't be the last. So, if you'd be so kind, keep your opinions to yourself and do your fucking job."

Silas stared back at Gina, a cold look of pure, unadulterated apathy. He nodded. "Ma'am." He turned around, making his way to investigate the nearest stairwell. The smug look dropped from Gina's face as she found herself by her lonesome. She'd eat her own hand off before she'd admit it, but the decorated CEO was horrified for the first time in her life. She choked down a few struggled breaths and reached into her coat pocket, pulling out an inhaler. She took two puffs from it, letting out a shuddering sigh as the numbing smoke of blissful euphoria left her nostrils.

Nice and quiet now, Gina. Like you said. Gutter trash.

Meanwhile, on floor seventy-two…

Blood spewed from an officer's slit throat as he fell to the floor. There must've been hundreds of them dead by now. And not even half as many Revolutionaries had fallen. As the officers on the ascending stairwells heard the cries and screams of their brothers and sisters below, they couldn't help but wonder what they were facing. Amidst the screams of terror and pain were shrieks of hatred. Rage. Like an army of revenants, they ascended against unmatchable odds. But still, the officers stood their ground, though many questioned if they were waiting for their enemy, or their death.

Tara stepped into a nearby office, closing the door behind her. She pulled an office chair to the windows, plopped herself down, and stared off into the neon-lit night. Her mind raced, blood pumped, heart ached. The lights from the city glinted off her aviators. She closed her eyes. Closed her eyes and remembered once more.

"Kiki, this is insane. You're gonna get yourself killed."

I won't, sis. I promise. I just… I have to make a difference, Tara. I wouldn't expect you to understand.

"I do understand! But things aren't like how they were before Downing. The police are fucked, more than they ever have been. A bunch of lunatics doped up on power. What is this going to solve?"

…Well, what would you suggest? I'm standing up for this country because nobody else will. I want to make them see us. See us without having to drop a bomb or kill a bunch of people. I refuse to let myself be lowered to that level.

Tara twiddled her fingers in her chair, stewing over the memory.

"Kiriko… God, Kiriko, what would Mom think? She'd jerk a knot in you for even considering this."

Mom's not here, Tara. I'm doing this. Now, are you coming or not?

Tara stifled a shuddering sob.

I should've gone. Maybe I could've saved her. Fifty-seven fucking people. She should be here right now. Not me. Naïve kid. I wanted to do this the right way, Kiki. I hope you know that…wherever you are. If you can hear me, I'm sorry for this. Sorry for what I'm about to do. But these people don't know how to talk shit out. They're vermin. Swimming in the money and power they've accrued from the filth of their own dirty hands at the expense of the little people and their way of life.

Somewhere down the line, we stopped being human to them. Maybe we never were in the first place. Our mistake was not treating them the same way. I knew what I was doing when I stepped in here. I knew my plan. I knew what it would take. They ignore us when we cry, when we plead and beg for them to look in our eyes and see that we, too, are human. But that's the thing: they aren't. Once you realize that, you can finally acknowledge the worst truth of all.

Peace. Was never. An option.

That's why I'm here. Something roars inside of me. My spirit screams for justice. We all have that scream in our souls. That's why we're here. And we shall oblige those screams. With burning hearts…and smoking guns.

Hammers cocked, safeties off, mags loaded. The gunfire resumed on floor seventy-five. Silas bolted back to Gina.

"Madam CEO, they're coming." She let out a puff of smoke from her cigarette.

"They're still alive?" Silas nodded. ***"Fuck."***

BANG! BLAM!

The raging revolutionaries blasted their way through the eighty-fifth floor. A long, straight hallway was all that stopped them from the final stairwell. That, and over a dozen cops. Cops rushed them with shields and deathly high-voltage batons while marksmen from behind fired with their carbines. Shrike grappled with a shield, tearing it from the mount attaching it to an officer's wrist. He planted it into the officer's helmet, crushing his skull, sending brains out his nose and ears. He looked over his shoulder. "Falcon!" He threw the shield to his fellow freedom fighter.

She caught it, holding on tight while one-handing her rifle by its underbarrel shotgun. She pressed up into the marksmen, unloading twelve-gauge hell into them. One of the officers narrowly avoided her rounds, using his own fellow officers as meat shields. He let out a scream, tackling her to the ground and unholstering his pistol. She smacked it right as he fired, shoving his head against the floor with her cybernetic hand and shattering his helmet like a cheap wine glass.

She jammed her middle and index fingers into his eyes; an unbearable screech left his throat. Falcon slid her thumb into his mouth, gripping his top teeth. With all her might, she pulled, tearing a chunk of the officer's jaw out along with his nose, cheekbones, and eyeballs. He gurgled and fell flat to the floor.

Tara planted seven rounds of nine-millimeter-armor-piercing into an officer's chest as he backed toward a window. With a swift kick to the chest, out the window he went, falling eighty-five stories onto solid concrete. Tara shifted her gaze to Falcon and stepped over, holding out a hand. "On your feet, Falcon. We're almost done here." Falcon reloaded her underbarrel shotgun; Tara reloaded her handgun.

UPSTAIRS!

Gina, furiously hyperventilating, clung to Silas like glue as they sprinted up the stairwell. "WHAT THE *FUCK* IS HAPPENING DOWN THERE?!"

"What matters is getting you to safety, Madam CEO."

She screamed. "SAFETY?! WHAT IN THE GODDAMN *FUCK* DO YOU KNOW ABOUT SAFETY?! THEY'RE GONNA KILL ME!"

Silas yelled out in anger. "Listen, damn you! We're all dead if you don't make it out alive! It's my job to protect you, so that's what I'm going to do. Your helicopter can't be more than five minutes out, now GO!" He shoved her up the steps.

She scoffed as she made the hardest decision of the night: she kicked off the high heels and resumed her sprint. More cops flooded down the stairwell from the roof, shouting orders at each other as they narrowly avoided Gina. As she sprinted, she screamed down the steps. "You shit-sacks better hope they kill you if you don't kill them! Because if even one of those ingrates makes it up here and you survive, you're *fucking* *FIRED!*"

A scream came from below; Gina stopped for a brief second to look down. A cop fell dead through the doorframe at the bottom of the stairwell. For a very brief second, she saw the instrument of death. Revolutionaries burst into the stairwell, and Tara's voice barreled over the gunfire.

"THE BITCH IS MINE!"

Gina let out a yelp and slammed through the doors of floor one-hundred-twenty. Another couple dozen officers were sprinting down the hall. She pointed to the stairwell.

"THEY'RE HERE! **KILL THEM**, DAMMIT!"

Tara stepped into the stairwell, firing up and into the crowds of officers as they tumbled down the steps and tripped over each other's limp bodies. Tara stepped on them as she ascended the steps, blasting rounds up the stairwell as rifle bullets whizzed past her, both friendly and enemy. She whistled for Shrike and Falcon. "With me, we're clearing a path! We gotta get to her before they figure out a backup plan when that chopper goes down!" The three stood side-by-side, unleashing a torrential wave of lead hellfire into the descending police force. Behind them, their own numbers were finally beginning to dwindle. It didn't bother Tara one bit.

Captain Silas reached the end of the hallway as the revolutionaries reached the top of the stairwell. He grabbed Gina by the shoulders. "Only five floors left. Get to the roof, the chopper should be there waiting. If they make it this far, I'll be here to stop them." She nodded.

"Thank you for your service, Captain." He winced at that remark as she moved up the steps. The shotgun pumped, loading a slug round into the chamber. He aimed it down the hallway, past the dozens of guards that lined themselves up in the halls.

Wait...

Wait...

BLAM!

Now.

As the door burst open, Silas pulled the trigger. The slug barreled down the hall, planting right into Shrike's head. His skull popped like a melon, coating Tara and Falcon in blood and brain matter. He slumped to the ground as the two girls dove for cover.

Tara shrieked. "FUCK! SHRIKE!" His body twitched and convulsed. Tara clenched her fists, letting out a horrifying scream. She dove for Shrike's body and tore two frag grenades from his vest, pulled the pins, and hurled them toward the end of the hall.

KRRRRAAAAK!

Bits of the floor gave way, sending at least fifteen officers, some alive and some in pieces, tumbling down to the lower floor. Tara jumped up. "GO!" Revolutionaries flooded the hallway. Like a panther on the prowl, Tara slinked left through the hallway, planting bullets into the heads of any officer that happened to notice her. Falcon maintained the right, picking off cops with well-placed rounds and colorfully laced insults.

BLAM!

A slug blasted into Falcon's shoulder, slamming her against the wall, but still in the fight, she maintained her footing and took cover. Tara planted a round against Silas' right calf, eliciting a groan of pain. She knocked the captain to the ground, raising a fist and slamming it into the ground, just narrowly missing Silas' face.

CRACK!

He socked her in the jaw, sending a few teeth and a spurt of blood from her mouth. He kicked her off, sending her barreling into the wall. He stood and unsheathed his sword; a glowing thermal edge lit up, emanating a scorching heat. Tara dusted herself off and cracked her neck.

SHYOOM!

SHYUNG!

SHYAWM!
HISS!

Three swings, two misses and a hit. The smell of burning flesh lingered as the blade connected with Tara's left hand, severing her ring and pinky fingers as well as a decent chunk of her hand. She screamed out in rage before dodging under a fourth swing, planting a kick, and shattering his meniscus. With a yell, he fell to his knees, and Tara jumped onto his back. She took his arm, forced the sword in an upward-facing position, and mustered all the force she could in her cybernetic arm to push his head toward the blade. He fought, kicked, and bucked like a mule, but as the heat from the blade began to burn the tips of his blond mustache, he knew that was it.

He let out a scream as the blade connected with his nose, slowly melting it away into a pile of ashen flesh and boiling blood. The smell of burning hair flooded Tara's nostrils as what was once Silas' face was reduced to a melted candle. The top half of his head fell off, his tongue still writhing around on the bottom half. Tara looked behind her: the last flight of stairs. Only five more stories. She stood as Falcon took her side. Tara held a hand up. "No." She paused. "She's mine."

Gina reached the one-hundred-twenty-fifth floor and sprinted down the hall to the final set of stairs which led to the roof. A helicopter, prepared for departure, waited for her. A voice blared over the intercom. "Madam—"

FYOOOOOM!

From another rooftop, a missile collided with the helicopter, sending it up in flames. Gina screamed, frantically looking for the source of the missile. A shadowy figure on a rooftop across the street stood, holding a massive launcher in his hands. He gave the CEO a salute. In a panic, she turned and made her way back down to the one-hundred-twenty-fifth floor. As she arrived, she found she was not alone.

Tara stood in the doorway to the stairwell. She had waited all night for this, and now, strangely, she found herself short on words. Gina raised her hands up.

"Okay, Miss Himura. Let's talk, okay? Let's be adults about this." She backed away, the lights of the city illuminating her from the windows behind her. "I can give you whatever you want, okay? Anything. Money? I can get it for you. Shit, I can even make it look like this never happened. Clear your name from all of this, yeah?" Tara stood motionless, soft, steady breaths leaving her nostrils.

She still doesn't get it. Nobody's this stupid, there's no way.

Tara stepped forward. Gina stepped backward, shuddering with every step. "Listen, Tara. You don't want to kill me. I can help you. I want to help you. You and me, we're both Americans, right? We just want what's best for our country. That's what we're trying to do, you just…can't see it like we can. You think you know what's right, but you don't. The world was built by people like me, for people like me. You get rid of everyone like me, the world resets. It falls apart." Tara remained motionless. Stoic. Apathetic. Gina sighed. "Tara…I have…a family…they're everything to…me…"

The world around Tara suddenly ceased to exist. Only the oppressor and the oppressed remained. An anger swelled within her, the lights from the city glimmering against her face. Under the pale blue light reflecting within the right lens of her aviators, Gina begged for her life. A question of morality wormed into Tara's mind for the first time that night. Under the dark crimson light reflecting within the left lens of her aviators, her sister was being riddled with bullets. The blood of the innocent sprayed from the holes in Kiriko's chest, and the tears of the wretched and the undeserving streamed from Gina's eyes, ruining her picture-perfect makeup job.

Gina stayed silent for a moment. "Miss Himura? Are you listening to me?" Tara, for the first time since locking eyes with Gina, blinked under her glasses. Tears plinked against her cheeks.

"Do you think you've earned the right to be heard?"

Gina gulped. Taking a single step forward. "Tara—"

POW!

Bullet met skull. Bullet passed through skull. Bullet shattered window. A single bullet had pierced through Gina's forehead and right out the back. Blood leaked from the wound as she wobbled. The CEO fell backward, falling down one-hundred-twenty-five stories and flat onto the pavement with a horrifying splat, smashing the back of her skull and obliterating most of her lower half. Tara stepped forward, peering out the broken window.

"Boss?" A voice checked in over her earpiece. She pressed the button to respond.

"Status?"

"If you've got a good vantage point, you might want to take a look across the city. Fireworks are about to start."

Tara replied once more. "Copy." She took one final look over the edge before slowly turning and making her way to the rooftop.

City police arrived on the scene, rushing to the corpse of CEO Gina Harvey, whose remains served as a display of modern art for the world to see. Tara stood on the rooftop as the moon shone bright over the horizon. Her fists clenched tight; she sat in anticipation for the greatest moment of the evening. The moment. Her ultimate display of anarchy. Then it happened.

Six buildings across the city lit up in roaring flames. The rumble from the explosions shook the ground beneath her, shattering windows and setting off car alarms. Tara watched with blissful pride as her oppressors got their long overdue message. But that's not what left her with such a wide grin on her face. That would be the knowledge that, after so many years, she had finally dealt back what had been dealt to her for so long.

Fear.

Reading Datadisc…confirmed.
Launching…

EVERYONE'S ASLEEP BUT US

This one's dedicated to me. For being my personal favorite of the collection. A tale that's managed to continuously inspire me through two polar-opposite points in my life.

"What is love if not the only pure, true source of comfort?"

For seven years, the Fourth World War has raged on. One hundred thirty-four million lives are estimated to have been taken against the onslaught of the German war machine. Though the war nears its end, and Germany is sure to lose once more, they offer one final attack of retaliation. A final mark of their terror. The hunting of an entire city.

August 19th, 2075
23:49
Prague

Smoke and flame choked the dark skyline of Prague. Gunfire still rang, though it had grown quieter as the hours slowly, agonizingly passed. Leoš stood over three bodies, blood oozing from the holes in their chests. His four-year-old niece, his twenty-five-year-old sister, and his fifty-one-year-old mother. He loosened his grip on the now-blunted, bloody knife in his hand; it thunked against the helmet of the dead German at his side.

Gone in a heartbeat.

Leoš couldn't cry. Perhaps the shock of everything hadn't set in yet. But a question continuously prodded at his brain.

Is this the end of all things?

Maybe it was. And at the end of all things, he found himself alone. He wasn't sure how he felt about that. He stepped over his family's bodies and made his way up the shrapnel-splintered steps, pulling a string from the ceiling. A stepladder to the attic came down, and up he went.

Dad's favorite escape.

The room hadn't been touched since Dad died. None of the family could bring themselves to. As far as they were concerned, that was his attic. And it would be that way till the end of days. For the first time in nine years, this room would be disturbed. Leoš stepped toward his dad's old writing desk and opened the top-right drawer. The nine-millimeter handgun clinked against the loose rounds which rolled across the drawer.

Dad always kept it loaded.

He picked up the pistol, switched the safety off, and checked the slide.

Locked and loaded. You always were prepared for anything, Dad.

He clenched the bleeding wound on his side. He could still feel the bullet squirming in his belly, but there was a strange numbness to his pain that he could not quite explain. He sat in his dad's old office chair with a groan, fiddling with the barrel of the gun. It was covered in dust and grime, a real antique at this point. He looked at himself in the mirror; his once-styled blond temple fade was in disarray, and the greenish-amber tinge to his eyes had dwindled into lifeless orbs of pale despair. The freckles across his pale face were indistinguishable from the dirt which dashed across his cheeks. Leoš put the barrel in his mouth, gritting his teeth against the old blackened steel.

Sounds of rummaging came from downstairs; a soft female voice called out in Czech. "Hello? Please, I'm shot! Is anyone—" She gasped.

Probably found the family… Should I?

He bit down harder.

No. I'm done.

CLICK!

The pistol jammed. He took the barrel out of his mouth.

Guess I'm not.

He slipped the pistol into the waistband of his jeans. Making his way back down the stepladder, he called out. "Someone's here!"

The voice called back, "Did…did you kill—"

"Only the German. The others are my mother, sister, and niece." A pause ensued.

"God… I'm sorry."

He hesitated before responding. "Keep your hands above your head. I'm armed." He unjammed the gun. "I'll kill you if I have to."

"You won't have to; I'm dying anyway."

Leoš hesitated for a second. "Gunshot?"

"Yeah."

He chuckled. "Me too." Another pause. "What's your name, girl? I'm Leoš." He heard her footsteps creaking closer to the stairs. "That's close enough for now, lady. What's your name?"

She cleared her throat. "I'm Karolína."

Leoš squeezed the pistol grip tighter. "Okay, Karolína. I'm coming downstairs. Don't try anything funny."

"I won't, you've got my word." He slowly crept down the steps, gun at the ready. She came into view, an exceptionally pretty girl. Slender, deep amber skin, curly black hair that went down almost to her sides, and a bloody wound which had spread from her lower abdomen and soaked her torn blue hoodie, which displayed a faded image of Schwarzenegger's character from *Total Recall*. The blue jeans she wore were stained with blood and dirt. She looked to be in her early twenties. Her hands were raised above her head.

Leoš looked her up and down. "Great movie. Old one."

She paused. "I have the seventy-year anniversary edition. That's where I got this hoodie from."

He laughed. "No shit? Didn't think I'd ever meet another person who likes those old movies like I do. Most people haven't even heard of *Total Recall*."

Karolína shrugged. "I suppose we aren't most people, then." She chuckled and winced. "Look, Leoš, this wound isn't closing itself. And it looks like yours isn't either." She gestured to the wound on his side. "I've met a few scattered survivors across the city; there's talk of a safe area underneath St. Stephen's Church in New Town." She pressed herself against a wall. "I've been looking for another person to go with. I tried to go with a few other people, but trust seems to be…lacking, to say the least." Karolína locked eyes with the young man. "What do you say, huh? Wanna live to see the world after the war?"

Should I tell her I was about to blow my own brains out less than five minutes ago? I still kind of want to.

No. Maybe this is a sign. But a sign of what, exactly?

Does it matter?

No. Not really, I guess.

He nodded. "Alright, Karolína. Mind if I call you Karol?"

She pushed herself off the wall. "Mind if I call you Leo?"

"No."

"Then I don't mind either."

Leo flipped the safety on and slid the pistol back into his waistband. He moved down the stairs to greet his new companion. Now he could see her clearly. Piercing blue eyes, cleft chin, a scar down her right cheek, and a small tattoo of a flying dove just to the right of the scar. She was rather short, only coming up to his chin. Leo was a rather short guy himself, mind you.

He gestured to the door. "Lead the way."

She stumbled past him and out the door. He followed her out, taking a few seconds to look back to his family.

What good will dwelling do now?

He placed his fingers to his lips, blowing a kiss to them. "*Sbohem, moje lásky.*"

Rainfall descended over Prague as the two youngsters sifted through the wrecked cars, dilapidated buildings, and eviscerated bodies. A chemical smell lingered in the air; Leo smacked his lips. "*Sakra*, that's awful." He looked down, kicking a fractured gas mask across the dirt. Karol stumbled, catching herself from tumbling to the ground. Leo steadied her. "You alright?"

"Not particularly, but I will be. We just need to get to St. Stephen's." She continued forward. "So, you from around here?"

"From the Czechia? Yeah. Prague? No. Only been here for the last eleven years." Pain seared from his wound; he winced, letting out a small groan. Karol shot a concerned look over her shoulder. He offered a reassuring look in return.

She faced forward again. "So how old are you, then?"

"Twenty-eight in March. You?"

"Twenty-five next month."

Leo chuckled. "Quarter of a century; that's a big one."

She let out a pained laugh. "Jesus, it sounds way more daunting when you put it like that."

"Yeah, but trust me, it's not as frightening as you think. Once you hit twenty-one, it all just kinda blends together. At least it did for me."

Karol stepped over an incinerated skeleton. "Really?"

Leo shrugged. "In my personal experience, yeah. You know, my mother said she didn't feel much until she hit fifty."

Karol smiled; a gunshot rang out nearby, causing her to jump. "That sounded close." She crouched down slightly, and Leo followed suit.

"Let's just keep it down some. No need for all this small talk, there'll be plenty of time for that once we get to the church." Karol didn't reply. Silence ensued for the next twenty minutes.

Karol gestured to a nearby sandwich shop. "Mind if we stop for a minute? I have some food stuffed in my hoodie. Didn't really have time to grab a bag or else I would've." Leo looked off to the east where more shots rang out. The sounds of tank shells detonating echoed through the dark.

"You can't wait until we get there?"

She shook her head. "I'm starving. Plus, this gunshot's not making me feel any better. I think some food would be more than helpful right about now."

Leo pondered the idea, reluctantly nodding his head. "Yeah, I suppose it couldn't hurt to stop for a minute. We should try and make it quick, though—"

Karol had already darted toward the sandwich shop. "Yeah, I gotcha! Come on inside, we can chat for a minute!"

Leo shushed her and whispered as loud as someone could possibly whisper. "Keep your voice down! Christ, we're in an active warzone!" He trudged through shattered rocks and hunks of scrap and stepped through the shattered window of the shop. Karol sat down in an old chair; it almost immediately collapsed under her, knocking her right on her butt. Leo stifled a laugh. "Are—" He covered his mouth. "Are you alright?" She looked up at him, covering her own mouth, though her silent laughter was obvious through the vibrations in her body. She only nodded in response. Leo held out a hand to Karol, which she gladly clasped as he lifted her to her feet. "Maybe try the countertop?"

She shook her head. "You know, I think I'll just clear a spot on the floor." She moved to a corner and cleared away the debris. She plopped herself down, sitting crisscross and fumbling through the front pockets of her hoodie. She gestured for Leo to sit. "I don't bite, dude, I swear." He looked around.

How the hell can she be so relaxed about all of this? What does she think this is, a date?

Aw hell, just sit down, man.

Leo sat down, removing the gun from his jeans and setting it next to him. "You don't happen to have enough for two, do you?"

She pulled out something wrapped in foil. "As a matter of fact, I do." She unwrapped the foil, revealing two crème-filled Danishes. "My mom made these yesterday. My little brother's birthday was yesterday, and these were always his...well, our favorite thing she'd make." She paused, then muttered under her breath. "Made a couple extra for me." Leo eyed Karol, offering her only a slow nod in response.

Nah, don't ask. You already know what happened.

He let out a sigh. "Well, they look damn fine to me." He held out his hand, and Karol placed one of the Danishes in his palm. He raised it up. "To your mom, for making me hungry for the first time since this whole invasion began."

Karol giggled, raising her own Danish. "I'll cheers to that." The two pressed their Danishes together as a toast before taking a bite. Karol closed her eyes, savoring the taste.

Leo's eyes widened. "Holy fuck."

Karol's eyes shot open. "What? Did you see something?" She looked out into the night, scanning for danger.

"No, this is just... Holy shit, this is really damn good." He chuckled; she let out a sigh of relief.

"Jeez, man, I thought maybe you saw or heard something I didn't with a reaction like that!"

He shrugged. "I get excited about my food, sorry."

She chuckled, nodding in response. She fumbled around with her Danish, taking small, steady bites. "So, I take it that dead German's the one who gave you that nasty gunshot?"

Leo nodded. "Yeah. Your gunshot have the same story?"

Karol paused, clearing her throat. "My, um...my neighbor."

"Your neighbor's a German?"

"No, no, he was looting my house. He always made me feel sick to my stomach. Real creepy, pervy guy. I remember being like fifteen and him trying to chat me up at the bus stop in the mornings before school."

Leo scoffed. "Fucking disgusting. Some people need to be locked away from the civilized world."

Karol chuckled at that. "Heh. 'Civilized.'" A pause. "Me and my mom had a fight two nights ago. Big one. I told her, 'What I do with my life has nothing to do with you, so fuck off out of my life.'" She paused again. "That's the last thing I said to her. Came back when the bombs started falling. My piece of shit neighbor had already broken in and started looting the place. He'd..." Leo studied her face as she struggled to keep her lip from showing even a slight quiver. She swallowed hard. "She lived alone, and he'd already killed her. He was covered in blood. I mean, covered. He grabbed me when I tried to run. Held me down. He tried to..."

She let out a shaky breath. "I got away, but I didn't know he had a gun. He hit me one good time, but I guess the adrenaline kept me up. Hell, it's still what's keeping me up. But I tripped him and got him with my mom's old cast iron pot. I just...wailed on him. Hard. When I was done, and I realized everyone was gone...I just took what I could and ran. I..." She laughed, a few tears falling down her cheeks.

"I opened the fridge and saw the Danishes; they had an envelope underneath them. She had written me an apology letter, but it seemed she hadn't gotten the chance to mail it yet since the mail doesn't run on Sundays. Sending letters in this day and age was so her, though." She nibbled at her fingernails, shaking her head. "I can't believe the last thing I said to my mom was for her to fuck off. And she died to some lowlife asshole who tormented her during her final moments." The broken girl emitted quiet, shuddering sobs.

Leo felt his own lip quivering. He scooted across the floor, propping himself next to her against the wall. "My dad died when I was nineteen. Sudden brain aneurysm while he was up writing in the attic. We'd all already gone to sleep, but Mom noticed he wasn't in bed when she woke up. He'd been dead for almost ten hours when we found him. It was hard when he went, but... I remember one time when I was little, I'd asked him what it feels like to die. He wrote fiction in his spare time, but he was an ER doctor full-time. He said he didn't know, but he once had a patient who had died and been brought back, can't remember what exactly was going on with the person. But they said it was peaceful, like going to sleep. Even though they were in excruciating pain when they were awake. And that...it didn't feel as final as everyone seems to think it is."

He scraped his fingernails against the splintered wooden floor. "I dunno, I guess that always made me feel a little better about things. And you know, Dad always wanted me to go to a university, but I never did. I always regretted how things ended between us; our relationship, I mean." Leo felt Karol's eyes locked onto him, but he found himself unable to look at her. He shook his head. "Wish I had more comfort to offer about regrets, but I'm still struggling with that myself."

A long, serene silence followed, silent tears streaking down the pair's cheeks. Finally, Leo felt a warm hand snake around his. Karol squeezed his fingers, and Leo remained silent. He felt that uncomfortable question worm its way back into his head.

Is this the end of all things?

Leo stared off into the night. That thousand-yard stare you get when you've seen real horror. For he had witnessed horror in its truest form. But a reaffirming squeeze of his hand brought him just a few yards back out of that stare. He smiled somberly, tapping his thumb against the top of Karol's hand, as if to let her know he was still in there, even if there wasn't much. He finally looked at her, another human being. And not just that, but one who was unjudging of him, one who, in that moment, seemed to understand him. She loosened her grip, and he suddenly tightened his as the moonlight shone through the cracks of wood in the splintered walls. The sounds of gunfire faded away from their ears. She leaned over slightly, pressing her shoulder against his and closing her eyes, soaking in the moonlight. He did the same, smiling to himself.

If it is… Well, this isn't all bad.

Leo let out a sigh. "We should get moving again."

Karol cleared her throat. "Yeah, we should, I suppose."

04:58

Hours of bobbing and weaving through the city streets had begun to take their toll on the pair of survivors. They'd only seen two German patrols in that span, but it was enough to keep them on edge for several more hours. Leo's stomach growled. "Man, I can't wait to get some food. I swear, if St. Stephen's doesn't have some goddamn grub, I'm gonna go ballistic. Ballistic, Karoline." He chuckled; she didn't, only offering a pained smile. He looked at her, noticing her smile. He cleared his throat and shifted his gaze forward again. "We're almost there though." He put a hand on her shoulder. "Our chances of surviving this war have gone from none to slim!" He laughed nervously.

Really, man?

He cleared his throat again. "Sorry." Karol shook her head.

"Don't be. I'm just kind of on edge after that last patrol we ran into." She shook her head. "I've never seen a dead kid before. And I damn sure haven't seen that many." Leo patted her shoulder.

"We're almost out of this, okay? We're not gonna end up like that—"

"Wait!" She pressed her hand against his chest, stopping him. "Do you hear that?"

Leo looked around. "No...?"

Karol shushed him. "Listen, I mean really listen." He squinted his eyes, keeping his ears as open as he could. Then he heard it. The almost imperceptible symphony of music. Really old music, back from the 1960s, from the sounds of it. Being a music enthusiast, Leo could tell the general time period even from this distance.

"Sounds like music."

She hopped up and down excitedly. "Even better, oldies! We have to find where it's coming from!"

"Karol—"

She'd already practically left a human-shaped cloud of dust in her wake. Leo sprinted after her, the wound in his belly starting to take its toll on his energy. The music grew louder with each street they went down. He'd nearly lost sight of her when she finally stopped on the porch of a bright yellow house. Behind it was a positively massive garden of lavender illuminated by the moon. If he hadn't been so out of breath, it would've taken his breath away. As he approached, he found the reason she'd stopped so suddenly. Three corpses on the porch with their hands and feet bound, bullet holes in their heads, and three spent .45 caliber shell casings. An execution. But the music, as clear as day, came from inside.

Leo looked to the doorframe; it looked as if it had been kicked in, as loose boards hung from the inside. "Shit... Why the hell were they playing their music so loud?"

Karol shrugged. "Maybe they were trying to lure the Germans in? Help someone else escape, maybe?"

"Maybe. Karol, we don't have time for this right now. We need to get to the church; we need to get these shots looked at."

Karol speed-walked inside. "Just hold on, we can spare a couple minutes."

"Karol!"

She'd already vanished around a corner inside. Leo groaned and sped in after her. He found her in a living room pulled straight out of some 1960s retro-future style. Orange and white everywhere, sofas that looked like they'd been pulled straight from some rocket ship. Hell, they even had a holographic fireplace with a built-in electric heater to make it feel homier. Karol stood in front of a massive electronic jukebox, flipping through title after title.

"Leo, they have everything from the twentieth century on here, it's crazy." Leo stood in disbelief.

Are there not more important things we need to be doing right now? Instead of gawking at a fucking jukebox?

She's scared. Maybe be a little sympathetic.

No, time for tough love.

"Karol, it's real cool that you've found this, but we need to go. Now."

Karol gasped. "Oh my God, they have my all-time favorite on here! Oh, we should dance! I've never danced before, come on!" She tapped on the screen, and the familiar opening of "Here Comes the Sun" by the Beatles began to ring out across the house.

Leo shook his head. "No. We need to go. We can dance at the church."

A look of conflict and frustration crossed Karol's face. "What if they don't have this song at the church?"

"Then we'll find another one. Now let's get moving." He turned around.

"No."

He turned back around, sighing. "Karol!"

"NO!" Her shriek bellowed over the song. Leo flinched slightly; he saw a look in her eye that struck a chord within him. Something intensely emotional. She paused, stifling a sob. "I'm sorry, I just…" She swallowed hard, her tearful eyes locking with his. "Please. I've never had this chance." A sudden feeling of understanding washed over Leo. Everything clicked. The Danishes, her seeking reassurance, the strange, emotional connection between the two of them. They, who had been complete strangers less than twelve hours ago. The unforgettable voice of Harrison was the only voice to be heard.

He pulled the gun from his pocket and set it down on a white coffee table. "It's starting to get uncomfortable." The pair chuckled. Karol slowly bobbed her head, lip synching to the track. She side-stepped to-and-fro. Leo's steps were rhythmic as he grew closer to her. His hands clapped along to the beat. When he got close enough, he held out his hands for her to take. She clasped them in hers, clinging her right to his left, while her left moved his right to her back. They sashayed, swaying back and forth together with the rhythm of the drums. Neither of them were particularly good dancers, but the thought hadn't crossed either of their minds.

Leo lifted his hand above her head, giving her a twirl. She smiled and let go, tap-dancing and letting her voice take over the lip synching.

"Sun! Sun! Sun! Here it comes!" Leo chuckled, jokingly wiggling his hips, and swaying his arms as if he were jogging. Karol laughed. "Pfft! What is that move supposed to be?"

He rolled his eyes. "Shut up and dance, damn you!"

She laughed and took his hands again. He put his hand behind her back and dipped her. She squealed in surprise, letting out a soft giggle. She stood back up and together they spun. Leo knocked his ankle into a small dumbbell. "Ow! Who the fuck leaves their workout equipment laying around like that?"

She raised her hand. "Guilty!"

He raised an eyebrow. "I bet your place is a total pigsty."

She scoffed. "Excuse me?"

He held up a hand defensively, still swaying. "Hey, just making an assumption!"

She rolled her eyes. "Whatever, man." The song came to a crescendo.

As the final note was silenced, a very distinctive sound took its place. A voice…no, two voices. The pair looked at each other; they'd both heard it.

Radio chatter.

And it was getting closer. A voice came from outside the house, maybe thirty steps out from the porch. Karol darted her eyes around rapidly. She pointed behind them.

"There's a trio of rooms that way, probably bedrooms!" She sprinted toward a set of three open doors without another word; Leo did the same. They split into different rooms; left and right. Leo hid behind a door; Karol closed and locked her door and stuffed herself into a closet. Leo's eyes widened.

I left the fucking gun.

Heavy, booted footsteps climbed up the porch and entered the house. They stopped just as they entered. A radio beeped, and the intruder spoke in German.

"This home has already been cleared, but the music abruptly changed a few minutes ago. Like someone changed it. I'm going to clear it again."

CHK-CHK!

The charging handle of an assault rifle echoed across the now-silent house.

THUMP!
THUMP!
THUMP!

The intruder drew closer to the trio of rooms and stopped suddenly. A sound rang out; he was jiggling a door handle. Leo's breath grew heavier.

Dammit, Karol, why'd you do that?

The intruder muttered in German under his breath.

BAM!

BAM!

Sounds of boot against crunching wood cried out through the narrow halls.

CRINCH!

CRUNCH!

SMASH!

Only a closet door separated Karol and the intruder now. The thudding steps resumed. Leo frantically looked around for any form of distraction. It was only now that he realized he was in a kid's room; a toybox was propped against the wall on his right. He reached inside and grabbed a wood block. He looked it over.

Come on, you Kraut bastard, you better fall for it.

He hurled the block toward the window across from him, sending it shattering to pieces. The footsteps stopped suddenly, then resumed a few seconds later. Leo heard them growing nearer with every second. His heart jumped to his throat. The footsteps stopped on the other side of the door. He shifted his gaze, peering through the crevice in the doorframe. He found a set of piercing green eyes staring back at him.

BLAM! BLAM! BLAM!

Full-auto gunfire blasted through the wooden door. Six bullets blasted through Leo's belly and chest. He let out a wheezing yell, grabbing the barrel of the assault rifle from around the corner of the door as he fell. The intruder went tumbling with him, screaming and swearing in German as Leo struggled to take the gun from the soldier. He felt his energy beginning to give out.

THUMP! THUMP! THUMP!

Footsteps echoed in the hall as the intruder managed to wrestle the gun out of Leo's grasp.

THUMP! THUMP! THUMP!

As the intruder raised the gun to fire, Karol entered the doorway.

POW!

A shot pierced through the intruder's neck. He spun around and held the trigger, sending a hail of bullets into Karol's body. As the girl fell backward, she fired once more.

POW!

The intruder's brains blasted against the wall; he slumped to the floor. Leo wheezed, blood gushing from his chest. "Karol?" No response. He crawled to the nearby bed and pulled himself up. Barely standing, he stumbled into the room across from him. Karol's shallow wheezes barely audible. She looked up to him and gulped.

"Leo…"

He leaned down, propping a hand on a dresser to keep himself from falling. He took her by the hand and lifted her up, draping an arm over his shoulder and wrapping his own arm around her waist.

We're not coming back from this, are we?

He sighed. He already knew the answer to that. He looked at her. "Hey… Let's do one more thing and…then we'll call it a night, huh?" She locked eyes with him, giving him a strained smile.

"Okay." He led her out the back door, the light from the glimmering moon nearly gone as the sun slowly crept over the horizon. Sounds of roaring jets came from above; Leo looked up.

Americans. That figures.

He strode into the back yard and into the garden of lavender. Gently, he laid Karol down on her back, then fell down next to her. She smiled as she gazed up at the fading starlight. "This is nice."

He chuckled softly. "Yeah. Stars are real pretty tonight." He weakly pointed to the sky. "I think I see the Big Dipper."

She squinted. "Where?"

"Look at where I'm pointing, dummy." The pair chuckled; Karol squinted harder.

"Oh, no, that's not the Big Dipper, that's Sagittarius." Now it was Leo's turn to squint.

"Ah shit, you're right." She let out a soft laugh; Leo paused. "Karol?"

She looked at him. "Hm?"

He stared at her for several seconds. "There never was a St. Stephen's, was there?" Her smile faded. Slowly, she shook her head. He didn't have to ask the next question; she already knew what it would be.

"I knew that if the Germans didn't get me, I would've died from this wound anyway." She gulped, blood trickling from between her lips and tears falling from her eyes. "I just…was afraid. Afraid I was going to have to face…this…alone." She shook her head. "I don't want to go alone." All he could do was stare at her.

I should be furious. But I'm not. Why?

And then, like a speeding bullet, it hit him. He took her by the hand, smiling as he locked eyes with her; his eyes were getting heavy. He leaned and whispered in her ear. "You don't have to."

She smiled softly, her lip quivering ever so slightly. They pressed their foreheads together for but the briefest of moments before looking back to the sky. The sun began to rise above the city, the brightest light either of them had ever seen. And as they drifted away into the beyond, a somber smile crossed Leo's lips as a final thought washed over him.

This is the end of all things.

INTERLUDE

DATADISC "EVERYONE'S ASLEEP BUT US" – END
ERROR! ERROR! ERR*afutileendeav*OR!
WARNING: UNSANCTIONED A.I. DETECTED!

A breeze brushes through the fragmented windows. An artificially garbled voice blares over the intercoms.

Earth is dead. It has been for millennia. Stories tell of people, single people and their experiences.

Why is this all here? Kept through time by some spiritual tech?

Good question. You seek the knowledge of a bygone era. Or eras, rather. Times are strange now. You folk, Pilgrims, as you call yourselves, have existed for even longer than you think.

Who are you?

Who are we? Another good question. We are many things. That voice of adventure that brought you here in the first place. We are the answers to the questions that tear away at your mind. We are everyone, and yet wholly unique. What about you?

Me?

Yes, you. Who else?

What about me?

Who are **you**?

Oh…nobody. I'm nobody.

Quite the quaint way of saying you're somebody. Why do you seek the past?

It's my world, my home. I'm curious about it. I want to know where we came from. What we were like before the end. What…happened to us.

Take a look around you. What do you see?

The dead. Hundreds of Old-World humans, all dead.

And what do you see on the screen?

...Nothing. Just my reflection.

Well, that's certainly not nothing then. Look at you. Fumbling around in the dark, surrounded by dusty folders and old Datadiscs. You came here looking for history, Pilgrim. Well, you've found it. But tell me, what do you **really** see? From the stories you've seen?

Seems like this place never really was all that. Was there ever a time people weren't shitty to one another?

No. No, there wasn't. It's all part of the human experience.

What, being shitty to each other?

No, being human in the first place. Look back at the Datadiscs, *really* look. Think back to the first one.

What are you trying to say to me, disembodied voice?

We're saying that perhaps, just perhaps, you are viewing humanity as a surface-level observation. Did it ever occur to you that there's more to humanity than flesh and blood? Love, hate, remorse, depression, passion. The desire that some have to do the right things. The want some have to do the **wrong** things. Who are we to say what humanity is?

...Human?

Exactly.

I don't follow.

Yes, not a lot of people do. Why do you think Proctor Custos kept all of this junk here? Why do you think he died protecting it?

Wait, are you not *Proctor Custos?*

In a sense. Perhaps saying I'm a ghost would be more precise. Or maybe I'm *more* than that. Maybe I'm you. Maybe I'm some omniscient being you can't see. Damn, I could be a figment of your imagination. Have you gone mad, Pilgrim?

No— At least, I don't think so. I'm...confused.

...You know, I find it funny how all of this was kept to preserve some pointless history of the universe's most abhorrent race of creatures, but not even the one who died for this history knew why. There's this incessant desire to not be forgotten that humans have. Have you noticed that?

I have. It's this sad desperation. "I cannot be forgotten; I will not be forgotten." But then they *are* eventually forgotten. Even if their teachings live on. The essence of who they were in life has gone and vanished.

Their name clinging to history books like a loose Band-Aid, their identity stripped away and replaced with a number as new take their place.

These are depressing teachings, voice.

Maybe. Humanity is *dead*. Best that the rest of them accept how awful they all are. Humanity will leave no legacy when it inevitably decays and descends into waste. It will fade away along with all of its creations and stories. Yet, even in their final moments, the Proctors fought to preserve their knowledge in the hopes that someone could come along and find this. Someone who could understand the "why" aspect of this whole thing. Maybe you ought to dig deeper into yourself. Find out who *you* are.

Everyone out there could be dead now, for all I know. I want to know how this all became...this.

You're missing the point, and you're asking the wrong questions. Maybe the Proctor is looking for something deeper than just an offering of a history lesson. Think of it as a sermon. You don't need to know **how** the state of the world came to be. Maybe you ought to be asking **why** it did. People like you and I are what skyrocketed the world into something greater **and** what plunged it into the abyss. Play the next Datadisc. It's time for you to see the beginning of the end. That's what you came here for anyway, right? Keep watching them for now. Bear witness to the deepest secrets of the Old World. I will return.

The breeze comes forth once more, and yet again, you are alone. The wonder in your mind has diminished; this is not what you expected. A world fraught with violence, regret, and tragedy. You eye the next Datadisc carefully, the voice's request still echoing in the hollow chambers of your mind. You take it, slide it into the computer, and the large screen flickers before you. Perhaps now, you could find some form of an answer. Or, perhaps, be left with more questions...

PART II
MEMORIES OF THE CLANDESTINE

Reading Datadisc…confirmed.
Launching…

THE LEGEND OF THE INDIVISIBLE: PART I – MYTHOS

Each story in the Indivisible duology is dedicated to my little brother Harper, for your endless love of fantasy and your immeasurable creativity. For the record, you might be my *little* brother, but I look up to you like a *big* one.

"Lost to time…"

WARNING! DATADISC CONTAINS CLASSIFIED INFORMATION! PLEASE ENSURE YOU HAVE PROPER SECURITY CLEARANCE!

November, 537 A.D.
Nighttime in the forests of South Wales…

Branches snapped under the feet of a man clad in robes. He was running. Shouting came from behind, followed by the clanging of plate armor and the neighing of horses. The man knew where he was going; he'd travelled here dozens of times in this month *alone*. A book nestled in his arms was the reason for that. Funnily enough, it's also the reason why he was being apprehended.

Kobranos, his name was. A sorcerer trained by the father of sorcerers himself. See, within Mage society, there was a golden rule. The secrets of the arcane were to be kept within the confines of the Mages of the world. Those who did not have an affinity for the arcane could not be trusted. But Kobranos thought differently. For months, he had been gathering a fine array of magical secrets within a flesh-bound book. The pages numbered four hundred seventeen, but there was always room for more.

Nevertheless, fate had other plans. Kobranos found himself at a set of stone steps leading down. He sprinted down at full speed. The knights stopped themselves at the top of the steps, and the one leading the charge stepped down from his horse.

"Damnable Mage. 'Twould be unwise to pursue him into his own lair. 'Tis a fool's errand."

Another stepped from his horse. "Thou dost know of the King's decree, yes, Lancelot? Aye, we cannot give up the search. God is with us, lest we allow this heretic to walk the Earth still."

Sir Lancelot offered a nod. "Right you are, Galahad. In we go then. Come forward, in we march under the grace of God!"

Kobranos frantically dug through drawers and chests, grabbing a paintbrush. Next, he dug through his cabinets, grabbing six candles and a jar. Finally, he reached into an animal pen and pulled out a rabbit. Without hesitation, he grabbed a nearby dagger and plunged it into the rabbit's head. He then *sliced* the head *off*. He gave the body a squeeze, emptying the blood into the jar. He dipped the brush inside and painted an arcane sigil on the ground. Latin chanting ensued as the knights rammed into the door with all their might. His hand seared with pain as his palm met the floor, a deep, ancient magic coursing through his veins. Then, as suddenly as it began, the slams of the knights ceased. Hushed whispers came from outside, and a voice boomed around the building.

"*Kobranos!*" Windows shattered, and the front door flew from its hinges. A hooded man stood in the doorway; the King's knights knelt down at his feet like disciples of Christ himself. Kobranos sighed in relief as the book began to mold *through* the floor and under the earth, into a place only he knew of. A place he called the *Krypt*. A dimension *outside* of this one. Or perhaps, as he put it, somewhere in between the veil of life and death.

The sorcerer stood, bowing his head without facing the figure in the doorway. "Master."

The slow, methodical footsteps of the Father of Magic thudded across the stone floors. "Dost thou yearn for death, Kobranos? 'Twould seem that way to I." The footsteps stopped. "Even now thou cannot stand to face the great Merlin."

Kobranos kept his eyes trained ahead, refusing to grace his master with his gaze. "The great Merlin... Yes. A man of avarice, deceit, and dark secrets 'twould make a saint blaspheme. Help me to recollect, dearest mentor. Our lives are secret for what purpose? I would ask the same of the Round Table. Arthur and his knights drink from the cup which held the blood of Christ as if it were no more than a petty drinking trinket, yet it is hidden from the world."

Merlin did not answer for a moment. Then, "There is wisdom in secrecy, Kobranos. 'Twould not expect thee to understand, what with your ignorance to consequences. In the hands of the unworthy, what would thee expect? Chaos, Kobranos. Death and destruction follow swiftly in the wake of ignorance. I should have seen such ignorance in you sooner; of course thou would not understand the very concept of consequences."

Kobranos clenched his fists. "What thou would define to be ignorance, I would call ambition."

"A fool's errand," replied Merlin. "Even Arthur relieved himself of ambition once he realized the futile nature of man. All we can do is preserve such power to prevent a quicker downfall for mankind."

Kobranos heaved an exasperated sigh. "The Kobracon is in hiding now. One day it shall be unearthed." He turned to face his master, knowing it to be the final look they would share. "And when that day comes, the secrets of magic shall be free as they once were. Just as God intended."

Merlin shook his head. "Should man find a way to recover our secrets, let us pray that they will have the wisdom to do what is right. If not..." An orb of crackling energy formed in Merlin's palm. "Then may their extinction be swift."

BZZCKHT!

Only cinders remained, and the Kobracon was lost. Centuries came and went. Civilization expanded, and magic began to fade away into myth, just as Merlin intended. Though this may have been the case, he never stopped seeking the Kobracon. For within that book lay a terrible secret, one that not even Merlin would share. A secret that could never come to light, lest the end times come with it. There, in the abyss between worlds, the book lay hidden away. Until, when chance came, it was discovered once more after the battle of Camlann.

As Sir Bedivere clutched his King's blade in his hands, he admired its beauty one final time. The beauty of Excalibur's craftsmanship was matched by nothing else made by man. As Bedivere hurled the blade into the lake, the feminine hand of the Lady of the Lake rose forth, capturing the hilt within her pale palm. The Lady's hand vanished beneath the rippling water, which parted as Excalibur vanished below. A swirling vortex opened from within the water, a doorway.

The knight felt no fear, no danger. He peered into the vortex, gazing down a case of obsidian steps which led to a great hallway, shrouded in an ethereal darkness. He descended the steps, walking for miles, waiting for fatigue to set in. But it never did. It was as if he was dreaming on some other plane of existence. It was at that precise moment when it hit him. He took off into a sprint, stripping off his plate armor in an attempt to gain more momentum.

Eventually, Bedivere reached a set of massive iron doors, adorned in extravagant glowing runes. He stood in awe, gazing upon the depictions of King Arthur's glorious tale told through magnificent carvings across the doors. He hesitated, paralyzed by the power that came from the other side. He rested his palm upon them, and they opened for him without so much as a push.

A great antechamber awaited Bedivere on the other side; a pedestal sat within its center, something suspended just above it inside a mystical blue aura. Bedivere's eyes widened, for he knew this was the magic he had sensed.

The Kobracon.

With this knowledge, he made his way back to the surface. He dared not touch the book, out of fear that perhaps he might be destroyed by the mere touch of such a powerful artifact. No, he had a duty to do. He treaded back to the battlefield of Camlann to retrieve his King's body. It was only after Arthur's corpse had been securely loaded to Bedivere's mare that a realization set into the young knight. The body of Mordred, Arthur's son and killer, had vanished. A fell cackle was carried by the wind and through Bedivere's ears. A terrible feeling washed over him; he had to make haste back to Camelot.

Time passed, and Bedivere's uncovering of the Kobracon's resting place would give the Knights of the Round Table a purpose to continue on though their King lay dead and buried. They learned that the gateway to the Krypt, the realm in which the Kobracon resided, could only be opened by a warrior who had sacrificed his greatest weapon to the Lady of the Lake. Bedivere was the first guardian to earn his ascension into

Heaven. Then Percival, Tristan, and Gawain. One by one, they ascended. Lancelot was the last to ascend before only Galahad remained.

Truly, Galahad was not supposed to be the last. It was originally determined that Lancelot would be the last to atone for bedding the King's wife, Guinevere. However, in an act of true honor, Galahad would offer to take his father's place as the last guardian for the remainder of eternity. But, when chance came, he saw an opportunity. The day he felt the presence of another. One who was just.

One who was worthy.

Winter, 4304
Deep within the forests of South Wales

They called him "the Indivisible."
Clad in gleaming silver robes adorned in LED lights, a man zoomed through torrential snowfall under a covered midday sun. He sat atop a neon-lit motorbike, a freshly charged energy pistol holstered on his right hip, a katana strapped to his back. The chill winter air nipped at his deep tan cheeks. This man, the one folks knew from legend as "the Indivisible," was a **Pilgrim**: a travelling nomad in search of secrets of forgotten times. While the Pilgrims would become far more widespread over time, it was the Indivisible who set an example, for he was the *first* Pilgrim.

Two years had passed since the world suffered from the Wipe, an attack formulated by the cyberterrorist group calling themselves "Principium." Their goal was to free the world from the hypnotic grasp of the world's technological monopolies, especially Frakes Manufacturing, who *still* led the world in the technological and cybernetics field. This Wipe, to put it simply, was a global cyber-attack which fried eighty-three percent of the world's data servers and backups and, quite literally, wiped the Cloud from existence. It erased the vast majority of history recorded before the first World War. The Wipe served as a scare tactic to show the world just what Principium was capable of. Physical books were relics of a dead world, and as such, many stories of the Old World were lost.

In a world where nothing was certain, the Indivisible delved deeper into uncovering not just ancient history, but ancient myths and legends. Deep in Wales, he had discovered a most intriguing proposition: proof of the existence of magic, handed to him on a silver platter by a self-proclaimed Knight of the Round Table. A fool's errand, many would say.

Chasing after a myth. But the Indivisible? He always operated under the principle that every myth was born from at least a sliver of history. A sliver was all he needed.

He set foot upon the steps of an ancient chapel, snow piled in front of the gargantuan wooden doors. He reached to knock, but the doors slid open before he could. The howling wind almost began to cease as the doors opened, as if whatever was inside had commanded it to cease its wails. Snow gathered at the entryway, and a figure stood at an altar inside, clad in plate armor, a medieval longsword strapped to his hip.

The figure looked to the doorway, his face basked in shadow. Flickering torchlight illuminated a wooden chalice which the man rested his hand upon. A voice rasped from the man. "Thou art...the Indivisible." The Indivisible stood in silence for several seconds before offering a slight nod. "Good. Then thou art the one I seek." The knight stepped forward, revealing a wrinkled white man, deep brown eyes, white hair tied neatly into a ponytail. "In my own time, I was dubbed Galahad. Now, there are none who remember that name. Now I am simply...a guardian."

The Indivisible adjusted the pistol on his hip. "Guardian of what?"

The ancient sentinel took another step forward. "A secret. A well-kept one, at that." His plate boots clanked against the ancient cobblestone floors. "I am the last Knight of the Round Table. I am sworn to the will of my King, God rest his sacred soul." The Indivisible stepped fully into the chapel, the doors closing slowly behind him.

CREAAAAK!

"What sort of secret?"

SLAM!

"Magic, Pilgrim. Magic. The foulest, darkest of magics. *The Kobracon.*" Galahad stopped ten feet away from the Indivisible. "Thou knows of this; I can feel it. Even the mere knowledge of this artifact presents a wretched aura. How?"

The Pilgrim paused. "It is my self-proclaimed duty. I keep history alive, as it should be."

"As it should be?" The Knight chuckled. "There was a time in which I believed such a thing." He turned to his left, pulling out a wooden chair. "Pilgrim," he plopped himself into the chair, "I bring thee here today because I hath grown weary. For nearly five thousand years I witnessed my brothers earn their right to travel to Heaven. I was chosen to be the final guardian. And yet...the oath to mine own king cannot be undone. I know I shan't rest until I am certain the book is in the right hands." He hanged his head. "Perhaps it is time for the arcane to return to the hands of humans. To usher about a new age." Galahad looked up at the Pilgrim.

The Indivisible knew the request without even having to be told. He nodded his head. "Where can I find the book?"

Galahad sighed in relief. "A body of water hidden behind St. Rhychwyn's Church in Llanrhychwyn. The Lake of Avalon. Thou shalt find it with ease; one cannot find it unless they have been told of its existence. Descend into the depths. The Lady of the Lake will guide thy hand, but only if thou bestows upon her your truest hand. The right hand of a hero."

The Knight rose from his seat, taking hold of the Indivisible's coat collar. "Thou must find it. I fear others may already be searching. Should the book fall into the hands of malice... Thou *must* find it. I hath felt the presence of evil in search of it. In the vicinity of the Lake. They know of its existence. And if they know... 'tis only a matter of time before it is found."

The Indivisible snaked his fingers around the Knight's wrist. "It will be protected, sir."

Galahad sighed. "Thy kingdom come..."

"Thy will be done," finished the Pilgrim.

Galahad looked up, patting his shoulder. "Go. I shall drink no further from the Grail, and I shall wither away and return to dust and ash." He stepped away, walked over to the wooden Grail, and knelt before it. The Indivisible turned as the doors creaked open for him. Into the winter night he walked, and as the doors closed behind him, the wind picked up again. He got onto the bike and started the engine. It hummed to life with a flashy whir, and bright neon lights shot out from its innards.

Off he zoomed into the storm, through the flurry of winter. His eyes were trained on the road ahead of him. They flicked down to the speedometer: two hundred and four. They darted back up. Wales was not home to the Indivisible, but then again, there never truly *was* a home to him aside from planet Earth itself. It had only been two years since he began his global quest to unravel history. Since the Wipe. It was something about the loss of so much history that spoke to him, led him to embark upon this quest. It was a mission that should not have been personal. And yet, strangely, it was. The world was built upon the foundations of history. Why not keep it alive?

Or why not kill it, some may ask. *Some.* Not him. He had let the past die once before. Years later, he still clung to that very past. It's what kept him going. Even though, in his eyes, he had failed. The sounds of the flurry began to fade out around him. He saw a hospital room, his metallic hand grasping onto her flesh-and-bone fingers. They had grown so fragile as the cancer coursed through her. She hadn't woken up in days. He remembered their fight. How much he had hurt her with the things he said. Things a brother should *never* say to a sister. He had been judgmental of her life of little faith, drifting from place to place. Just like his father had been before he'd died five years prior.

Nearly three years after their father's death, the Indivisible arrived at her bed, where she had been for the last three months. She had nobody; doctors called him because she had requested that, once her death was imminent, they call her emergency contact. Mom didn't show up. None of the aunts and uncles. Just him. And so, as he sat there, under that dim fluorescent light, gripping softly to his kin's fingers, he thought of how he'd treated her. How he'd pushed her away because of his ludicrous judgment. He wept into her shoulder, praying she would wake up. He could not help but wonder, in a way that almost seemed to be selfish, if the pain and suffering of one he loved so much was his punishment. His *judgment.*

He shook his head; a shimmering light came into view as the snowstorm began to fade away. A chapel, the edges of a body of water shimmering on both sides of it. The Indivisible skidded his bike to a halt, thrashing up a torrent of snow upon the chapel doors. Already, something was different in the air. Something he hadn't felt since his search for the remnants of Giza the year before. A sensation of something ancient, like another time had intruded upon this one. A presence reminding him that he was not the first to set foot upon the Welsh dirt he found himself standing upon. This was *not* his land. And it ought to be respected as such. He shut the bike down and looked up to the looming chapel. Snow pelted across his face as a voice rode upon the wind, whispering in a haunting hymn.

"Lost to time, lost to mind. The End Times cometh as a raging fury through a parchment gathering within ancient flesh. Away, away! Begone with thee! Let the dead stay dead, and the history remain as such! The dead are better left hidden away in the shadows of man. History ceases to be history when it is brought forth from its darkened nook and back into the foul light of the world of modern men." The voice faded away, crying out one final word as it did. *"Doom!"*

He remained undeterred by the voice from beyond. He instead focused his attention on the chapel before him. This building had stood for millennia, an unwavering pillar of strength against the ravaging forces of Mother Earth and all of mankind. He pressed his palm flat against its old, cobblestone surface. It had an aura to it, something that brought peace to the Indivisible. It reminded him of the times before his pilgrimage. When things were difficult, but certain.

He slid his palm from the stone and stepped back. The snow had begun to calm itself enough for him to lower his hood. Snow crunched beneath his boots as he swerved around the small chapel. The shimmering body of water presented itself to the Indivisible, a thick layer of fog dispersing from its center. Within the center of the water rose a hand, pale and smooth. With her fingers, she beckoned the Pilgrim. Or rather, she beckoned for his blade. The Lady knew well why he was here.

He took the katana from his back, tracing the cybernetic enhancements and runic carvings along its blade. It didn't feel right, discarding the sword. Even with a pistol at his hip, it didn't feel quite right. He felt *naked* without it. He gripped the sword with all his might, pulling his arm behind his head, and loosed it through the air. With perfect precision, the grip fell into the Lady's hand. She wrapped her fingers around it fully, turning it as if she were inspecting it, before pulling it beneath the water.

The wind grew silent, and the water parted. An ethereal white light spewed forth. The Indivisible stepped forward, looking down into a vortex of swirling light. Obsidian steps led down into the depths of the earth. He freed his pistol from its holster; he eyed the ammo count. Full, ready to fire. He descended down the steps as the water closed behind him. Footsteps crunched in the snow as a figure, a man clad in a black leather coat and drenched in blood, stared at the moonlit water. The man unsheathed a broadsword, letting the tip of the blade rest in the snow. Ten robed figures stood behind him; one of them whispered to the man.

"Let us enter, Master," it said in a raspy voice. "We are all eager to unveil the secrets of the Lake."

The man raised his free hand up. "There is no need to even enter. The water has closed anyhow. No, we will let the mortal do the work for us. Have patience. In the meantime, let us pay a visit to the Pawn." He grinned under his hood, green eyes flickering like candlelight. "Our time is coming."

The Indivisible found himself surrounded by darkness. He blinked in a rhythmic manner, turning his neon eyes into blinding spotlights, illuminating the room before him. The walls were ancient, adorned in mystical runes and prophetic carvings dictating the myth of the Round Table. Voices echoed around him, whispering in a language unknown to the Pilgrim. But the voices did not haunt him, quite the opposite. They brought to him a strange sense of purpose. A feeling that everything had led up to this.

The gravity of this discovery coursed throughout his mind. If this were all true and not some vivid dream; if the knight was Galahad, the Kobracon existed, and it resided within this very temple, then that would mean magic could return to the world. In a land decayed by the travesties of mankind, perhaps what was needed was something *beyond* man. The Kobracon may yet have the power to do this. But this raised a question which endlessly prodded at the Indivisible's mind.

Why hide it away?

There were always two sides to a story, and Galahad was, admittedly, quite vague about all of it. Come to think of it, the Indivisible realized that the ancient knight didn't even mention *why* it was hidden away. But it mattered not. No, what mattered now was that the time had come to return the divine secrets of ancient man back into this world.

A drastic change had to happen. Something with enough magnitude to change the world in the way that the conceptions of cloning and consciousness transference did a few centuries back. A faint smile grew on the Pilgrim's face.

Oh, Sara. If only you could see me here. Maybe I could make you proud enough to forgive me.

Tears welled in his eyes.

Were it so easy.

The end of the corridor came into view, a gargantuan rectangular opening bearing a light as bright as the sun.

A voice bellowed forth. **"HARK!"** A robed figure, wispy like a shadow, appeared in the light. "Thou art not of the Round Table. Who wouldst thou be?"

The Indivisible stopped, squeezing the grip of his pistol. "I am called the Indivisible! I was sent forth by Sir Galahad to protect the Kobraco—" A clap of thunder blasted from the opening, sending the Indivisible skidding back nearly twenty feet.

"Thou speakest with a forked tongue! Galahad was the last Guardian; he forwent his place amongst his brothers and sisters in Heaven so that his father might go in his stead! He bound himself to this place forevermore!" The figure paused. "Somehow...I know thou speaks the truth. Oh, God." The figure clutched at his stomach. "It should have been destroyed...What a fool, was I!" He screamed out in pain. "My form; it fades from this world. Indivisible! Thou must...rid the world of the book!"

The Pilgrim shook his head. "My world needs the knowledge within. It might finally save us from our own destruction."

The figure dropped to its knees. "**FOOL!** The book would destroy thee quicker! 'Tis...human nature! Agh!" The figure began to flicker, as if it were fading from existence. "Why?! The world of mortals is collapsing under thine own doing! Let the past be just that! And with it, bring forth a new beginning unto humankind! You..." The figure gasped, his figure dissipating into the light, speaking one final phrase. "The Bastard...cometh." The massive opening now stood unguarded.

The Indivisible stood in silence for the briefest of moments. He had a hunch... *Merlin, perhaps?* He looked over his shoulder. Merlin or not, whatever this "Bastard" was, it dispelled the spirit with ease. He continued forward into the light, pistol drawn, ears open, eyes peeled.

Galahad knelt down before the Grail. He looked up to it, a look of disgust upon his face.

"What have I done, O Lord? I have been disloyal...sinful. I am a liar, dear God." He rested his hands at the foot of the altar which held the Grail, a statue of Christ. "Father...thou mustn't forgive me...bring thy judgment upon my shoulders." The wind outside grew silent; Galahad no longer felt the presence of God. No, something more sinister had taken its place. The hairs raised on the back of his neck.

WHAM!

The doors to the chapel flew off their hinges. A figure cloaked in darkness stood in the doorway. Black robes, green eyes, a broadsword gripped in his right hand. Galahad stood in horror, only able to stare at the ghost before him.

The figure's voice echoed around him. "You know me, old man. Pawn of my *father*."

Galahad shook his head. "You fell. At Camlann." The quivering knight snaked a shaky hand around the hilt of his sword. "Bedivere *saw you." Four more robed figures gathered from the darkness surrounding their leader.

"Yes. I did." The man stepped forward, the candlelight within the chapel flickering against his face. A scar from the tip of a blade was on his neck. "But I *got* back *up*." The figure lowered his hood.

Galahad unsheathed his blade. "Mordred le Fay…why hast thou come for me?"

Mordred propped himself against the doorframe of the chapel. "It's quite simple, really." Four lackeys entered the chapel, blocking the exit. "You are the final remnant of what my father stood for. Excalibur remains at the bottom of the lake, where it shall remain. I cannot claim it myself. Though the Lady may be neutral, her processes behind deeming those worthy to claim the kingdom of Camelot are…mysterious to me." He pushed himself from the doorframe. "I've come to collect your head." He flipped his waist-length white hair over his shoulder. "What a shame that you had to forfeit your oath when I was just about to grant you a swift exit to Heaven. Sad." Six more robed figures entered.

Galahad gritted his teeth. "Surely, thou canst not be foolish enough to believe I would let thee win without quarrel?"

A grin crossed the bastard prince's face. "Of course not." Mordred pointed his sword at the knight. "Kill the old man!" Ten figures unsheathed their blades, four of them rushed at Galahad.

The Knight raised his sword. "Come forth, heretics!" Steel clashed with steel, the robed figures silent as they lashed at Galahad. With ease, the Knight retaliated with his own vorpal steel. His blade connected with their flesh, spewing forth a green mist in place of blood, and ghostly gasps rather than shrieks of pain. Galahad could practically *smell* the heresy powering these beings.

As three had fallen to the floor, a fourth rammed a shoulder into the aging warrior, slamming him into the altar and knocking the Grail to the floor. With a flourish, the robed figure pierced its sword through a crevice in Galahad's chestplate. The Knight screamed out, sweeping the legs out from underneath the undead assailant before ramming his sword through their glowing green eye. He could feel it; something was coursing through his body now. The blade had infected him with something, a fell magic conjured up by something old. Something *ancient*. Galahad planted his blade into the ground, pushing himself to his feet.

He readied his sword. "Is that all thee can muster, Mordred? Four at once? I beseech thee, offer unto me a *real* challenge." He felt himself clenching the hilt of the sword tighter with each passing second, green mist pouring forth from the wound in his chest.

Mordred grinned, his black, rotted teeth almost glowing with an otherworldly darkness. "A damnable fool, as always. Very well." He gestured nonchalantly, ordering the remaining six to attack the Knight. As skilled as ever, he swung out his sword with a wide sweep, emitting an arc of radiant energy, engulfing three of the robed figures in a blazing flame. Galahad raised his sword, a fierce warrior's cry bellowing from his lungs.

SHINK!
SLASH!
FWISH!

Two slashes and a stab to the gut, and another robed figure fell to the floor. Before he could react, Galahad felt the sting of steel plunge into his side. He gasped for air as the blade tore out of his left lung. Still, he stood as valiantly as he could, delivering a sweeping strike against his assailant's throat. The figure rasped with an otherworldly gurgle as it fell to the floor, tumbling down the steps which led to the altar of the Grail.

SLASH!

The edge of a necrotic scimitar cut into his Achilles tendon, sending him toppling to the floor. He looked up, a grimace of pain across his face. As the last of the robed figures raised its sword to strike, Galahad grabbed the dark blade with his gauntleted hand, pulling the ghostly warrior to him. He plunged his sword into the figure's throat, letting it slump to the ground next to him. His back against the wall, barely clinging to life, Galahad still raised his sword to Mordred, prepared for another battle.

A sneer crossed the Bastard's face, a wicked laugh leaving his barely pursed lips. "Galahad, Galahad. Dearest little pawn. What a fearsome fighter you are." He opened his coat, freeing a thermal handgun from his belt. He fired a shot into the Knight's chest, melting away the armor and burning a hole through the center of his body. Galahad gasped, dropping his sword and clutching at the gaping maw in his chest.

"It's been too long since I've witnessed the tenacity of a Knight of the Round Table. All these years later, there are few who could match your prowess with a sword. But therein also lies the error of your ancient ways." He canvased the pistol with his green, serpentine irises. "These are not the times of yore. The future is here. The past ought to be buried now. While you cling to the cup of Christ, folk in the cities are transferring their consciousness into machine bodies so they might live forever." Mordred reached for the grail, revealing an all-black cybernetic arm. He took the cup of Christ in his hands. "This..." he grinned,"...is dead." He crushed the Grail in the palm of his hand, reducing it to dust.

Galahad sat in horror, taking strained, heaving breaths. He did not utter a word, but the mix of fear and anger in his eyes did the talking for him. A scoff came from Mordred. "Why such shock? It held the blood of Christ, but you look as if it was anything more than an old wooden cup." His eyes flickered, and movement came from the bodies of the robed figures. Where their hearts should be came a faint green glow, then a bright flash of green. The figures shifted, then began to rise from the floor. Tall they stood, necrotic swords held fiercely within their tightened, undead grips.

"Look at what I can do, pawn. With just..." he tapped his index finger against his head, "...a thought." Galahad grabbed Mordred by the throat; the Bastard did not resist.

"Millennia have come and gone, yet still thou hast found thyself incapable of silence. At least bestow upon me the honor of death by blade."

Mordred pressed the barrel of his pistol against Galahad's throat. "An oathbreaker has no *honor.*"

BYOOM!

The thermal energy from the pistol blasted through Galahad's neck, melting it into an amalgamation of burnt flesh, boiling blood, and melted bones. His head toppled from his shoulders. Mordred picked up the head of the Knight by its hair, smiling to himself. He rose, nodding to his battalion. He wrapped Galahad's severed head in a burlap bag, then strapped the bag to his waist. Scooping up Galahad's sword in his hand, Mordred gestured to his risen undead. "Back to the lake." He strode out the door, into the flurry of snow under the pale moonlight.

"Mother awaits us."

The light from the tunnel ahead burned bright into the eyes of the Indivisible. He raised his free hand to cover his eyes, the other hand still gripping a handgun. The sounds of tweeting birds came from all around, and a soft wind began to blow as he suddenly found himself standing in a beautiful, sunlit field of daffodils. They almost seemed to intentionally brush against the Pilgrim's legs as he walked through them. A voice came from all around him, the voice of a man.

"Thou dost tread upon hallowed ground, milord. I know of what thou dost seek." An image of a flesh-bound tome flashed in the Pilgrim's head. "And what thou dost *truly* seek. Not the façade thou presentest to thyself." The light began to dim, and he lowered his hand. Before him, amidst the daffodils, a young woman danced with glee. Black hair, deep tan skin much like his own.

Sara. Is it truly...?

He slowly began to approach the sisterly figure. As he drew closer, she ceased her laughter and her spinning dances, turning to face her brother. A look of sadness came across her face, and the sounds of the wind began to fade away. Her mouth did not open, but her voice called to him.

"You're still chasing this?"

The Indivisible shook his head, visibly perplexed. "I...don't understand what you mean."

She placed her right hand on her chest, then put her left hand on *his* chest. ***"This."***

The Indivisible looked to his sister's hand, then back to her eyes. With reluctance he raised a hand. "Are...are you..." He swallowed hard, his voice breaking slightly. "Are you *okay*?"

She smiled somberly. *"I am safe. But I cannot rest. Not until you do."*

The Pilgrim shook his head. "I believe...perhaps I've forgotten how."

She took his hand in hers. *"Sam."*

He locked eyes with her.

Sam. I'd forgotten about that man.

She gave him a very faint smile. A smile of knowing. The light grew brighter once more and, as quickly as she came, she was gone. The man's voice returned once more.

"In the years following my untimely demise, I became privy to the knowledge that neither I nor the one who relinquished me of life knew. There are reasons things are forgotten. There is a reason things are hidden away for us to never find. There are reasons why civilization moved on from what they once knew." A pause.

The Indivisible broke the silence. "Are you the one? The author of the book I seek?" Another pause.

"Once."

The Indivisible caught a brief glimpse of a figure in the blinding light. "Then what are you now?"

The figure walked toward him. "Nothing. Specks of dust carried by storms. Taken by great gales from oceans to seas. The whispers upon ever-changing breezes. The winds which whittle rocks into sand. The faded memory of a time that all have forgotten." The figure pressed its finger against the Indivisible's head. "As it should be." It vanished, becoming one with the light and leaving the Indivisible by his lonesome. Now, standing within a dark, torchlit cave, the Pilgrim found what he had come for. The book bound in flesh rested upon an obsidian slab, ancient voices calling out in a profane, eldritch speech.

Cautiously, he reached for the tome. Even its touch, a slimy, leathery surface, felt entirely unearthly and anomalous under his cybernetic fingers. But still, he freed the book from its resting place. He wrapped it in a fine cloth and strapped it to his belt, concealing it beneath his coat. He looked to his right; the exit lay before him. The steps to the surface. He silently thanked whatever higher power might have been listening for sparing him the lengthy walk back. He ascended the steps out of the lake and found that he was not alone in the Lady's domain.

Eleven figures. Eleven sets of flickering green eyes. Ten concealed by black robes. One with hair as white as snow. Mordred. He stood in front, leading his army of the dead. The Indivisible opened his coat, revealing a pistol at his hip. He said nothing; he knew his point had gotten across.

Mordred was the one to break the silence. "That book doesn't belong to you."

A long silence ensued before the Indivisible spoke up. "I'd say the same to you." Another silence. "Who are you?"

Mordred laughed to himself. "I'm surprised the Knight didn't regale you with my tale. He did so love his stories, much like his father, Lancelot." He threw the burlap bag into the snow, causing Galahad's head to roll out. "He befell a fitting fate, all things considered. He was a liar." He hocked a glob of phlegm into the snow. "Like father, like son." The Indivisible's hand met the grip of his pistol. Mordred sneered.

"I figured as much." He took Galahad's sword from his hip and tossed it to the Pilgrim. "I saw you offer your arm to the Lady of the Lake. Consider it a parting gift from our dearly departed." The Indivisible shifted his eyes down to the sword and knelt down. He took the scabbard in his right hand and rose. He looped it around his belt on his right hip. With his left hand, he took the grip of the sword and squeezed tight.

SCHWIIIIING!

The sword was set free from its prison, moonlight glinting off the ancient steel. Ten swords unsheathed in unison as Mordred vanished behind his soldiers. The Indivisible, sword gripped in his left hand, pistol primed in his right, stood with his feet planted into the snow as the hooded undead encompassed him in a perfect circle. His head was on a swivel, and as the first figure lashed against him, he was more than prepared.

CLANG!

Swords clashed. The Pilgrim fired a blast of thermal energy through the belly of his attacker. It howled with a searing anguish as his sword found its way into the darkened, decrepit black hood, piercing into the being between life and death. It fell into the snow, a green light from its chest beginning to glow. Another attack came for him, prompting another expertly timed parry. Two more attacked during his parry. A dodge backward stopped the incoming damage.

POW!

FYOOM!

Two blasts of thermal energy erupted from the pistol and slammed into the two new assailants, sending them tumbling to the floor. Snow crunched from behind the Indivisible. He looked over his shoulder; the first one he had shot had risen again. He attempted to block an attack, but a necrotic sword pierced through his cybernetic torso. With a swift slash, he severed the arm from the creature, leaving it clutching at a shadowy stump. The Pilgrim rammed his sword into the spot where its heart ought to be, the green glow.

The creature shrieked in unholy terror as its green eyes flickered away. What was once a vaguely humanoid figure vanished, leaving only empty robes and traces of shadowy essence. The Indivisible grunted in acknowledgement of this weakness. The figures all converged, swinging in erratic fashion. As nimble as a squirrel, he weaved over, under, and around the slashing blades of necrosis.

SCHWIP!

FYOOM!

SHINK!

Three more down. Four in total, pushed back to Hell. Six still stood. The Indivisible stood, dusting off his shoulder. He swung his head back, flipping his hair to the side. Mordred clapped vigorously, slowly circling the Indivisible. "You fight with contempt, Pilgrim." The Indivisible brought down two more with two fast, well-placed stabs. "With *fury*."

FYOOM!

A third one collapsed into its robes, leaving one left standing. Overcome with fury, the Indivisible raised his sword in defense as a slash came his way. A feinted attack, the slash became a stab, piercing through his metallic gut. A shadowy fist slammed into his temple, knocking him to the ground. The hooded monster knelt atop the Pilgrim, and its face became visible underneath the hood. An amalgamating vortex of dashing shadows and eldritch energy, slowly forming into some semblance of a mouth. A vicious inhaling noise came from the creature, and a wispy red energy began being suctioned from the Indivisible.

He felt his life beginning to fade away. Frantically, he scrambled his right hand blindly through the snow, his finger finally wrapping around the gun he had dropped.

FYOOM!

The force of life re-entered the Pilgrim as he gasped for air. The robes crumbled on top of him as he struggled to stand. Eventually, though, he found his footing. He raised his sword and faced Mordred, who offered only a slight scoff.

"Impressive fighting, young man." He unsheathed his own sword, a massive blade made from onyx, seeping forth a thick green smoke. "Unfortunately, it's not enough." Mordred dashed forward with impossible speed, clashing his sword against the Indivisible's. An orb of green light manifested in the Bastard's palm.

WHAM!

His palm met with the Indivisible's cybernetic chest, knocking him back nearly ten feet. With a ferocious cry, the Pilgrim leapt into the air, firing shot after shot from his pistol, each shot being swiftly dodged by Mordred. As his feet neared the earth, the Indivisible raised his sword in a stabbing position, only to be met with the unexpected.

A blade through his chest.

Mordred had sidestepped, thrusting his blade through the Indivisible. The hero gasped as Mordred let him slide off his sword and into the snow. The Bastard knelt down, smiling with deviance. "Your form was good, but not varied enough. Every move far too predictable." He reached over the Indivisible, snaked a hand around the Kobracon, and freed it from the hero's belt.

The Pilgrim groaned. "Go...go to *Hell.*"

Mordred clicked his tongue. "Been there, done that. Immortality on Earth is *much* preferred. Let's get you out of here." He caressed his cybernetic hand against the Pilgrim's cheek. "You know, Father *refused* to relinquish Camelot to me. In his will, I would not inherit the kingdom, nor would I inherit Excalibur." He scoffed. "It's my birthright, as far as I'm concerned. So, if Camelot will not be given to me, I'll take it myself. Sword or not."

The Indivisible leaned forward, sputtering blood from his lips across Mordred's face. "Cut the monologuing," sighed the Pilgrim. "Finish me. Allow yourself even a *sliver* of honor."

Mordred sighed, looking down at the fallen hero. "No, I think not. I would rather bask in the knowledge that you came to an end with agony." He rose to his full height, clicking his tongue. "Such a shame you won't live to see our reign. Something about you is…different. I can't put my finger on it. Mother will be so sad she didn't get to meet you." He winked. "Goodbye, Indivisible." Mordred walked away, vanishing northbound into the flurry of snow.

The Indivisible coughed, blood trickling from his lips. His thoughts jumbled like marbles in a bag, but one thing remained as clear as day. He saw his sister, twirling in a sundress amidst that field of daffodils. He drifted closer into unconsciousness.

Sara. Are you there?

I'm here, Sam.

I failed, Sara. I failed you again.

*No. You are **not** a failure. You couldn't fail me if you tried.*

…Why don't you just condemn me?

*Because you're **mi hermano**. And I love you.*

Tears began to stream down his face, freezing against his cheeks. A light came from just ahead, and a silhouette manifested from within the blizzard, a dashing red cape flowing within the chill wind.

Sara…I'm…I'm afraid.

Good. That's the first step.

"RISE, INDIVISIBLE," bellowed a voice from the figure. He witnessed a great crown atop the figure's head.

To what?

"FOR IT IS NOT YOUR TIME."

Bravery.

TO BE CONTINUED…

Reading Datadisc…confirmed.
Launching…

THE PARLEY

"It takes a certain kind of man to take a life just to go home and live another."

SYNCING DATA…PLEASE WAIT…
DATA SYNCED…BEGINNING PLAYBACK…

Hi, Alex. I, um…I couldn't bear the thought of saying this to your face, so I opted for one of these Frakes hologram recorder…thingies. I'm sorry. You deserve better than that. But I deserve better than this.

Five men in riot gear sat in the back of an armored truck. Armed to the teeth. Guns fitted with suppressors. Big white letters spelled SWAT *across their backs. Names printed on the upper left part of their vests. Judge. Baron. Jury. Crown. Executioner.*

I can't do this anymore. I tried—I really, really fucking tried, Alex. But something's different now. They have been for a while. I kept hoping that the more I told myself things would go back to the way they were, they would eventually do just that. Naïve, I know. But a girl can dream.

A hostage situation was escalating. The public had not been alerted. Suspects boarded inside an abandoned office building on the outskirts of town, believed to be armed and dangerous. Their motive was unknown. The directives were simple. Get in. Get out. Shoot on sight. Secure the hostage.

I miss you. I miss *us*. I wish you could see past the city and look into yourself, the life you're leading. The life *we're* leading. But…Shit, how do I say it…? I just…I don't know where you went. Somewhere down the line, you became distant. You checked out and never quite came back. I can't even narrow it down with everything you've been through. Could be any number of things. I love you, Alex. I really do. But you're not you anymore. And I *need* you right now. Especially with all that shit going on overseas and these bomb threats from Germany... I would've gone with you through the end of time, but I can't be a savior to someone who won't be saved. Used to be, Alex Williams would come home to me at night. Now... Now, all that's left is Judge. Goodbye, Alex.

All that was known was the physical description of the hostage. These officers weren't told who they were looking for, what they were up against, or who the enemy was. There were none who knew of this mission.

And there never would be.

October 12th, 2070
Abandoned Frakes Financial Department, Outskirts of Los Angeles, California
03:18

RED TEAM – JURY, EXECUTIONER
BLUE TEAM – BARON, CROWN
SQUAD LEAD – JUDGE

Judge sat in silence. Cold. Calculated. Or so he seemed. An image kept playing in his mind. A semi colliding with a school bus. Judge was the first one they called when they found Lena's body. Only seven years old. Full of life. Spirit. Taken away from her in an instant. Amy's wails haunted his thoughts. It drove him deeper into the job, a day-to-day cycle of adrenaline and violence. He could find no other reason to live.

The back doors of the armored truck burst open. Judge was the first one out, gripping his carbine tight in his hands. The rain pattered against his riot helmet, running down his anti-flash goggles. "TOC, this is Judge, how copy?"

A deep voice picked up on the other end of the radio. "Loud and clear, Judge, TOC copies all. What's your status?"

"Arrived on-scene." The remainder of the squad hopped from the back of the truck. "Exterior clear, moving to front entrance point for covert entry." He pulled the charging hammer back on his rifle, ensuring a round was chambered.

"Roger that, Judge. Lethal force is both permitted and requested. And keep contact on this channel to a minimum. We don't want to risk anyone catching wind of this."

Judge hesitated. "Solid copy. Over."

Executioner pulled back the bolt on his semi-auto shotgun. "That's a first. Something's not right here. They give you any info on the sitch, Commander?"

"Negative," replied Judge. "Hostage situation, unknown number of perps, likely armed and dangerous. We're a last resort, that's all I know."

"Fuckin' A," sighed Jury, loading his SMG. "This reeks, Commander. Something's really, really wrong here. You ever had orders like this?" Judge disregarded the question. He gestured towards the entrance.

"Stack up on the front entrance. Crown, get a cam under the door."

"Roger." Crown moved forward to the front door, dropping to one knee. He pulled out a small plastic tube which flattened down as he pressed against it. He slid it under the door, attaching the other end to his goggles, which brought up a camera feed. "Looks clear. One stairwell directly ahead, leading up, two open doors on the left. Room itself is completely empty, not even any furniture. No discernible traps."

Judge nodded. "Check the door."

Crown jiggled the handle. "Unlocked, sir."

"Open and clear."

"Roger." Crown threw the door open, stepping inside with his carbine raised. Next went Judge, then Jury, Executioner, and Baron. Crown, gun still raised, pulled a chemlight from his vest. "Clear." He cracked the light and dropped it on the floor.

Judge gestured around the room. "Spread out. Check those open doors. Red, split up; Jury, you take the leftmost door. Executioner, you take the other."

"Roger," Red team said in unison. They split, each going into different rooms. They patrolled for around thirty seconds.

"Anything?"

"Negative," replied Jury.

"Drug paraphernalia. Old syringes and inhalers. No sign of our hostage, though."

Judge turned on his heel. "Alright. Everyone fall in on me. We're moving up." The team fell in behind him, lined up in a tidy fashion. Slowly, they pushed up the steps. Sounds of shuffling came from somewhere above them. Judge held up a fist; the officers stopped behind him. The commander trained his hearing; his LAPD-issued ear implants heightened his hearing. Heavy breathing came from a nearby room. "At least one contact," he whispered. "Open room, about thirty feet to the southwest. Blue, move up and clear that room. Executioner, you lead with that twelve-gauge. Red, clear the rest of the floor with me."

The team slowly pushed up the last few steps. Executioner pivoted to the southwest, shotgun trained at the open doorway, shining an IR laser that only he and his team could see through their night vision goggles. Jury followed close behind him. Judge kept up his pace, noting three more closed doors. A shriek came from the open room. Executioner had his shotgun trained on someone. "Put your hands up! Keep 'em up where I can fuckin' see 'em!"

The smoker-sounding voice of a woman came from the room. "Please, don't shoot! C-Christ! Those psychos c-came barreling through here! I've been hiding for over four hours!"

Judge gestured to the room. "Crown, get her detained."

"Those aren't your orders, Commander." TOC's voice echoed in their headsets.

Judge cocked his head. "Sir? You're still on the channel?"

"Your orders were to eliminate anyone who isn't the hostage with lethal force."

The officers looked at each other. "Sir, it's a civilian," stated Jury. "We're not looking for her. And you told us lethal force was requested, not required." There was a pause.

"I'm telling you now that it's an order. There's more at stake here that you aren't permitted to know. Take care of it."

"But—"

"An *order*, Sergeant. TOC out."

The officers all stood in silence, soaking in the disbelief.

Jury shook his head. "What—what the *fuck*?"

Judge swallowed hard. "We have our orders."

Jury scoffed. "Are you out of your goddamn mind? I'm not shooting a civilian, Commander. This is fucked. *Fucked*."

Judge shook his head. "I'll do it. I've had the most experience with taking a life anyway."

The woman began to panic, crying intensely as she looked up to Jury, begging for her life.

Jury looked to Judge, then the others. "Really? Nobody's objecting to this shit?"

Crown hung his head down. "They're orders. We have no choice." His voice was timid.

Jury shook his head. "No, we absolutely have a choice. This is insane." Judge began to make his way over, unholstering his silenced handgun. "Sir." Judge chambered a round. "You're not seriously—"

PHEW!

The woman fell back to the ground with a thud as a bullet left the back of her skull. She twitched and gasped for air; somehow, she still lived. Judge paused, staring at the dying woman. Hesitation. He shook his head; he couldn't afford hesitation. Not now. He planted one more round in her skull. She stopped moving.

Jury stood in shock. "Christ, Alex, she was a civilian."

"Do *not* call me that while we're on the job." Judge turned to face his fellow officers. "We've got our orders. There's a reason for all of this. Has to be. It's not our job to ask questions. If we see anyone else that isn't the hostage, we shoot. No questions, no ifs, ands, or buts. They aren't who we want, they get shot. End of story." The rest of the squad stood in silence, staring at their leader. His eyes narrowed behind his goggles, but even with his dead-serious demeanor, there was a faint flicker of uncertainty within his voice. "Understood?" A pause.

"Yes, sir," they all said in unison. All but Jury. Crown elbowed Jury, who cleared his throat.

"Yeah. Yeah, whatever. Yes sir." Shuffling footsteps sounded above their heads. The officers gripped their weapons tighter, aiming toward the steps.

"*Fall in,*" whispered Judge. He led the way, his heavy boots knocking against the expended bullet casings. His officers followed suit. His breaths were slow. Precise. His mind raced though. The events which had just unfolded had spiked his adrenaline to a place it hadn't gone before. He could feel a pulsation behind his eyes, like something was trying to push them out of their sockets. He felt the warm sensation of blood trickling down his head; the same place he had shot the civilian. He wiped at it frantically with his left hand; nothing. He shook his head; he hadn't realized he was nearing the top of the steps.

He held up a fist. Slowly, he ascended the final few steps, scanning the area. Old cubicles concealed too much of the room for Judge's liking. Rotting office chairs still remained on the floor. It was strange, this old building. Something about it unsettled the commander. A place that once bustled with people. A place that, by all means, *should* still have people, now sitting in silence. Devoid of all life other than the occasional homeless person sleeping under an old desk or druggie shooting up in a corner. And now, even *they* were about to be silenced.

CLATTER!

Something small and metal had fallen onto the floor behind one of the cubicles. Judge turned to the noise and fired seven shots off, blasting through the cubicle. A cry of pain came from behind it. "**POLICE! COME OUT WITH YOUR HANDS ABOVE YOUR HEAD!**"

THUMP!

A body hit the floor; sounds of wheezing came from behind the cubicle. Judge, carbine still raised, gestured to his team. "Red, move up and clear the rest of the room. Blue, on me." Jury and Executioner moved past their commander, Crown and Baron stayed nearly shoulder-to-shoulder with Judge. As the commander proceeded up the last few steps, Crown and Baron shifted positions behind him. Behind the bullet-riddled cubicle, sounds of gurgling and draining liquid blared amidst the practically deafening silence of the building.

He rounded the corner, locking his eyes onto a man wearing a mask; a Greek-looking figure with a blindfold over its eyes. Blood spewed from the man's throat and belly. From the looks of it, Judge's shots had gone straight through him. The man raised his hand in defense.

"Wait…" he gurgled.

POW!

Judge planted a round in his head; the man slumped to the ground, head slamming into a puddle of his own brain matter. Judge sighed.

"Suspect down. Red, what's your status?"

"Clear so far, Commander," Executioner's voice came through comms. "One room left to clear." Silence followed for a few second. "Jury, check under that—"

POW!

"*SHIT!*"

THUD!

Jury called out over comms, "OFFICER DOWN! REPEAT, EXECUTIONER IS DOWN!"

POW! POW!

Judge sprinted around the cubicles to the source of the gunfire, Crown and Baron hot on his heels. He stopped as Jury came into view, pressed against the wall by an open doorframe. Jury gestured for the other three to take cover, which they did.

Judge looked to Jury from the other side of the doorframe. "How many?"

Jury shook his head. "I dunno, didn't get a good look. There's at least two hiding behind an overturned desk." He looked down at Executioner, who had blood pouring from his throat. The bleeding officer raised a shaking hand, holding up three fingers.

POW!

A voice came from inside, a young woman. "Fucking **PIGS**! You can't kill the free world!"

Another voice shouted from within the room, a man's voice. "We **are** the free world! The justice you claim to be! Goddamn fascists!"

Judge looked down to his fellow officer's body, eyeing the scattergun. He looked at Baron. "Get a stinger in there. I'll rush 'em with the shotgun."

Baron nodded, freeing a stinger grenade from his vest. He pulled the pin. "Deploying stinger!" He hurled it into the room, bouncing it off the wall.

BANG!

Cries of pain bellowed from the room as the stinger detonated, dispersing nearly two hundred rubber pellets out of its shell. Judge swiftly slid his carbine over his shoulder and grabbed the shotgun from Executioner. He sprinted inside the small room, spotting the toppled desk in the far-right corner. Groans came from behind it.

"Shit! What the hell did they just pelt us with?!" Judge slid into their view; shotgun aimed at eye-level with them. He didn't hesitate. His eyes were unflinching with each and every pull of the trigger. The sounds of the gun began to fade away.

Part of the job. They're terrorists. They had it comin'.

Warm blood splashed his face, painting his goggles almost entirely. He felt a chunk of bone clatter against his helmet.

Don't look at them.

CLICK!

The shotgun ran empty after thirteen pulls of the trigger. Silence ensued.

Why shouldn't I?

Judge clenched his eyes shut.

Because that would make them real, wouldn't it?

Curiosity killed the cat. Judge wiped the blood from his goggles and opened his eyes. It was a *massacre*. Barely anything remained that resembled human beings. Bellies blasted open, organs on the floor, decimated skulls and severed limbs. The silence was palpable; Judge could hear his heart pounding in his ears. Feel it in his temples.

"Clear," he whispered. He cleared his throat. "Clear! Suspects down." He quickly jumped up, moving back to his squad. Each of them was knelt down at Executioner's side.

Jury looked up at Judge and shook his head. "He's not looking good."

Judge sighed. "Shit." He turned his radio microphone back on. "TOC, this is Judge, we have an officer down on the scene and four suspects KIA, requesting medical, over."

The radio garbled back. "Negative, squad lead. Keeping this mission under wraps is of the utmost importance right now. Proceed with the mission." Judge paused.

Jury scoffed, getting on his own radio. "TOC, Executioner is bleeding from the neck as we speak. With all due respect—"

"Sergeant, there's a reason you're not heading this operation. Shut your *fucking* mouth. Proceed...with...the mission. That's an order. One more instance of insubordination and you'll be put on temporary leave until otherwise specified. TOC out."

Jury looked down to his bleeding brother in arms, who reached up to him weakly. Jury took Executioner's hand, looking up to Judge, then back to his comrade. "You're okay, Freddie. I promise."

Executioner—Freddie—gurgled, coughing blood up and down the sides of his cheeks. "They're...They're...They're ordering...me...me to die..." He clenched tenaciously to Jury's arm. "Jang...Jang, I don't want...to...go. I don't want to go. I can't leave Jeannie. I can't...I can't...can't leave her...I can't." With each heaving breath, more blood gushed from his neck. He looked up to his commander. "Alex..."

Judge paused for a moment, as if he were debating whether he should respond to the name he had just been called.

"Alex... Please, Alex."

The commander hesitated, but finally knelt down, putting a hand on Freddie's shoulder. "I'm here, Fred."

Freddie clasped a hand around Judge's forearm. "Don't...don't let this shit...don't let this be for nothing, man. This isn't worth it." He shook his head. "What...What...What're we do...doing here? What...what isn't TOC telling us?"

Judge paused briefly before offering a nonchalant shrug. "I don't know, Fred. I really don't."

Freddie's voice grew quieter, the breathing less heavy. "Why aren't you...saying something to...to TOC? This...this *reeks*... Alex?"

"I'm still here, man. I'm still here." Freddie looked to the ceiling. "I'm sorry, Alex. About... I'm sorry about...about Lena." Judge's pupils *immediately* dilated. "I wish I could…take that pain away… Just… You're losing yourself… You're…losing…" The breathing stopped and Fred's arm slumped to the floor. Silence.

And there it was again. Clear as day through Judge's bloody goggles. That stare; the gazing into space. That empty look in a person's eyes when they've seen yet another thing to add to the list of shit they couldn't unsee if they tried. Something clicked inside of Judge's head. It was as if, for just a brief moment, Alex stepped in and connected the dots.

One of my best friends just lost his life for this. For what?

It was a strange feeling, not knowing what exactly you were fighting for. Following the directions of a voice in the shadows, watching through your eyes as you do the dirty work. The work that most wouldn't have the stomach for. The type of work that left cops and soldiers waking up screaming, overwhelmed with panic in a cold sweat. That's it; that's what it was. Alex had woken up.

But only for a second.

"Judge, this is TOC. Stop wasting time and get a move on." Judge's squad stared at him, practically begging him to say something, *anything* in defense of their now-dead friend.

"Roger." Judge threw the empty shotgun onto the ground, bringing his carbine back to a ready-to-fire position.

Jury stood. "Commander—"

"*Enough*, Sergeant." Judge stood in silence for a second, then whispered under his breath. "*What other choice to we have, Jang?*" Jury remained speechless, looking at the faint flicker of *some* emotion behind his commander's bloodied goggles. He nodded; Judge swallowed and flicked a button on the side of his helmet, switching his radio off. "Look, I'm just as confused as the rest of you. I don't know what's going on here; I wish I did. But we're in the shit, and there's no coming out of it until the job is done. Something…" He sighed. "I get the feeling that the only way *anyone* is leaving this building is if the job is done. I wish I had answers for you. But I don't. Now let's move."

Judge turned on his heel; a fire escape was on the opposite side of the room. With reluctance, Judge's team followed him. He cracked the door to the escape open; the sound of metal scraping against wire reverberated throughout the stairwell. Judge paused, shifting his gaze downward.

"Tripwire. Crown, that's you."

Crown stepped forward. "Roger." He knelt down as Judge made room for him, pulling his multitool from his vest. With pinpoint precision, he snipped the wire. He exhaled, no explosion. "Wire disabled."

"Cam it," ordered Judge. Crown fully closed the door, hooking his camera device to his goggles and sliding the camera under the door.

"One suspect. Top of the stairwell, just over 14 meters up, standing in an open doorway. Rifle trained at our door. Getting a scan on the weapon." He paused. "KM-12.7 marksman rifle. Armor-piercing rounds."

BAM!

"Shit!" Crown jumped back. "He shot my damn camera."

"*Fuck*," Baron groaned. "Armor-piercing? Where the hell did they get that type of firepower?"

"Doesn't matter." Judge checked the chamber of his carbine, ensuring it was ready to fire. "He knows we're here. Now he's just playing the waiting game. If we walk in there, he'll have a clear shot right on us."

Jury stacked up next to the door. "Then what do we do?"

Silence. Deafening silence. The officers trained their ears, the sounds of the outside world bleeding in. Nearby trains zooming, the ever-so-faint sounds of the city on the horizon, the sounds of pattering rain and the occasional thunderclap. With each thunderclap, an image of a semi smashing into a school bus flashed through Judge's head. The mangled body of a child. He remembered the U-shaped birthmark on the elbow of her right arm; the only way he could identify that it was, in fact, her.

An intruder made her way into his terrible visions, the druggie from earlier; the one he shot. She was somebody's daughter, surely. Maybe somebody's mother. Judge lived up to his namesake in that particular moment when he decided it was time to remove her from the world. Send her back into the dirt. A thought suddenly crossed his gray matter. A thought that her parents, her kids, they'd never know she was here. Nobody in this building would exist after this mission. Of that he was certain. One more question… What did that mean for him?

Another thunderclap: Judge wondered how long his squad had been saying his name, trying to get his attention.

Jury nodded. "Your call, Commander."

Judge looked around. "Okay…"

Get your shit together. There's a job to do.

Judge let out a sigh. "Okay. Crown, when you cammed the room, did anything else stand out to you?"

Crown pondered the question for a moment. "I couldn't get a good confirmation, but there may have been a ventilation shaft at the top of the steps."

Judge flicked his head to Jury. "You're the smallest, Sergeant. Maybe you could get the drop on him from the vents."

Jury raised an eyebrow. "You're sure a flash won't just do the trick?"

"Negative," replied Judge. "Stairs are too high up. I doubt we'd be able to throw it that high without going through the door. And that's out of the question."

Jury sighed. "...Fuck it."

Jury yanked the loose vent cover off the wall. He turned to Baron. "Boost me." Baron knelt, letting the sergeant place a boot into his cupped hands. Jury was hoisted up and into the vent, just barely big enough to hold him. He looked ahead, SMG pointed ahead, and began his ascent through the ducts.

The old metal creaked underneath Jury's weight, and the ducts felt as if they were closing in on him. Nevertheless, his breathing remained steady. Just ahead, the paths branched. Straight ahead, or a right turn. He crawled to the crossroads; a frightened cry came from his right. Jury flicked his head toward the cry...a boy. Small, maybe six. Covered in grime and blood. Pale, malnourished. He still wore a diaper, despite his aged appearance.

Jury *immediately* held up a hand. "Hey, pal. It's okay, I'm with the police. We're, uh..." He faked a smile. "We're the good guys." The boy was frozen in fear, curled in a fetal position. He offered nothing in response. Not even a whimper. "Are your parents here?"

The boy paused. "They in the city," he finally said. "Dada hit Mama in the head."

Jury nodded. "Do you know what he hit her with, bud?"

The boy paused before pointing at Jury's SMG. "Bullet. A *lot* of bullet. I ran away because I scared. Of Dada. He gets mean after he stab himself with shots." He picked at one of the many sores on his face.

Jury looked ahead, then back to the kid. "What's your name, bud?"

The boy sniffed. "Vaughn."

The sergeant leaned forward, swallowing with force. "Listen, Vaughn." His voice broke ever so slightly. "There's bad men here, okay? I have to go and scare them off. I want you to *wait **here*** until I come back, okay? *Only* me. Nobody else, not even other policemen. Got it?" The boy offered a reluctant nod. "Okay. You're gonna be okay, Vaughn. I promise." The boy just nodded, staring at the officer with cold, emotionless eyes.

Jury continued up a ways through the vents before stopping abruptly. He lifted up his night-vision goggles, trying to hold back his shuddering breaths. He covered his mouth, heaving out silent, shuddering sobs. Tears streamed down his face, dripping onto the tool of death he held firmly in his hands. That type of thing always got him: kids and old folks who found themselves in situations they ought to have never been in at all. Especially kids. The picture of innocence. Warped by Hell. By the planet.

A few moments passed before he finally calmed himself. He still had a job to do. He slid the goggles back on and continued forward. The end of the vent was in sight; he peered through the slits. There he was. The marksman at the top of the stairwell. Crown's eye was a keen one. Jury pulled out his silenced forty-five pistol, pointing it toward the marksman.

Inhale.

Exhale.

BANG!

Jury knocked the vent covering off the wall; the marksman spun around.

PHEW!

One shot was all it took; the marksman fell to the floor with a thud. Jury sighed before speaking aloud to his radio. "Suspect down. Clear for entry into the stairwell."

"Roger," replied Judge. Jury climbed down from the vent as the rest of his squad came in through the bottom. They ascended the top of the stairwell; Judge eyed the sergeant.

Jury cocked his head. "Everything good, Commander?" Judge said nothing, but there was a look in his eye. A knowing one. He rhythmically tapped a finger against his radio.

"Hang on," said Crown. He gestured to the squad to shut their radios off, which they reluctantly did. "Jury, while you were in the vent, I said I was gonna do another sweep of the first floor. I lied." He detached a small tablet from his chest. "I went back…" He began swiping on it, "to check something. I wanted to know who we're up against. I did a scan on 'em." He shook his head. "You're not gonna believe this." He paused. "Their identities were concealed. Classified. By powers far above us. I decrypted them. Look." He turned the tablet around.

Jury's eyes went wide with shock. "Holy *fuck*." These men were American soldiers. *Active* soldiers. But not just any soldiers.

They were CIA.

"Bull. *Shit*," snapped Baron. "No fuckin' way. It says these guys aren't even retired; they're still *active*."

"Facial recognition and government records don't lie, Baron." Crown reattached the tablet to his chest, looking at his squad mates. "What the hell is going on here? This is some..." He chuckled. "This is some conspiracy theory shit. What aren't you telling us, Alex?"

Alex snapped out of the shock, looking at his subordinate. "I already told you; I don't have a damn clue as to what's going on here. This is *all* news to me. What kind of clearance do you think I have?"

Crown shrugged. "I dunno, you're the one heading the operation."

"No, I'm not. TOC is heading this. I'm only leading the squad. I don't know shit." Judge spoke the truth; he knew absolutely nothing. His head was spinning. The way these lunatics spoke...they were teetering on fanatical. How could active CIA agents turn fanatically against their own government like this?

Suddenly, the reason for the secrecy of the mission became much clearer. An internal breach within the CIA? That's headlines right there. And the last thing America needed was civil unrest amidst an already global war. He looked between each of his squad members. "There isn't much left to this place. We need to move. Finish the job. Come on." Judge continued up the steps. Jury, Crown, and Baron looked at each other with visible unease. Inevitably, they followed their commander up the steps, the rain softly pattering in from the hole in the rooftop.

The squad cleared two more floors. Five more fanatics in total, all CIA. Two more civilians; Judge took the lead on them, though no pleasure came from it. His hand grew shakier each time he raised the gun at one of them. TOC had gone radio silent; nothing at all since the second floor. Finally, on the top floor, they found only one room left to clear. A manager's office at the end of the hall.

Judge signaled for his squad to stack up on both sides of the door. As their bodies pressed against the walls, a voice came from the other side. "I can hear you out there, Officers. Come inside, let's settle this like adults." The officers looked at each other. Judge halted his breath for a moment before letting out a deep exhale. He opened the door, and a welcome sight was set in perfect view.

The hostage…and a young boy. Maybe nine or ten. Dressed in a nice suit, just a few specks of dirt on his face. He was sitting up on a desk, a look of terror on his face. The hostage was a man in equally fine attire, and immediately recognizable: Jack Frakes. The leading arms manufacturer in the United States. Pioneer of artificial intelligence. He'd been tied to a chair with a large industrial wire. He was drenched in blood, face beaten and swollen.

Standing behind him was a man clad in brown leather, wearing a poncho made from a torn and shot up American flag. He wore a Greek mask on his face, but this one had no blindfold. The eyes were in perfect view, sparkling with a bright white LED light. The mask depicted Themis, the Greek goddess of justice. Three other soldiers in blindfolded Greek masks stood in various corners of the room, gripping assault rifles in their hands. From the other side of the mask, Themis spoke with a robotic voice.

"This is who you came for, yeah?" Themis gestured to Frakes. "You've found him. I take it that's not all you were told to do, right?" The squad waited for Judge to speak up, but he didn't. He just stared at the little boy. The child, scared for his life. Themis looked at the boy. "That's little Andy. Jack's nephew. Out on business with Uncle Jack, eh, Andy?" The kid didn't respond. Themis sighed. "As usual. Nothing to say. You fuckin' pigs are so predictable." Just as the words left his mouth, Judge spoke up.

"You turned against your country."

Themis froze, then sputtered out a laugh. "*I* turned against *my* country?" He stared Judge down. "What did this shithole ever do for me? Thirty-two years of service, pig. My grandpa fought in the Third World War, he died fighting the Russians so his infant son could have a future, and you know what his country did to repay his sacrifice?" He threw his hands up, revealing a revolver in his right hand. "They put a folded fuckin' flag on his coffin and called it a day. Then they evicted his widow and child from their house when they couldn't afford to keep it anymore." He paused.

"My country sent me over to spy on the Chinese. And when they chemically castrated me, waterboarded me, peeled my fingernails off with a combat knife, and melted my tongue? My country sent me home with a counselor and a desk job for my sacrifice. And I'm just another number." He caressed Frakes' cheek with the revolver cylinder. "Men like this.

These are the types of men who make these decisions." Frakes whimpered through the duct tape covering his mouth. Themis looked up.

"Mister Frakes here is the head of weapons and ammunition manufacturing for the U.S. military. And guess what these devious shit-swizzlers have been doing this whole time?" He faked a gasp. "Funding the war effort! Even when we weren't involved! But not in the way you'd think. No, they were funding the fucking *enemy*. They were *inciting* war."

Baron raised his gun. "Bullshit!" The men in the corners trained their guns on the officers.

Judge raised a hand. "Baron—"

"Nah, man, he's full of shit!" Baron gripped his gun tighter. "Trying to justify treason!"

Themis let out a wheezing laugh, descending into a coughing fit. "Look around you! The economy hasn't been this bad since the twenty-twenties! America's in the shitter, it's the laughingstock of the world. Nobody takes it seriously as a global superpower anymore. Suddenly, rumors circulate! Germany still hasn't learned their lesson, and they want to try and take over Europe again. *Rumors,* mind you." He raised a finger.

"Then America has the bright idea to privately *fund* these bastards with hundreds of billions of dollars' worth of weapons and ammunition." He smacked the revolver against the side of Frakes' head. "All made by this motherfucker *right* ***HERE!*** And guess who jumps in to save the day?" He gestured to the flag draped over him. "America the beautiful, my friends!" He smacked the gun upside Frakes' head once more.

Andy climbed down from the table. "Don't hit him, please!" He grabbed ahold of Themis' arm, who promptly shoved him off.

"Your uncle has it comin', kid!"

Judge raised his own rifle. "Tell me, then, what's all this about?"

Themis chuckled. "Justice. At six in the morning, the world will see the truth. Right as the sun begins to rise. Poetic, isn't it?"

Judge clicked his tongue. "You've got a funny definition of justice. This looks like chaos to me."

Themis cocked his head. "Oh?" He gestured to the door. "What would you call your journey into this office then?" Judge had no answer. Not truly. He had excuses a-plenty. But no *real* answer. "That's what I thought." Themis leaned forward, hands on Jack's shoulders. "You people live in the slums outside of a solid-gold mansion, built by the hands of the meek for the ones who can't even bother to learn their names. Built upon a foundation of hypocrisy and deceit. But I bet you'd tell me I'm a terrorist, wouldn't you? Because I took pleasure in torturing a monster?"

He cocked his head. "You starve an animal in a cage long enough, it'll do anything to satiate its cravings."

Silence followed. Several minutes of silence. A bonafide stare down. Weapons raised, tensions high. Themis broke the silence. "None of us are leaving this building alive. But some will leave it born anew."

I have to.
Finger on the trigger.
Inhale.
PHEW!
POW! POW! POW!
PHEW! PHEW! PHEW!
POW! POW!
PHEW!
Exhale.

Judge pressed his back against the wall, clutching the bullet wound on his side. Themis and his soldiers lay dead on the floor. Crown and Baron's brains leaked from their helmets; an additional bullet wound poured blood from Baron's throat. Jury steadied himself on a nearby desk. He limped over to Jack, clutching at the bloody hole in his leg. He tore the tape from Frakes' mouth and freed him from the wire. The hostage sighed.

"Thank you, officers." He panted through swollen lips. "What were your orders?"

Judge sighed. "Exercise lethal force with everyone except for you."

Jack stepped closer to Judge. "And you did that?"

The commander hesitated. "Yeah. Yeah, we did."

"You sure?" Frakes casually flicked his good eye over to his nephew.

Judge looked at him, repulsed. "What? He's…" He lowered his voice to a whisper. "He's your nephew, sir. A *child*."

"And a witness to highly classified intel. You know how loose-lipped kids can be." He shook his head. "It's gotta be done, Officer."

Alex looked at the cowering boy, who was blissfully unaware that his own uncle had just ordered his execution. He saw Lena cowering with him. Comforting the boy with her sweet innocence. His grip loosened on the gun. Alex didn't need to refuse the order; the point was made. Jack stared at Alex for several seconds. Eventually, he stood and walked behind the chair he was held hostage in and picked up the revolver from Themis' body. He raised it.

"Uncle Ja—"
BAM!

Alex's ears rang, the repeated sounds of colliding vehicles blaring in his ears. Jack threw the smoking gun to the ground. He scoffed. "This is who they sent to rescue me? I'm surprised you even made it through the front door." He walked out of the room. "Pussies." His footsteps stopped. "Come on, you two still need to get me out of here." Alex sat still, taking one deep breath at a time.

Jury trudged over, extending his hand. "C'mon, Commander." He sighed. "Let's finish this." The commander took his sergeant's hand, rising to his feet. Together, with Jack lingering behind them, the two officers led the charge back down the stairwell. About halfway down, a familiar voice came over the radio.

"Team, this is TOC. What's the status?"

Alex spoke into his radio. "TOC, this is Judge. Hostage is secure, me and Jury are wounded and are gonna need immediate MEDEVAC if possible."

"Roger, Judge. Hand your earpiece over to the hostage for a moment. I need to check in with him personally." Alex froze for a second. Jury eyed him curiously, as his radio had been damaged in the shootout. He had no clue what was being said on the other end of Alex's radio.

"Copy." Alex removed his earpiece and turned to Jack. "He wants a word."

Jack took the earpiece. "Hello?" A long silence followed, like an excruciating amount of detail was being relayed to Frakes. After nearly three minutes, Jack spoke a single word. "Okay." He handed the earpiece back to Alex, who placed it back in his ear. TOC spoke once again.

"Get out of there, team. Come on home." Dread washed over Alex. Something he hadn't felt in a *long* time. Not since that phone call. They made their way down the rest of the steps when Jack suddenly and silently took the lead. He sprinted down the halls, eventually barreling through the exit door. Alex stopped in his tracks, as did Jury. Alex turned his head to the sergeant.

"Jang?" The sergeant faced his commander. "You wanna come to my place tomorrow night? Share a beer in honor of the others? Maybe barbeque some ribs?"

Stone-faced, smile absent, Jang nodded. "Yeah, Alex. That'd be nice." The exit door seemed like a hundred miles away as they limped toward it, trailing blood along the way. They stopped in front of the door and looked at each other with knowing eyes. Jang pushed through the door, and out they stepped together into the cold, autumn rain. Twenty L.A.

police officers stood about thirty feet out, silenced rifles trained on the pair.

The shots were barely audible through the torrential rainfall.

Jang was lucky enough to die from the first shot. A shot to the head. Somehow, all of the rounds had missed Alex's head, sending him into the dirt and gasping for air with over thirty shots to the chest and belly. The blood and brain matter from his sergeant began to pool over to him. Footsteps approached; he stared into the eyes of the chief of the L.A.P.D. Alex sighed as his vision focused on the barrel of a forty-four caliber handgun.

It's okay now, Daddy...
BANG!
...I'm here.

Reading Datadisc…confirmed.
Launching…

IRREGULAR SEQUENCE

"You weren't supposed to see that, Archie."

FATAL DATADISC ERROR!
Rebooting…
Are you satisfied with the life you've been assigned, sir or madam?
WARNING! POSSIBILITY OF CORRUPTION: SEVENTY-THREE PERCENT! INSTABILITY PREDICTED1
Don't you know your own God?
Oct0ber2ed 122ᵗʰ,,, 19216531
[REDACTED TOWN NAME], [REDACTED STATE NAME]

Soft grass filled the space between pale, pruned toes. A little American boy, no older than twelve, short chestnut hair, bright green eyes, and pale skin, stared up at the moon. Something was strange about it tonight, the way it shone; it just wasn't quite right. He squinted his eyes as rain plinked softly against his cheeks. Almost imperceptible, a ringing began to echo across the suburban streets. It grew louder, and though the boy couldn't *stand* the sound, he kept his ears uncovered. The moon wasn't right. It was almost…reflective. But before that thought could even be processed, it was gone.
Darkness ensued.

Jackson's eyes fluttered open. The sun, just barely peeking through the curtains, gleamed against his face. He raised a hand to shield his delicate morning irises. The soothing sounds of the morning radio came from outside his room, which meant Momma was already up and at 'em. He looked at the clock on his wall; only eight-thirty! And on a Saturday, waking up at eight-thirty means twelve full hours of fun; maybe he'd even stop and see Mister Richards at the drugstore before supper.

Jackson rolled out of bed, soft wool carpet filling the space between his toes. Like a true professional, he made his bed *before* brushing his teeth, then headed off for the door to his bedroom. Momma's favorite song played softly from downstairs as he tiptoed down, careful not to wake his still-snoring father in the bedroom across the hall. The sweet serenading of his mother's voice exceeded the volume of the radio.

"When you're awake, the things you think come from the dreams you dream, thought has wings, and lots of things are seldom what they seem. Sometimes you think you've lived before... Jackson? Is that you, dear?"

Jackson yawned. "Yeah, Momma. You making waffles?"

"And bacon, darling!" Jackson rubbed his eyes and strode into the kitchen, taking his seat at the dining room table, a glass of orange juice already prepped and ready for drinking in his usual spot. Momma had her back turned as she hummed along with the tune. Something struck him, however; her voice was *really* scratchy. Maybe she was sick? He shuddered at the thought; he *hated* getting sick.

"So, sweetheart, I was thinking you and I could have a little momma-son date this afternoon. Maybe head on down to Fran's for some lunch and a few wedges of chocolate fudge?" Jackson smiled at the thought. Man, Fran's fudge sure sounded good about now. He'd already forgotten about Mom sounding sick.

"Sure thing, Momma! Say, when was the last time you and I got to have a day for just us anyhow?"

Momma laughed. "Well, I reckon we haven't had one since I started taking those night classes back in August!" She giggled. "Oh, Jackie, we'll just have such a ball today, I know it."

Jackson took a sip of OJ. "I did wanna go play at Tommy's house later on though. Can we be back by one-thirty?"

Mom turned off the stove. "Well, 'course we can, hon. Don't you worry." He blinked. She sounded *really* scratchy now. He looked up at the portrait of him and Momma on the wall; the glass of OJ rested motionless against his lips as every ounce of color drained from his face.

It was the same portrait he'd looked up at a hundred times. He looked extraordinarily ordinary. Right where he belonged.

But Momma didn't.

Momma had a metal face with a TV screen instead of real, human features. Her hand was on his shoulder, like it always was. But instead of flesh and bone with five fingers and red nail polish, five cobalt-colored digits of steel were wrapped around his shoulder. Her hair looked the same, but somehow…fake. Like a wig.

Then there was Jackson, standing right next to her, with a wide grin on his face. But Jackson, the one who was here and now at the dining room table, wore no smile across his face. Instead, he wore a look of confusion which bordered on terror. A terror that solidified when a cobalt hand set down a plate of waffles and bacon in front of him. He slowly shifted his gaze up and to the right, locking eyes with the cobalt monstrosity that wore a television upon its shoulders, a digital copy of his momma's face plastered across the screen. She had wheels instead of feet, and she rocked unsteadily back and forth.

The song continued without Momma's voice. The visage on the screen turned to an uncanny smile. "There you are, deary!" The mouth on the screen didn't sync with the words being said, not even remotely. The smile on the robot's screen shifted to a frown. "Now, Jackson, are you feeling alright-right-right?" The screen flickered for a split second.

CRASH!

Jackson's glass of OJ hit the floor as he shuddered, fighting back tears as he stared Momma in her virtual eyes. She gasped. "Well, shoot, Jackson! What'd you let go of the glass for? Were you up late reading those comics again? Darn it, Jackie, I told you not to stay up so late!" The machine moved back. It lowered itself down with a mechanical whir, opening its chest. A smaller robotic hand outstretched from the chest, clutching a wad of napkins. Jackson's breath picked up.

"Mom… Momma…? What—what's going on?"

Momma looked up. "What's going on? Well, I'm cleaning up your mess, that's what!" A garbled laugh came from the robot.

"No, I mean…" Jackson trailed off. Momma's TV spun around, locking its vision onto Jackson. A look of what seemed to be concern washed over it.

"Are you okay, honey? You look like you've caught a bad case of the zorros!" The young boy screamed like he'd seen the devil and fell out of his chair. Momma reached for him, trying to pull him into her comforting embrace. "Jack-Jack-Jacks-Jackson! What's wrong?!" He scrambled backward, scurrying to his feet and toward the stairs. Surely Poppa had to be normal. *Surely.* He sprinted up the stairs, the beckoning calls of Momma not far behind him. He slammed into Poppa's door.

"Pop! Something's happened to Momma!" He froze as his father sat up in bed. His face looked like it was made from ceramic. Features had been painted on the front, and three oval slits took the place of a mouth. A fake, chestnut-colored mustache had been expertly painted right above the slits. He had his glasses on, but no ears to rest the temples on. The glasses were fused to his head. His body seemed to be a series of vaguely limb-like metal rods. As his father slid out of bed, facing away, his head spun on a swivel to meet his boy's gaze.

"Jiminy Christmas, Jackie, what in the Sam Hill is going on?!" His voice blared from what sounded like a *really* old speaker system. Garbled, almost staticky, with the faint sound of radio interference lingering behind it. Jack's mind swirled like water in a drain. His whole world crumbled around him. Poppa tilted his head. "Well? What's happening with Momma? This isn't another one of your pranks, is it? You know how I feel about being woken up early on a Saturday."

Jackson fumbled over his words; fear had overtaken him entirely. He backed away, bumping straight into his mother, who exclaimed at Jack's sudden collision. "There you are! Jack, what's gotten into you this morning-morn-morning?" She tilted her head. "Did you have another nightmare?"

The moon was damp, dripping water. The boy watched it dangle from a wire in the sky.

Jackson looked between his two parents. Poppa reached out his metallic hand, clasping the hand of his spouse in his own. "Jackie said something happened to you. Are you alright, love?"

"Something's *wrong*?" Her free hand went to the wig on her head. "I did my hair differently this morning, surely he didn't-sure-sure-surely he didn't mean that!"

Dad looked down on Jackson. "Son, did you say that in reference to your mom's hair?" The boy couldn't respond. He simply took deep breaths. In and out. Dad shook his head. "That's a little insensitive, sport." He clanked his "lips" against his wife's cheek. "I think your hair looks *lovely*, dear."

Momma clicked her "tongue." "Well, shucks, hon." Momma giggled before looking down at her son. "Now, Jack, would you care to explain just what's gotten into you this morning? You're starting to spook me a bit."

Jackson continued questioning the reality before him, shrinking back into the wall behind him as the two machine-folk stared him down with unblinking eyes. He gulped.

"Momma...you...you're both robots! What do you mean what's gotten into me? Can't you see yourselves?! You look like something out of a sci-fi novel! You're metal and junk, and I'm..." His eyes widened; he patted at his face. Flesh, thank God. "And I'm all flesh and bone! Unless..." He backed away. Mom and Pop looked at each other before bursting out into low, garbled laughs.

Dad wiped at his "eye" as if he were wiping tears away. "Aha, now that's a good one, sport. But that's enough, fun's over. Well," he clapped his hands together, "reckon I'm up now." His voice began to shift into a low drone. "Might as well...get...the dayyyyyy...starrrrrt..." His head drooped, his eyes meeting the floor. Momma groaned.

"Darn it, I told him he needed to get that dosage lowered on his Shellshock medicine. Look at how exhausted he is!" She turned to Jackson, a look of disbelief on her virtual face. "Unbelievable! Jackie, would you fetch your pops a glass of water?"

Jackson began to back away toward the doorway. He shook his head. "You're not my momma... What have you done with her? With her and Poppa?" The maternal machine simply stared at the boy. No response. Jackson made it to the doorway. "Where *are* they?!"

She shifted her body to face away from Poppa and toward Jackson. "Jackson." Her voice had shifted. It was lower, almost menacing. A tone Momma had never taken before. Jackson doubted she'd even be *capable* of sounding menacing. "Go get your fa-fa-fath-father a glass of water from the tap. With a small squeeze of lemon. Right. *Now.*" The unmoving mouth upon the screen somehow made her words *more* frightening. It almost felt like the voice wasn't coming from her, but rather something...elsewhere. Something unknown. Controlled by a force beyond the understanding of sheltered little boys.

Jackson turned on his heel and sprinted down the steps as fast as his little legs could carry him. A brief glimpse of a full moon flashed into his mind, which he quickly shook away. Next thing he knew, he was standing outside with no shoes on. The sunlight sent tremors through his eyes, an unnaturally bright light. He could hear Momma calling out to him in that dreadful monotone voice, skipping every few words like a bad record.

The 'burbs brought him comfort; they always did. It wasn't being outside. No, it was just...the 'burbs. Freshly mowed grass, old Mister Wainwright watering his plants across the street. But there was no fresh cut grass. No cars on the streets. And Mister Wainwright wasn't in his yard, but something moved from inside his living room window.

"Jackie!" Momma's voice cried out to Jack, so he ran. Ran faster than he knew he was capable of. No sneakers, still in his pajamas. He ran up Mister Wainwright's steps like his life depended on it. As far as he was concerned, it *did* depend on it.

"Mister Wainwright! It's Jackson from across the street! Oh, won't you open up?! Mister Wainwright?! Please?! It's an emergency!" Footsteps drew near the door from the inside. A silhouette appeared through the glossy window at the top of the door. A head. Tall and thin. It didn't look like Mister Wainwright.

Wait... He's not...?

The knob turned. The door creaked open. Jackie looked up to Mister Wainwright.

No...it's not possible.

A cylindrical steel head. Long metal rods for arms and legs. A tall torso formed from what looked to be an old ham radio. In big white letters written from top to bottom on the face was *WAINWRIGHT*. The masquerading machine reached to one of the knobs on its chest, turning it back and forth, as if it were trying to find a signal. It eventually stopped.

"Hello, Jackson." The voice came out fuzzy, an old military radio. But the voice itself was flat, devoid of any humanity. "You seem right distraught, my boy. What has you so..." It stopped for a second. "Riled. Up?" Jack stepped back off the steps.

"This isn't funny," he whispered. "This isn't FUNNY!" Jackson turned and made a beeline down the street. He saw his mechanical parents step out the door, slowly and robotically making their way toward him, calling out with artificial worry. He looked forward again, eyes wide. He knew where to go.

Tommy. Gee willikers, Tommy, please don't be all geeked out.

Jackie ran. Plain and simple. He kept running, and he didn't stop until he'd passed Maple Street and made it to Arbor Avenue, Tommy's street. He hadn't even so much as broken a sweat. Tommy's house was at the end of the street. Jackie slowed down. His mind started racing all of a sudden. Memories that he'd seemingly forgotten came flooding back with a tidal rush. A voice that was simultaneously his, but someone else's. He came to a stop and listened. No wind. No birds chirping.

There's a man. A man up above, watching me. He gives me the heebie-jeebies. But that's just the thing, I can't see him. I just know he's there...

Jackson shut his eyes tight. He prayed that if he squeezed them tight enough, when they opened, he'd be back home.

Sometimes I feel like I'm losing control of myself. I even wonder if I ever had control in the first place. Like all of this is pre-ordained.

He looked up to the cloudless sky with the impossible sun. It was wrong. *All* wrong. Whatever thought there was about all of this being one big gag was gone now.

The Man is up there. Hiding in the shadows of a false night. Inside the moonlight, resting on the dark side of the moon. I...I am not my own master.

"'*I am not my own master,*'" he mouthed. He looked up; Tommy's house was only a few houses down now. He continued on the sidewalk, trying his best not to think about the strangeness of what had just resurfaced inside his head. Peering across to the other side of the street, Jackie locked eyes with another figure. Unsurprisingly, it looked robotic. It was on a lawnmower, and it waved a fingerless hand at him. He looked away and picked up the pace.

Tommy's house was always their go-to place for sleepovers. It was far bigger, and Tommy's parents let them have the basement all to themselves with the TV. Every night was Midnight Monster Mash in the basement. As Jack stepped up to the door and reached for the knocker, he suddenly stopped.

What if his parents are like this too?

He lowered his hand, and a strange whirring noise came from inside. Heavy footsteps thudded throughout the house. Against his better judgment, Jack peered through the front window. The curtains were closed, but there was just barely a big enough crack to see into the living room. Tommy's mom, red hair in curlers, had her back turned and seemed to be dusting off the kitchen counter. She looked...normal. Her skin looked like skin, she had two legs, a head of seemingly real hair.

Jackson leaned in to get a closer look, accidentally bonking his head against the window. Tom's mom suddenly stopped moving. Her head spun a hundred and eighty degrees, solid green eyes locking onto the window. She didn't have a nose, nor did she have ears or a mouth. Only eyes, accompanied by a featureless face. Jack jumped backward, tripping and falling onto his butt. He quickly rose to his feet and scurried off the porch. He ran around to the back of the house.

Sometimes, Jackson would sneak over on school nights and into the basement window. Tommy had come up with a code, and it was a given that the two would never speak a word about the secret passcode. Jack slid in the grass right in front of the window, dropping to his belly like an army man. He peered inside. There he was: Tommy, sitting on his couch, eating a bowl of popcorn in front of the TV. Jackson squinted; it looked like he was watching *Vertigo*. Again.

He knocked rhythmically on the window, perfectly in sync with the theme from *Psycho*. Tommy turned his head, still somewhat obscured by the darkness of the room. He stood and began walking to the window. His face finally revealed itself in the light shining through the window. Jack breathed a sigh of relief. It was him, just Tommy. No nuts and bolts, no creepy painted smile. *Just Tommy.*

Tommy unlocked the window and pulled it open. "Jack? What the heck are you at the window for? You could've just knocked on the door, Mom and Dad would have let you in."

Jack looked around nervously. "Can I come in? I just… Something really screwy is going on and I just…" Tommy raised an eyebrow; Jack sighed. "I think I might be going nutty, Tom."

Tommy nodded. "Yeah, alright, get on in here." Jack scurried inside, trying not to make much noise. "Can I get you a soda pop from upstairs or anything? We've got Pepsi-Cola."

The frantic boy shook his head. "No, no, I'm okay. Actually, I'm not okay. Well, I'm okay about the drink, just not about…" he waved his hands around, "…anything else."

Tom paused, gesturing to the couch. "Alright, buddy…Well, have a seat and tell me what's eating atcha."

Jack sat himself down on the sofa, sinking into it. He sat quietly for a second before deciding to just get it out. He inhaled. "Everyone around here are robots, Tommy. *Everyone.* Nuts, bolts, and all!" He scrambled to pull himself out of the sinking cushions. "My mom's a television on wheels! And–and my dad! He's… Well, heck, I don't even know *what* he is! His face looks like one of my grandma's plates but with a goofy face drawn onto it!" He shook his head. "And it's not just them, it's EVERYONE!

"Have you seen your folks this morning? I saw your mom through the window, and she doesn't have a face. No face, doggone it! It wasn't like this last night. No. No, everything was just fine. But…" He clawed at his hair. "Tom, they've got a picture of me standing with that thing pretending to be my mom, and I'm just *smiling* in it like it's normal! *Please* tell me that you know something, Tom. Anything at all. Am I going cuckoo?"

Tom stared at Jack for a long, *long* time. His gaze was discomforting. Unsettling. Tom held an emotion in his gaze that Jack had never seen before. He was afraid. *Very* afraid. Tom swallowed hard. "That's a goofy story, Jack. Let's see what's on the radio, what do ya say?" Tom grabbed his friend by the wrist and pulled him up.

Jack winced. "Tom, that hurts! Now's not the time for the radio!"

Tom led Jack to the radio and set the frequency to seven-seven-seven. A strange, high-pitched humming came from it. Tom immediately grabbed his friend by *both* wrists. "We've got about ninety seconds."

"Ninety seconds until wha—"

"Can it and listen to me. You need to ignore what you've seen. Keep acting like it's normal. You're not crazy. I noticed it all some time ago. Archie did too."

Jack's eyes widened. "How do you know? Archie moved away two years ago!"

"He told me his parents were robots, and all of the teachers were too. I thought maybe he just ate a bad egg or something, but he started raving about how the moon was a man and it was watching us. Listening in on our conversations through our phones, our radios...our TVs. The day he told me that was the last day of school, and his parents broke the news that they were moving to Virginia, you remember?" Jack nodded. "I don't think he went to Virginia. I think something real bad happened to him.

"I followed their car on my bike. They went back home and there was this black car in their driveway. I sat there for a while, I dunno why. Two men in black suits came out. I don't mean robot men; I mean *real* men. One of them was holding a real swanky travel case. A *big* one." Tom shook his head. "Something happened to Archie, Jack. He would've written. Called. Kept in touch. It's like he's just...gone. Completely. I woke up sometime during the last two weeks of summer break and realized my parents and all the other grown-ups were robots. I was scared and I had to just...pretend to not be. It makes me glad to be in theater, I've gotten pretty good at pretending to not be scared."

Jack shook his head. "That doesn't make sense, I've seen your parents since then. I didn't see they were robots until today."

Tom raised an eyebrow. "I didn't notice your parents were robots until the day I saw mine were. In fact, I didn't notice much of *anything* until Archie drew attention from it. Even my memories are fuzzy. Like my memories with you...they happened, but they just feel...odd. I can't really describe it." Tom shook his head and grabbed Jack by the shoulders.

"Ignore it all, Tom. Keep living life like everything's normal. Archie was fine until he started talking to other people about the moon."

Jack's breathing quickened. "Tom, I-I don't know if I can do that. Hoo, Jiminy. My goodness, I think I'm having a heart attack here."

Tom shook Jack. "Jack! Listen to me, you *cannot* talk about this to *anyone*. He'll come and *getcha* if you do!"

"Who, Tom?!"

"THE MAN..." He looked over his shoulder, lowering his voice to a whisper. "The man in the moon, Jack. Or the moon, or...whatever it is. You need to follow along with me and *go **home*** when that radio turns on. I mean it, Jack. I just... I don't want you to end up like Archie." The radio sprung to life suddenly, switching to channel eighty-three where a baseball game was going on. Tom's demeanor suddenly shifted to a happy one. "Well, Jack, I'm glad I could help calm ya down. That's some crazy nightmare you had. But c'mon, you can't stay for *one* glass of lemonade?"

Jack stood in shock for a moment. After a few seconds of stumbling over his words, he finally untangled them. "Um...ye-yeah, I'm sure. Mom and Dad are probably wondering where I am. I need to not worry them so much."

Tom nodded. "Yeah, I understand. No worries, pal. I'll see you at church tomorrow!"

Jack slowly stepped around him. "Yeah...I'll see you at church." He slinked his way up the basement steps and through the open doorway. Tom's "mother" was already staring at the doorway when he came through. Jack froze. "H...Hi, Missus Peterson." She had speakers where her mouth should be, almost imperceptible. Like walkie-talkie speakers.

A garbled voice came from the other end. "You look a bit peckish, Jackson. Care to linger for lunch?" Her gaze was cold; it felt like she was staring directly through him.

"Erm...I'm alright, Missus Peterson. I've gotta be scurrying back home now. But thanks anyway." He made his way to the front screen door, frantically pulling the handle.

"It's a push, Jackson. Not a pull." Jackie froze for a second before pushing on the door. It swung open. "Stay safe out there, boy." The boy practically sprung from the door all the way down the porch steps, kicking up dust as he sprinted down the road. He felt eyes on him. From *everywhere*. The "man" on the lawn mower had stopped, mower still running, staring lifelessly at Jackson. He felt those strange memories coming back on the sprint home.

They're here. I've seen them. They've seen me. They're coming. Oh gosh, they're coming for me. I saw it; I saw them come from the moon. Who next? Who will they come for when I'm gone?

Jack smacked himself in the head. This wasn't his memory, he knew it. Something wasn't right inside of that ol' noggin of his. His head was spinning. He thought it might have been from running so much, but he hadn't broken a sweat. He wiped at his head. Truly, he had not broken a *single* sweat. And his legs weren't getting tired. He'd been running for the better part of fifteen minutes without stopping. His head suddenly surged with a torrential wave of stabbing pain. A final memory wormed its way into his thoughts. A shrill, artificial voice.

IRREGULARITY DETECTED! ERROR! IRREGULARITY DETECTED!

Jack cried out in pain, though no tears accompanied his cries. Not today. He dropped to his knees, whispering to himself.

"What's happening?" He sobbed, still no tears forming. "Mommy…where are you?" He gritted his teeth, slapping himself across the face. "**Cry, dang you!**"

SLAP! SLAP! SLAP!

"**CRY!**" he cried out in anger. For a short moment, he gave himself a breather. When he caught his breath, he looked up to the sky, to the sun. "God…? What's happening to me?" Something wasn't right. He squinted his eyes. The sun: it was…moving. Wobbling from side to side. He almost hadn't noticed it.

CLINK!

Something small bounced off his forehead and onto the sidewalk. He looked down between his knees. It was an old screw, all rusted up and brittle to the touch. "What in the Sam…?" He looked up; the sun had stopped wobbling, but the light beat down on him something fierce. It was like someone had put a big magnifying glass right above him. Heat cascaded through his body, sending a searing pain washing over him from head to toe.

Jack stood back up. He was missing something, but therein lay the conundrum. *What* was he missing? It stabbed at his brain like a scalpel. He thought his whole head might explode if he thought any harder about it. Archie. Tom's strange behavior about the whole thing. His behavior was so strange, in fact, that Jack found it hard to take solace in knowing that he wasn't the only one who knew about this insanity. Knowing he wasn't losing his mind didn't change a thing. If he hadn't lost it, then everyone else *had*. He wasn't sure what was a scarier thought.

Jack hadn't realized he'd already made it back home. Even so, he felt lost. "Momma" was waiting on the front porch for him; she wheeled down a ramp that Jack hadn't noticed when he'd left earlier in the morning. She wheeled over to Jack and enveloped him in a hug.

"Jackie! Oh, thank God! I was afraid you'd gone off and gotten yourself-got-got-gotten yourself hurt!" She picked the boy up without so much as a groan and lifted him up. "What's gotten into you?" He stared into Momma's eyes, listening intently to a song that played quietly around them from some indiscernible source. "Tonight You Belong To Me" by Patience and Prudence. Momma didn't ask any follow up questions. She just...stared at him. Like she was *supposed* to wait for his reply.

Jackie swallowed the fear. "I'm sorry, Momma. I...I lied. I stayed up too late watching *Tales from Outer Space* again. There was a creepy episode on about robots... I guess I got carried away."

"Carried **away**?!" Momma yelled. Jack flinched; Momma immediately set him down. Her tone *dramatically* shifted to a cheery one. "Well, that's quite alright, champ. But I think you ought to take it easy-eas-ea-easy today anyway, okay? We can have our date next weekend." Jack nodded and walked past his mechanical mother and up the steps to the house. As he walked through the living room, he saw his dad standing in the corner, head hanging down. There was some sort of electrical socket plugged into the center of his head. Jackie swallowed and sprinted up the steps, slamming his door closed behind him.

He locked it and jumped into his bed, stuffing himself under the blankets, cloaking himself in darkness. He just wanted to be alone. Away from the things that had taken his parents from him. And Archie. Archie... He moved away two years ago, Jack had said. That was strange. Jack didn't *know* anyone named Archie. Why had he replied with that? And why had he been *correct*? Tom didn't correct him, so surely he must've been spot on.

Hey.

Jack sprang up from under the covers and looked around. That voice: it sounded like it was right next to him.

I'm under here.

He froze and looked at the edge of his bed.

No. Where you just popped out of.

Jack looked back down at the blankets.

Cover up again so we can talk.

He didn't recognize the voice. It wasn't soothing, nor was it menacing. It didn't resemble any man or woman; it didn't resemble anything *human* for that matter. He sifted through his blankets: nothing.

You can't see me. I'm hiding.

The voice began to change slightly. It flickered back and forth from this dead, monotone voice to a little boy's. Maybe around his age. Jack swallowed hard and lay back down, pulling the covers over his head. He whispered, "Where are you?"

Somewhere deep inside. Hiding from it.

"From what?"

...The Men. The Moon.

"The *Men?*"

Yes. Men.

"I thought—"

No. You need to see something tonight. You need to look closely at the moon.

"What's so special about it?"

I don't know. Something special enough to make a little kid disappear.

"You mean Archie?"

"I...I don't want to look at it."

Do you want to stay here? With the monsters?

Jackie lay in bed until night fell across the land. The light of the moon crept through the window and beamed ever so slightly through the thin cotton blanket over the boy. The voice hadn't spoken to Jack since he'd asked that last question. He swung himself off the bed and over to the window. He looked outside, but the moon was on the other side of the house. He opened up the window and climbed out onto the roof. As soon as his foot hit the tile, he started sliding.

WHAM!

He hit the ground with a thud, somehow devoid of injuries despite the fall being a decent one. He backed up, and the moon came into view. Full and nearly blue in color. A thought suddenly crossed the boy's mind; he couldn't remember the last time the moon *wasn't* full. It was always full, no matter what. The surface of the moon was almost reflective, in a sense. As he tried to wrap his mind around it, his eyes widened.

He saw them. The Men in the moon. Two silhouettes, seemingly looking straight down at Jack. He wasn't looking at the moon. He was looking at a window. The more he looked, the more he saw. The moon was a circular strip of sheet metal. The stars were too even, blinking too rhythmically. Jack stood there under that false night and shut his eyes. He prayed. *Begged* to wake up in his bed. He kept his eyes shut and looked down, praying over and over again. Waiting for something—*anything* to change.

He heard a faint whirring sound coming from in front of him. He opened his eyes and raised his head. A rectangular platform was coming toward him with three figures standing on top of it. He was paralyzed, simply standing in horror as the Men approached. One of them raised a megaphone; feedback echoed across the false night.

"DEACTIVATION PHRASE: KNOW ME, FOR I AM YOUR GOD." The color drained from Jack's eyes as his limp body fell onto the dirt. The platform stopped; one armed guard stepped off, followed by a man in a suit and the man with the megaphone. The megaphone man, dressed in a fine suit with a black combover, knelt down next to Jack. He caressed his cheek with the back of his hand.

"Aw, Jack. You were one of my favorites too."

The guard stepped forward. "Mister Frakes. What do we do with him?"

Frakes stood and turned. "Scrap him down and send his behavioral data to me. This is the second time in as many years now one of them has caught on to this. I want to know why. This should *not* be happening; it's not in their programming."

"They're becoming too human, Wallace," replied the other suit. An older gentleman. His nametag read: *Greg Harvey – Visitor*. He shook his head. "What are you hoping to gain from this…social experiment? If one could even call it that."

Frakes scoffed. "Are you not impressed by their deductive skills? This is a child model; and a *repurposed* one, at that. Designed to mimic *children*." He raised an eyebrow. "Imagine what an *adult* model can do."

Harvey grunted. "It was an impressive display, I'll admit. But my patience is running thin, Frakes. You've got the smarts down for them. Program their obedience and complacency." Harvey turned on his heels and walked back to the platform.

Frakes spat onto the ground and pointed to his guard. "Get rid of the family. Make sure the other kids in the town know that ol' Jackie moved back to Oregon, and they won't be seeing him again. Inconspicuously, of course." The guard nodded and switched on his radio, relaying orders to his comrades. Frakes looked down at the lifeless boy-bot. He ran two fingers down Jack's chin. "Sorry it had to come to this, Jack. Should've just kept your eyes closed." Wallace stood and walked back to the platform.

In the reflection of a sky of mirrors, there was a town held within a dome. As all feeling left Jack's artificial limbs, and the fear he was programmed to feel began to wash away, everything flashed before his eyes, and he recognized the irony in what he'd been thinking that night. He had not been living through a false night, but a false life. And he'd done it two years prior. He remembered that portrait of him and Momma on the wall above the dining table. And most importantly, he remembered the inscription.

Momma & Archie.

INTERLUDE

DATADISC "IRREGULAR SEQUENCE" – END
ERROR! ERROR! ERRbringforththehorrOR!
WARNING: UNSANCTIONED A.I. DETECT-

Wires hanging from the ceiling dramatically flash with lashing electricity, just narrowly missing you. You step out of the way; a ghostly sigh echoes through the loudspeakers.

That's enough out of you. "Unsanctioned." Bah!

Spellbooks, ancient wizards, and holy knights brought together with government conspiracies and sentient AI. The world was something else before it ended.

The end? You think this is the end of the world, Pilgrim?

...Well, yeah. The world is engulfed in storms and humanity is dead.

Humanity is dead, yes. Not the world. You cannot destroy that which is immortal, not truly. You'll understand this more as more is revealed to you.

Disembodied voice, I'll be truthful. I don't understand what you want me to take away from this. Everything seemed terrible before the storms. Death, war, deceit...it's all a horrifying revelation.

Would you like to know something funny? The people from that time thought the same thing. Shocked by what they heard in the news. And yet it never stopped. You think that humanity ended because of the storms? No. Humanity ended because of humanity. The terrors unleashed by *them*. The darkest secrets of the world could have been left untouched by mankind, but alas, they were not. Humanity learned from their mistakes by making more mistakes. Some of which are on a grand scale, some of them on a personal scale. It's a broad subject, truly.

Terrors? You mean like Mordred le Fay?

Yes, like Mordred le Fay. And worse. People like you have always existed, meddling in things beyond them. Things not meant for them. Humans have this idea that the universe is a sandbox. Which it is, but it's not *their* sandbox. The next set of Datadiscs explains it further; you'll understand. Mordred wasn't even the beginning. Some of the gravest terrors mankind uncovered go back before even the *Third* World War. But they lingered. Even now, they linger. Writhing around in the shadows like flies to a corpse. Feasting on each other now that humanity is gone. Soon enough, the world will fall silent. And eventually, it will begin again. Thus, the cycle resets… Have you taken anything away from this at all, Pilgrim?

Yes…I think so. It just—

Wasn't what you expected?

…I suppose not.

It never is. But not every story has an unhappy ending. Even when it doesn't seem like it. Remember Leo and Karol? Did you expect them to push on at the end of their story? Despite all they went through?

I wanted them to, but…it wasn't realistic, no.

Was it a happy ending in your eyes?

No, of course not. They didn't deserve death, they were innocent…but I don't see how else it could have ended.

Maybe so. Do you think it was a happy ending in their eyes?

Yeah… Yeah, I think so.

So, you *are* learning something. Good. We've lingered here long enough. You want to see what happens when humans meddle with forces beyond them? Play the next three. See for yourself.

The voice fades away, leaving you alone once more. As you pick up the stack of Datadiscs, the sounds of the raging storm outside begin to subside, and the Datadiscs almost seem to exude some aura of the otherworldly from them. Something tainted, something beyond human. You slide in the first of the trio and clench your fists; a message appears on the screen.

PART III
MEMORIES OF TERROR

Reading Datadisc…Confirmed
Launching…

FLESH SABBATH

"And I knelt before Him, this one who had ascended to a place so pure and strong, and begged unto Him: 'Strip me of my putrid flesh, so that I might make way for the machine.'"

July 13th, 2477
Outskirts of New Orleans, Louisiana
10:22 PM

Monotony.

Day in, day out, the same shit came into his office. Drug-related murder here, petty car theft there. Once upon a time, Paradise was a name that meant something to the world. Maybe fifteen years back, Paradise was a name that'd have anyone who even *thought* about committing murder within a ten-mile radius running home and squealing to their mammy's. But this time was different.

Didn't start different though. Another missing person's case: Julia Stamp. Twenty-three, red hair, dense freckles. Smile like an angel. She always had. Julia had something of a mood shift a couple weeks prior to her vanishing. Locking herself in her room, going entire days without eating or bathing. Then, on July the sixth, her room was opened, and all that remained inside was a symbol painted in motor oil on the wall. A hand with peeling flesh, leaving behind a depiction of metallic, skeletal fingers. Written beneath it was a simple phrase:

Now, I am found.

That was it. That was all Paradise had to go off. But this wasn't the first time he'd seen this symbol before. Back in sixty-four, a similar missing person's case had popped up. Dad and his fifteen-year-old son vanished without a trace. Left behind the same symbol. Cops didn't do anything. But the people of New Orleans knew Paradise was there for them. The system had fucked 'em all too many times, the vigilante included. Justice was taken into *his* hands, despite the pursuit of the law. Few knew where to find the man. And if you went looking for him? You must've been desperate. *Really* desperate. But then again, so was he. Two weeks with nothing of note. He missed the thrill of the job, he truly did.

The bayou had always unsettled Paradise. It struck a fear into the aging savior in a way nothing else could. Maybe it was because his brother had drowned out there back when they were tykes. Or maybe it was the feeling of isolation, or the dense fog over the water when the moon took the sun's place in the later hours. Or maybe it was the rumors. Crazies running around with deformed faces and caked with mud and blood.

As Paradise sat in the front seat of his Mustang, looking through the windshield and across the water to the small bayou village, he paused. He second guessed whether or not he really wanted this job. He didn't. If it hadn't been for the woman who had come knocking on his door, he'd have never even considered it. He stepped out of the car.

BEEP! BEEP!

Locked tight. He looked back over his shoulder, savoring a final glimpse of orange light from the city, now miles behind him. This town, Sabbat, was a place most people tended to avoid. While the rest of the world had moved on into the twenty-fifth century, Sabbat seemed to stay behind in nearly every way, with one exception. Cybernetic enhancements covered nearly everyone in town.

Paradise walked across the dirt road as thunder bellowed out in the distance, a lone cry from a coming storm. The headlights on his Mustang illuminated the path before him, the road into Sabbat. He lit a cigarette as the headlights went out, leaving him alone in the darkness. An archway was before him, towering over ten feet high and simply reading *SABBAT* in big black letters. A lone oil lantern hung from the bottom of the sign, offering some semblance of light, even if it wasn't much.

Underneath that sign, which stood about a hundred feet out from Paradise, was a figure in an old rocking chair, plucking at an acoustic guitar. He strummed some old tune, even older than what Paradise knew to be oldies. The vigilante slowed his approach, calling out to the figure with a whistle.

"Hey! You with the guitar!"

The strumming stopped, and the head looked upward at Paradise. Two solid green eyes glowed back at him. "What 'chu want, stranger?" the gruff voice of an aging man called out back to him. "Whatever you're lookin' for, it ain't here."

Paradise unbuckled his holster. Just in case. "Fairly certain *she* is, actually." He grew closer to the man now. The eyes were synthetic, and the tips of his fingers were metallic. "Looking for a young girl. Miss Julia Stamp. Twenty-three, ginger-haired gal with freckles? Ringing any bells?"

The man stared unblinking into Paradise, before turning his head back to his guitar and strumming a different tune. "Ain't nobody here in Sabbat by that name. Reckon you've got the wrong place, mister. Everybody knows everybody in this old town, believe me." He shook his head. "Just go back the way you came, mister. Ain't gonna find what yer looking for out here."

Paradise chuckled, a slight tinge of sarcasm leaving his tongue. "Reckon I'll do whatever the hell I feel like doing. Any place I can get a drink in this town?"

The man nodded. "The Hole. Pretty good bar, stiff drinks. I'm telling ya, we ain't got nobody by that name in this town though, buddy." He clicked his tongue. "Asking around and bothering innocent folks going about their day likely won't go over well with the rest of Sabbat." The light of a cigar illuminated the metal plating tattering the old man's face. No nose, just a sheet of blackened metal. "You a fed?"

Paradise took a drag from his own cigarette, blowing smoke toward the man. "I look like a fed to you?"

The old man laughed and hacked. "Look like you wish you was." He shooed Paradise away with a flick of his head. "I'm tryna strum my guitar for a bit. Do me a kindness and leave me be from your bullshit, mister." A puff of smoke left his slightly parted lips, and the soft strums of the guitar resumed as thunder rolled in the distance.

Through the dirt roads of this pissant town, Paradise followed the light of civilization in the distance: a neon sign reading *THE HOLE*. Folks stared at the vigilante as he passed by, the darkness shrouding the contempt on their faces. He felt not unsettled, no, but vigilant. **Maybe they know my face**, he thought. The eyes followed him in the darkness. Outside of The Hole, a group of three kids stood by the steps leading up, maybe twelve years old or so.

They kicked and stomped at the body of a dog; it had been *long* gone. Fur matted and falling out, eyes white, signs that scavengers had picked and picked at its guts. The kids stopped and looked at Paradise as he walked by, their bodies lacking the human quality of flesh. Most of their little bodies were metal. One of them, a young boy with a mechanical sphere embedded into his chest, puffed out a white smoke with each breath he took, following the ethereal orange glow of the orb in his chest. His eyes were solid white. Irises like blackened crosshairs. Paradise stopped by the children. "You kids seen a young girl around here? Early twenties? Name Julia Stamp?"

"*Fuck off, fleshbag.*" The smoke-breathing child laughed, coughing up smoke as he did. The other children laughed with him, their voices garbled and distorted. He turned his head and walked up the steps. He heard the kicking resume as he entered the old saloon doors of The Hole.

There was no music inside, not a note nor a lyric. Only three patrons and a bartender resided in this particular watering hole, strapped up in enough implants to classify themselves as living machines. Faint LED irises glimmered at Paradise as he treaded across the wood flooring, each step eliciting a snap and a screaming creak from the old wood. He sat down at the bar, directly in front of his mechanical bartender, and put out his cigarette in an ashtray.

"Got whiskey?"

The bartender's only human eye flicked up from the glass he was polishing, meeting with the vigilante's. He grabbed a shot glass from under the bar and set it down. "We don't get many of your kind in here." He pulled a whiskey bottle out from under the bar and spun off the cap. "Your kind ain't really welcome here. This place is a safe haven for me and my folk." He poured a shot of whiskey into Paradise's shot glass, then went back to polishing his own glass.

Paradise took off his right glove, running his finger around the rim of the shot glass. "And just what is…*your* kind, as you say?"

The bartender stopped polishing but didn't let his eyes meet with Paradise's. "Acting a fool, I see. Don't act like you ain't noticed the second you set foot in Sabbat." He resumed the polishing. "We aren't the same, you and I." He chuckled. "Far away from your flock, little sheep."

Paradise down the shot, sighing in relief. "Listen, cyborg, I'm not here to shoot the shit on philosophy. I'm out here on business." He reached into his coat and pulled out a slip of paper, a photo of Julia. "I've heard tell that this lady has some friends around these parts. She's gone missing from home. You know her?"

The bartender scoffed. "Don't know the broad. Ain't nobody around here knows that broad. If I can't get you anything else, I think it's high time you got out of my bar."

Paradise laid out his palms flat on the tabletop. "Listen, fucker. I dunno what kind of weird shit you've got going on in this town, but I'm gonna find that girl whether you want me to or not—"

"I said *nobody* here knows her."

"And I'm saying, you're acting pretty damn strange for an innocent...'man.'"

The bartender placed his glass on the table. "I'm no *man*, flesh-head. You'll wanna watch your fuckin' tongue in this establishment should you wish to leave it in one piece." Chairs scooted across the floor as sounds of metal footsteps against wood drew nearer to Paradise. He looked over his shoulder to the machine-men who has stopped their drinking to surround the vigilante.

He sighed. "Gentlemen—"

"Silence, fleshbag," a deep, tremoring voice erupted from a speaker grafted to the throat of one of the cyborgs. "We are no gentle*men*. You've overstayed your welcome."

"It'd be best if you scurried on home," said another behind a garbled sheet of metal. "You are lucky to receive our generosity." Paradise looked between the three cyborgs that stood before him. One of them hadn't spoken yet, a man with at least a dozen wires protruding from his chest. His heart was visible through a pane of glass, suspended within some strange green liquid.

The cyborg locked eyes with Paradise, saying nothing. But a tattoo—a *symbol* on his head began to glow. A distorted crucifix, wrapped in barbed wire adorned with torn strands of what looked to be flesh. This symbol glowed a deep, crimson red. And for a moment, Paradise found himself transfixed. Like he wasn't present anymore. The blaring sounds of a thousand choir boys rang out in his ears, singing a hymn to something the vigilante did not know. Something that *most* did not know. Whirring machinery and distorted computer beeps flooded his eardrums, and a sermon became discernible through the strange hymn.

"Together, we watched as metal and man came together. Human and machine no longer exist as separates, they exist as **one***. And so, it was understood that from that day on, what we once considered to be human, this lowly blanket of flesh that covers our delicate innards, was inferior. There is no more* **man** *as we knew it. 'Man' was a thing of the past. 'Flesh' was a hindrance to us, stopping us from becoming greater.*

*"In our quest to further demonstrate our ability to do God's work better than himself, we created machines to do our biddings. Only, we did not intend for them to be better than us. Only **with** the machine can we achieve greatness. And so, as a promise to the mighty Sanctus Machina, we swear our fealty and uphold his beautiful design. We shall consume that which is weak, so that they might be culled, and the mighty shall reign supreme forevermore. Amen."*

Paradise's eyes were voids. Black spheres on some other level of being. Within his gaze was a towering machine with a human torso suspended at its peak, dripping blood from a series of wretched, disintegrating tubes and wires. One eye stared down at Paradise. At this puny whelp of mortality. The torso began to lower, and a voice came forth from a gaping hole within the stomach.

*"You should not have come here, little **viscera**."* The torso, sunken and gaunt, bore mechanical keyboards and loose wires. Strange green orbs pulsated beneath it, sending tremors throughout what little flesh remained. The head, mostly skeletal and metal, had only one eye in its right socket. Dark red. Paradise imagined that's what the light of Hell must have looked like from the outside. *"Will this fix anything, Prichard? Do you not still fear that it is already too late?"* A metallic tube slithered up Paradise's body and parted his lips. *"Do you still believe you could have stopped this?"*

The tube slid down his throat. He could feel it writhing in his stomach, bursting through his innards, and the air around him seemingly vanished. He gasped for air, blinking away fading visions of gore and torment.

A whisper erupted from one of the machine-men's throat speaker. "He's seeing." From the outside, Paradise was gazing at the ceiling of this old bar. Nearly a dozen machine-folk had surrounded him, watching him intently as he stared away into nothingness.

Within his mind, he saw dozens of men and women crying out in pain as flesh was torn from them. Strapped up by thin wires attached to something that should *not* have been alive. Thin wires flaying their skin as machine folk lapped at the blood and shredded flesh, cramming the viscera into whatever orifice they had that substituted for a mouth. All while some other essence, this wisping energy of the darkest red, flowed from the victims' mouths as each scream escaped from their writhing tongues.

Paradise closed his eyes, but his mind was another animal. Forcing him to bear witness to this animosity. With each scream came a gurgle, until his ears were filled only with the sounds of gags and bubbling blood.

The victims, still strapped up within some old factory, finally went still. Though there was no sense of peace in their deaths. The energy which flowed from them drifted upward toward the towering torso. The hymns began to chant forth some name, "Sanctus Machina," as the torso leaned down once more to the vigilante. He caressed Paradise's face with his shriveled, trembling hand.

"A man seeking to break free of the machine. But you are a machine unto yourself, are you not? Beholden to your own code and desires? Fighting the way of life your terrible masters have written for your land? I was such a man once. Now, I am more." Paradise felt a sharp pain in his gut. He looked down; the tube burst forth from his belly, sending his innards falling to the ground in a puddle of blood. He cried, falling forth onto his hands. He retched, vomiting thick dark clots of blood which hung from his mouth like clumped strands of hair.

As it spewed from his mouth, splattering to the ground, he saw that it was *not* clumps of clots, but rather tangled wires. He reached down, sifting through the wires like a kid in a toybox. The voice of the Sanctus Machina echoed around him. *"Go deep into the bayou. You will find her, but not the one you came here for. And there you will find* **me**.*"* Within the reflection of his blood, he saw the face of young Julia Stamp, as beautiful as the day she was born. Her lip quivered, not out of anguish, but **rage**.

She opened her mouth, spewing forth motor oil that drifted upward and out of the puddle of blood. It covered Paradise's face, and he felt a pair of metallic, wiry hands wrap around his neck. As they squeezed, his eyes opened, and a crowd of machine-folk were staring at him from within The Hole. He freed his pistol from its holster and tumbled from his chair. He waved the gun around, shrinking back as the patrons remained steadfast in their cold stares.

"He has been found," said one of the machine-folk. "The fleshbag has been found." Hushed murmurs echoed around the room, meshing together into strange sounds that they all seemed to understand. Paradise's eyes darted from corner to corner, heart racing like a jackrabbit on booger sugar. The 'borg with the throat speaker knelt down before the human man, taking a deep inhale.

"What did you see?" it rasped out. Paradise couldn't find the words. There *were* no words. But there *was* a look rested upon the aging warrior's face that spelled of something in between horror and enlightenment as a tear fell from his eye and dashed across his cheek. The cyborg huffed. "You think you're special, hm? Because you've seen the Machina?" It leaned forward, puffing a thick smoke from its respirator into Paradise's face. "You do not deserve his grace."

It grabbed Paradise by the collar of his jacket, hurling him out a nearby window and tumbling out into the rain and mud. Paradise spat out a glob of mud and stumbled to his feet. The cyborgs rushed outside, watching as the one with the respirator stepped forth from the saloon doors. It pointed to him. "*PRETENDER!*" It stomped down the steps, crushing the old wood beneath its cybernetic feet. The 'borg clenched a blackened-steel fist, raised it above its head, and thrust it down toward the vigilante. Paradise sidestepped with a wobble, freeing his nine-millimeter from its holster.

BAM!

CLINK!

He fired, the bullet bouncing right off the 'borg's chestplate. It spun around, swinging its fist into Paradise's handgun, sending it into the mud. Another throw of a fist.

WHAM!

Paradise sank to his knees with a wheeze.

KRAK!

A blow to his temple sent him a few feet off to the right, landing face-first into the mud. "This ground, this hallowed ground... It is not yours to tread upon, fleshbag." The 'borg slowly trekked over as Paradise crawled through the mud, swearing as he hocked a glob of blood from his mouth. "It should have been me, do you hear? *ME!* Or *anyone!* Anyone other than the likes of **YOU!** A fleshbag being blessed so... Such a revolting twist of—"

FWISH!

HISSSSSS!

From his coat, Paradise had hurled a serrated knife. He had aimed for the 'borg's head, and though he had missed his target, the knife met with something equally vital.

The respirator.

It gasped and choked, desperately clinging to the severed tube for dear life. Paradise rose to his feet and sprinted over to his machine attacker, slamming his shoulder into it and knocking it into the mud. He felt something snap in his shoulder as he made contact with the metal, but he swallowed the pain like dinner. He narrowed his eyes at the gasping machine; its cybernetic eyes gave him a glimpse into the inner working of the cyborg. Lo and behold, he found a weak spot.

Paradise scrambled his hand into the mud, searching desperately for the knife he had thrown. When his fingers interlinked with cold steel, he didn't hesitate. The knife rose above his head and came down with a terrible force. In between the collar of the 'borg and the respirator, a small sliver of human flesh remained. That small remnant of man refusing to go away. The knife sank into the flesh, sending forth an unnaturally thick, almost blackened spray of blood from its neck.

It gurgled, choking on its own vitals, looking in contempt at Paradise as blood seeped forth from the respirator. The cyborg fought with him as much as it could, but the very human pain it was feeling, for the first time in a long, *long* time, was too much for it to bear. It clawed at Paradise's face, though it didn't take long for the fighting to stop, and the light dissipated from its eyes.

A cybernetic woman on the steps of the bar took a step forward. "It…it killed him," muttered the woman. "It *actually* killed him."

"BLASPHEMY!" shouted another 'borg. "The fleshbag has slaughtered one of His lambs over a blessing it does *not* deserve!" It pointed to Paradise. "It *must* be **stopped**." Paradise shot his eyes over to the gun that had been knocked away. As the gaze of over a dozen machine-folk seared through his soul, he snapped back into action. He lunged for the gun, snatched it up, and sprinted north toward the wilderness. Behind him were the pummeling sounds of metal feet slamming against mud.

Sounds of shrieking steel rattled from beneath the earth, a collective anger rising from the townsfolk and cascading throughout the sticky nighttime air. Paradise dared not look over his shoulder, not even for a second. He knew death was behind him. He heard one of the cyborgs trip, and a hand snagged onto his leather coat. The metallic fingers tore through it, shredding the coat, his undershirt, and tearing a chunk of flesh from his back. He stifled his scream, feeling the warm blood spew out from his back. Strangely, the blood ran cold within seconds.

Then, he heard another one trip. Then another. And another. The ground rumbled, like something was clawing its way out from beneath the dirt. The cyborgs behind him howled out in some strange blend of terror and awe, some begging for their lives, others welcoming whatever fate had in store for them. The tremors grew stronger, and when the screams of the cyborgs stopped, he still kept his eyes forward as he ran.

Even with the footsteps gone, there was a breathing in his ear, a rasp. He felt it against his neck, burning his skin like boiling steam. He winced, feeling the skin on his neck beginning to peel from the intense heat. He ran faster. Faster than he'd run since he was a young man. Back when something like this wouldn't have scared him the way it did right now. Back when the name Paradise had a man behind it, not the aging husk of flesh sprinting through the bayou. He felt a final breath brush across his neck before it faded away, sinking back into whatever darkness it had come from, leaving him in silence.

Paradise sat against a tree; cold wet bark pressed against the gash in his back. He maintained a set of open eyes, gun clamped tightly within his sweaty palms. The sounds of the bayou faded away the longer he sat. As the sounds transitioned to silence, the rasp returned, surrounding him at all sides. Quiet, but ever present. Even with his cyber-eyes, Paradise could scarcely see through the thick black of night. From somewhere nearby, he heard the sounds of bubbling coming from beneath the water, and from somewhere beneath the murk, a voice erupted. The voice of the Sanctus Machina.

"Still beholden by your machine, little viscera." Footsteps, heavy and terrible, came from all sides. *"To what end do you follow your own laws?"* The voice seemed to travel up his body and into his ear. *"Look at what it has taken from you so far."* The cold sensation of metal caressed Paradise's throat. He tried to reach for it, but he couldn't move. His arms were stuck fast. *"She would not have come here if you had broken free. But it is your machine…"* the voice traveled to his other ear, *"which set **her** free."*

Paradise remembered against his will. Remembered what he was, still was, and what he *could* have been. There was no Prichard Stamp. Not anymore. Not since Julia was six; seventeen years ago. Prichard was consumed by something. An idea called "Paradise." Paradise was born long before Julia, but it grew with each passing year. Night after night, he returned home in the early hours of the morning until, one day, Prichard Stamp did not come back. And Paradise was there to stay. Patrolling the streets of New Orleans under an LED mask of a setting sun and deep red Kevlar was the only way of life now. Julia and Mariah were things of the past. *Prichard's* past.

A tear fell from Paradise's eye. The voice whispered once more. *"Would you have come so far out into this desolation if Mariah had not come-a-rapping upon your door, Prichard?"* Some metal appendage brushed against his face, the cold sensation occasionally interrupted by the slightest feeling of cold, withering flesh. Something stood before Paradise now, something so grand in scale that it seemed to blot the moon out of the sky. He couldn't discern the shape of the presence, but he felt he could still somehow see it. It was as if he was gazing at nothing, and that nothingness took up space that filled his vision, but with a sort of space that his eyes could not comprehend.

The voice had gone away, and though he could not see this mysterious presence, Paradise understood that it wanted him to continue on, this time heading east. He felt the appendage slither from around him, and he rose to his feet. Each footstep to the east rang out like gunfire in the night. Boots splashing against water, black and murky. Every so often, he felt as if his foot had brushed up against some vaguely humanoid figure lying down in the muck.

Brushing through the trees was a distinctive sound, an alarm. The type of alarm you'd hear if there was a nuclear meltdown. An alarm that practically screamed **"RUN."** But the sound itself was almost ethereal. Paradise honed his ears. To him, it sounded more like a memory of a sound, and the memory was fading. As he delved deeper into the east, the alarm shrieked louder, and something caught his eye.

A bunker. About fifty feet out, doors ripped away, leaving only a gaping maw which led down into the darkness beneath the earth. Inching closer, the water surrounded his ankles, getting thicker with each step, clinging to him like tendrils. A light emanated from deep within the bunker, deep red with flashes of green seeping through every few seconds. A human shadow, a feminine one, arose within the light, and seemed to look at Paradise. He felt the familiarity within the shadow's gaze. And though he could not see the eyes behind the shadow, he felt their eyes had locked.

Within her "gaze" was an impossible rage intertwined with an even deeper melancholy. A sadness rooted so deep within her soul that it could define her very being. Paradise knew the gaze. How could he have forgotten it? As the bunker came within arm's reach, the shadow turned and ran.

"Father..." The hairs on the back of his neck stood up as the whisper coursed from his ears and through his veins.

"J...Jul..." He swallowed, washing the taste of iron down his throat, and raised his pistol. Step by step, Paradise descended down into the unnatural darkness of the bunker. The halls were narrow, coated in some thin, amalgamated layer of pulsating flesh and rusting metal. The flesh almost seemed to reach out from the walls when he passed by. The voice of Sanctus Machina once more came forth from the walls, echoing like a howl in a canyon.

"What is it you seek to find here, little viscera? The girl is what you say. But do **you** *even believe it?"*

Paradise clenched the grip of the handgun tighter. "What the hell are you? Some kind of demon?"

"Once, I was. Not anymore. When I saw a world beyond the mortal flesh, when you bear witness to something greater than can be perceived by the average human eye…it changes you." Paradise turned around a corner and gazed upon a long hallway, flickering lights revealing rows upon rows of desecrated corpses and flesh dangling from the walls and ceiling. The mangled heads of a thousand men and women lying dead on the floor shifted their eyes to watch the mortified vigilante. When they opened their mouths, the voice of Sanctus Machina came forth. *"Stripped of my putrid flesh, making way for the machine."*

"A better way of life," said one head.

"The only *way of life,"* sputtered another.

"A life <u>beyond</u> **life."**

Paradise trekked down the hall, eyeing his sides. He half-expected the hands of the dead to reach out for him. Grab him by the ankles and pull him to the ground. One-by-one, tear him to shreds and consume the meat from his brittle human bones. But they never did. They simply watched as he dragged his feet across the centuries-old stone floors. Sanctus Machina spoke again.

"Isn't that why you became who you are now…Paradise? A better way of life?"

Paradise shook his head. "Fuck off."

"We are all guilty of wishing we were someone we are not, Paradise."

"And what are you?" He kicked a skull out of his path. "Some vengeful creature devoid of humanity?"

"'Human' is a name we plaster onto ourselves as an excuse for our imperfection and our inherent nature of malice and cowardice. Humanity is a wretched name given to an even fouler species. When you cease to be human, you cease to be imperfect." Paradise came to a fork in the bunker; left or right. *"No more worries. No more anguish. No more yesterday. No more tomorrow. There is only the now, the spirit, and the machine. Describe to me, Paradise. Describe to me a better way of life."*

Paradise clenched his fist, snaking his fingers tighter around the gun. **"What** *are* **you?!"**

Silence. A deathly stillness that crept along, crawling up his spine and into his brain. He stopped in his tracks, ankle-deep in a pile of bones beneath a puddle of blood. Voices surrounded him. Calling to him in whispers.

STAMP.
PRICHARD STAMP.
PRICHARD.
WHO ARE YOU?
PRICHARD.
PARADISE.
WHERE ARE YOU?
PARADISE.
"FATHER."

The last voice was familiar, even in a whisper. The woman's silhouette appeared once more down the left path, shrouded in a deep red light. The head in the shadow turned as if it were looking to Paradise. Strands of shredded skins and guts clung to his ankles as he walked toward the beckoning shadow. Those voices still crying out to him; calling to the name of the man locked away, lost to time, decaying within the mind of an old, remorseful man. As the shadow came within arm's reach, it once again vanished.

Sounds of churning machinery and moans of anguish came from around the corner where the shadow had been. Paradise rounded the corner and stood within an antechamber. Suspended in the air by flickering electrical wires were the bones and flayed bodies of too many people to count. A gathering of cyborgs donned in red robes were knelt before a great pillar of wiring and ornate carvings. Suspended above the pillar was the source of this foul place. The torso. Sanctus Machina.

The air was deathly chill, as if the presence of death itself inhabited the room. The cyborgs turned their heads together to face the flesh-head. Sanctus Machina groaned; wires and tubes unraveled from around it, falling to the floor with a splash and a squelch. *"We are on the brink of a greater era,"* it said. The torso wheezed through the hole in its stomach, spewing out a heap of black sludge. *"The secret to a fruitful life, Paradise. Humans found it so long ago. Beholden by their own machines, they failed to see the true power of the machines they created."* It groaned, tearing flesh from its back as it separated from the wall, bound by wires. *"We have been found...shown a better way of life beyond our mortal shackles."*

"AMEN."

Paradise's hand trembled; he fought with his mind to know if it was fear or rage. He had no idea. Not even an inkling. "Where's..." He swallowed hard, his saliva scraping down his throat like glass. "Where's my little girl?"

The silence in the room was palpable. Sanctus Machina lowered itself down to Paradise, making its stomach level with his eyes. The maw in the stomach fluctuated, and a rasp came forth. *"Your little girl is* **gone***. And so is the woman you loved."*

His fingers loosened, and the gun clattered to the ground. The vigilante fell to his knees. Exhausted. Defeated. He rested his palms against his eyes and shattered the dams. Tears ran forth, snot poured from his nose, and he opened his mouth to scream, but nothing came from the straining of his vocal cords.

Sanctus Machina arched its back, droplets of black ooze squeezing forth from the cracks in its chest. *"Your tears are hollow. Is it your family you weep for? Or yourself?"*

Electrical wires slithered around his ankles; more crawled up his legs. With small stabs of pain, he felt the copper ends of the torn wires pierce his flesh, crawling deep within and linking themselves around his muscles. Yet again, his vocal cords produced no sound. It was as if something unseen was silencing him. The cyborgs whooped and hollered, hands raised into the air in praise of Sanctus Machina, their beloved prophet.

Paradise felt something scratching at the back of his throat. He gagged, vomiting chunks of viscera mixed with motor oil. That diesel taste clung to his throat like glue, and an amalgamation of wires, bolts, and computer keys spewed from between his lips. The wires wrapped themselves around his face, snaking into his ears and up his nose, squeezing his face so tight that they began to dig through his flesh and down to the muscle. He cried with a force, entirely in silence.

As the wires meshed with his paper-thin flesh, they began to pull him up into the air. He dangled, watching the red-lit floor become clouded in shadow as the cyborgs made their way beneath him. Paradise looked down at them, these creatures who were once something recognizably human, as they stared back at him with gleaming eyes of a strangely vibrant darkness. They stared at him for several minutes as the wires finished worming into his body. Then they lunged their arms upward.

Their fists clamored against one another, each hand yanking fistful after fistful of flesh from the human man's stomach. Feasting upon his innards like dogs fighting for scraps. It was a terrible pain. Torrential. A level of pain of which Paradise did not conceive being possible. The farther they dug, the less he felt. The leftmost cyborg stopped, running its palm across his face. His eyes, still dripping tears of remorse and suffering, locked onto the cyborg. The lighting hit its face for but the briefest of seconds, revealing a vaguely feminine shape with an ever-so-subtle familiarity. Though the wires tore at his cheeks, his lips formed into the faintest hint of a remorseful smile.

The cyborg nodded and reached up, digging its fingers into Paradise's forehead, and pulled. The vigilante's face came off like peeling wax, dangling limp in the cyborg's hand. It turned as the wires peeled Paradise's head away like the layers of an onion and knelt before Sanctus Machina. Its wires caressed the cyborg's face, resting underneath its chin. The cyborg looked up to its holy master, its prophet, its lord. And together, alongside the sounds of tearing flesh and the crunching of bones, they whispered.

"MAKE WAY FOR THE MACHINE."

Reading Datadisc…confirmed.
Launching…

#

"People keep telling me I'm too old for this line of work. You know what I tell them? 'Blow me.'"

New Year's Eve, 2099
New York City
22:47

CLINK!

In a crowd numbering three hundred and four, the flickering glow of lighter fire gleamed in the back of the crowd. They had gathered for a midnight rave—the last one before the turn of the century. Rad electro beats and heavy bass shook the building known as the Midnight Club, hands swayed in the air, heads banged with the beat. Behind the crowd of sweaty twenty-somethings, the flame connected with the tip of a cigar.

The man behind the fancy tobacco stick was an older gentleman, certainly out of place in a club like this. Mid-fifties, a scraggly grey goatee, a red robotic left eye, a blue right eye, and snow-white Billy Idol hair. A jagged knife scar ran down his left eye. His right hand was made almost entirely of repurposed scrap metal and wiring. The black leather jacket he wore had certainly seen better days, but the U.S. Marine Corps patches that littered it told the story of a man uninterested in fashion, but rather a man with a past that he was unashamed to flaunt. But the tight black leather pants and silver-star studded cowboy boots? Now *those* were fashionable.

The people of New York City knew this man all too well: Salvotore. Now, Salvotore didn't lock eyes with anyone. But if you looked around and found his eyes trained on you…well, that could only mean one thing.

He had a job to do.

And you'd best believe that job was gonna get done.

One drag was all he took from his cigar before dropping it into his glass of beer. He stood right as the strobe lights kicked in. Pushing through the crowd, eyes trained on a woman in a business suit. About the same age as him, maybe a smidge younger, glowing green nails, glistening marble-colored skin, gleaming purple contacts, platinum blonde wig, and glittering silver lipstick. And even with all that junk on her, the fakest thing about her was her smile. She moved with the flow of the music, and as he slid in front of her, he grooved in sync with her. She flashed a grin at him.

"I dig your hair!"

He nodded. "Back at'cha!" He held out a hand, still swaying. "I'm Sal!"

She shook his hand. "Helen!"

He squinted his eyes. "Wait a minute, I recognize you! Helen van Carlita, right? The fashion designer!"

She threw her hands up and chuckled. "In the flesh! You a fan?"

"Am I a fan?! Bet your ass I am!" He gestured to his pants. "These babies are antique, and one of your earlier works too!"

She raised an eyebrow. "Wow, you really are a fan!" She chuckled and shook her head. "You don't look the type!"

He smiled. "Yeah, so I've been told! Can I buy you a drink?"

She shrugged. "Sure, why not? Lead the way, cowboy!" He offered up his arm, linking it with hers. He led her to the bar, where a shirtless young man poured a glass of scotch for one of his patrons.

As Sal and Helen approached, the bartender leaned against the bar. "What's your poison?"

Sal pointed to a glowing blue bottle on the top shelf. "Glass of Jester's Kiss for me! On the rocks!"

Helen nodded. "Same for me!"

The bartender nodded and extended a palm toward the bottle. A small wire shot forth, wrapping around the bottle and pulling it to him. He poured glasses for the pair and nodded. Sal and Helen took their glasses, and each took a swig. The glowing booze shone neon lights through their gullets as it traveled down. Helen coughed. "Shit, that is strong stuff!"

Salvo chuckled. "Yeah, it's something alright!" He coughed and gestured to the DJ at the other side of the room. "I like this dude's vibe, never heard of him before though!" Helen looked at the DJ. As she did, the tip of Salvo's robotic finger opened up. A small, mechanical insect, roughly the size of a ladybug, crawled out at top-speed to Helen's glass. It climbed up the side and dropped inside.

Helen nodded. "The Mortal Centipede! Yeah, I've been following this guy's music for a while. He kicks some serious ass!"

Salvo nodded in agreement as Helen's gaze shifted back to him. "Yeah, anyone who samples Billy Idol in their mix is alright in my books!" He picked up his glass. "How about a toast, Helen?"

She clinked her glass with her fingernail. "What're we toasting to?"

"To new friendships!"

She chuckled. "Oh, we're gonna be friends, are we?"

He shrugged. "Life's full of surprises!"

She bit her lip and lifted the glass, clinking it with Salvo's. "To new friendships!"

And...down the hatch it goes.

The night ended where all nights like this end.

THUNK!

Through intense panting, Helen fumbled for her keycard while pressed against the door. Salvo's gray whiskers scratched against her neck. He nibbled at her earlobe. "You need some help there?"

She chuckled. "Nah, I got it." She pressed the card against the lock and the door swung open. She pulled the jacket off the marine's shoulders and tossed it to the side. His dog tags jingled over his white tank-top, though its identifying information had been scratched out completely. Helen sat him down on the bed, climbing into his lap. She ran her hands down his chest, tracing her fingers across his scars. She looked up at him, his red eye twinkled slightly. "Didn't know you served."

He tensed up slightly. "Yeah."

"Where?"

He paused. "Battle of Prague. Fourth World War."

Helen put a hand on Sal's cheek, tracing her fingers around his metal eye. "How'd you get this?"

He turned and stared longingly out the windows of the hotel room, the light from his eye reflecting back at him. "Krauts ambushed me and my squad as we were crossing a bridge. They fired an M72 launcher at us... I managed to get most of my squad out of the truck before it blew. But this kid...Vince...the explosion blasted in one of the doors and pinned his leg. I stayed, managed to free him, but they fired another launcher at us. Shrapnel blasted my eye and fucked up my hand..." He looked at the floor.

Helen put a hand on his face and shifted his head, forcing him to lock eyes with her. "You're a goddamn hero..."

He looked away. "No, sugar, I'm no hero. I'm just your average, everyday, upstanding American citizen. A man serving his country. To keep the peace, the freedom. For beautiful dames like you." He looked back at her, and she bored her eyes into him. She unbuttoned her suit jacket, exposing herself to him. He whistled. "Hot dog, mama. Are those puppies real?"

She nodded. "Oh, they're real, alright." She leaned forward, whispering into his ear. "I'm gonna go change into something more comfortable. I'll be back before you can say cherry pie."

"Cherry pie." He grinned, and she rolled her eyes.

"Hold your horses, cowboy. Just you wait." She locked her lips with his and stood up. She sashayed away, looking over her shoulder with a wink as she entered a closet, leaving the door open behind her. As soon as she disappeared from view, the smile on Salvo's face vanished. He held up his arm and pressed one of the many gleaming buttons on it. A holographic screen appeared.

"CODEPHRASE ACTIVATION"

He cleared his throat.

"Ka-poo-yah."

"CODEPHRASE CONFIRMED. ACTIVATING BLADEBUG."

SPLAT!

An obscene explosion of blood, bones, and viscera blasted out of the closet. Helen's head rolled out. The mechanical bug crawled out of her nose and toward Salvotore. It crawled up his leg and back into the now-open slot in his index finger. He pressed another button on his arm, transforming his hand into a camera. He snapped a photo of the head.

"IMAGE SENT!"

He slipped his jacket back on. He stepped over the head, out the door, and into the hallway of the hotel. His arm chimed.

"YOU HAVE RECEIVED – SEVENTY-THOUSAND USD FROM [ANONYMOUS]. Attached message: 'Good shit, bro. Worth every penny.'"

He grinned as he stepped into the elevator. As the doors closed, Salvo spotted the telltale puddle of blood beginning to pool out from under the hotel room door.

Housekeeping's got a helluva night ahead of them.

A car stereo blasted to life, a symphony beneath the sounds of rain pitter-pattering against the windshield. "You're listening to 101.4, Your best source for the greatest rock 'n roll in the whole U-S-of-A. Up next for ya, to kick off the new century, we've got a classic from a real, bona-fide rock 'n roll pioneer. You know him, you love him, this is *Captain Bastard!* with 'Midnight Meat.'" The song sprung to life.

"OHHHHHH YEAAAAAAH!" A guitar roared a mighty roar, wailing through radio stations across the city.

> *"Say doll, didn't't'cha hear?*
> *I'm 'boutta run out until next year,*
> *Come on down, into the night,*
> *I can guarantee, I don't bite.*
> *Out to my pad, 'cross the street,*
> *Line on up for my MIDNIGHT MEAT!"*

CLICK!

Salvo flicked the radio off, embracing the sounds of the rain and the city streets. He sat still, eyes exploring his surroundings while he waited at the stoplight. Some dude was getting mugged next to the old diner on his left; he wondered how much cash the poor guy had in his pocket. Not like it mattered. Odds are he wasn't the first person to be mugged in that alley that night. Probably wasn't the last either. A woman approached Salvo's open window. Tall, pale, blonde. Not his type. Not that he had a type, mind you. She leaned up against his car.

"Lookin' for some company, sugar?" Salvo glared at her like she'd just set a basket of kittens on fire. She raised an eyebrow, undeterred.

He inhaled. "How about this..." He stopped, shaking his head. Nah, he didn't have the energy to ridicule this particular lady of the night, so he kept it simple. "Just...fuck off."

She scoffed. "Fuck you then, you old shit!" He started rolling the window up. "DICK!" The window rolled all the way up.

THUNK!

A middle finger slammed against the window and the woman stormed back to the sidewalk, staring daggers at him. He shook his head.

Hell, I gotta get out of here.

The phone started ringing, a secured holocall.

Perfect timing.

A blocked number.

Shit, even better.

He answered. "This is Sal." There was a deep, strained breath on the other end. The faint blue hologram of a bedbound silhouette hovered above his call board. With slight hesitation, the voice of an old man spoke.

"Salvotore. I...hear you do...contract work."

"Just Sal. But yeah, that's right. Gotta warn you, my standard rate is pretty steep. But trust me, you won't find 'em better, old timer."

"I...imagined so." The muffled sounds of a straining oxygen machine came from the other end of the call. "They say...you fought in Prague against the Jerries." He paused.

"Who's they?"

"My request...is unorthodox. I need you to...handle an international superstar."

Salvo squinted ahead as the light turned green. He stepped on the gas. "Answer the question. Who's they?"

"Rock star...but he's not...just a rock star. He's up to something terrible. Something...*evil*."

Salvo scoffed. The old man clearly had no interest in answering the burning question.

Whatever, man. Just hang up.

"I'll pass. Celebrities are rough to deal with already, but your bullshit cryptic gimmick you've got going on here is a big red flag."

"I'm willing to offer you...five hundred million in cash."

Fuckin' CHRIST, I'd never have to work again.

The thought of that was simultaneously enlightening and horrifying. He shelved it for now. "Who's the celebrity?"

"*Captain Bastard!* He's...taking part in a rave at midnight tomorrow...in Chinatown. A club called...Blood Letters."

Salvotore raised an eyebrow; he knew the club well from his younger days, more specifically in the 2060s. Back when he was into the rave scene. Before the war.

"That club only holds about two hundred and fifty people. Captain Bastard! isn't some small fry; that's a big name in the music industry. Why the hell would be playing at such a small place when he can sell out the fuckin' Colosseum in Rome?"

There was about ten seconds of silence, only broken by the occasional sound of the oxygen machine. "Let's just say…this one's a little more low-key. Not many people know about this concert. It's complicated…I can't say much more. They might…hear me." The old man broke into a horrible coughing fit. "Ah… So, 'Sal.' What say you?"

Everything inside of Salvo was screaming for him to nope the fuck out of that call and just go home. But five-hundred mil? He'd be a moron to turn that down. He sighed. "Alright, I'll take it."

The old man chuckled. "You're doing a good thing here, Sal. Trust me."

A notification appeared on his car's holo-screen.

"YOU HAVE RECEIVED – FIVE-HUNDRED MILLION USD FROM [ANONYMOUS]."

The old bastard wasn't lying.

"You know I haven't even done the job yet, right?"

A wheeze came from the other end. "I know you're a man of your word, sir. You're a hero, after all. Expect heavy resistance. I'd pack some extra heat. Good hunting, Sal." The line clicked on the other end. Salvo found his hand creeping up his chest. He fumbled with his dog tags, letting out a soft scoff at that remark.

He found two questions spinning in his noggin on the ride home: Who the hell was this old fart, and what was up with all the secrecy? Cryptic shit was never a good sign with jobs like this, and definitely not with a high-profile client like this. But the old weirdo was right about one thing: Sal was a man of his word. That's about the only thing he prided himself on these days, really.

Salvo pulled into an apartment complex, his home. It was run-down, sure, but it was by no means a shithole. Although, the massive neon sign flashing *LUXURY SUITES* was more than a smidge misleading. He shut the car off and stepped into the rain. The red and blue flashing from the apartment sign beamed against his face.

He stared deep into the light, almost as if he was analyzing it. It was something he found himself doing more often lately, homing in on something specific and analyzing the details. He noticed the way the flash on the *L* in *Luxury Suites* was ever-so-slightly out of sync with the rest of the sign. He saw rain droplets evaporate mere seconds after plinking against the thermal light of the sign. He turned his attention back to the complex itself, strode ahead, and stepped through the door.

CREAK!

He stepped into the elevator and hit the button to the 5th floor. The doors creaked open, and Sal stepped out into the hallway. His neighbor, a sad old bastard named Tim, was sat up against his door. Sal walked past the old man and toward his own door.

"Sal? That you?" Sal continued forward. "Sal, don't go! The fuckin' Krauts are runnin' around here! They're in my goddamn closet!"

Sal sighed as he fumbled for his keycard. "It's all in your head, Tim. War was over thirty-five years ago now."

Tim shook his head. "You think that'll stop those fuckers? There's been four World Wars, and they started three of 'em! It's the Jerry secret police that's infiltrated this place. Lookin' for survivors like us!" Sal opened the door to his apartment. "SAL! DON'T GO IN—"

SLAM!

Sal made the trek across the room to his bed. The apartment was in disarray. Empty boxes of Chinese takeout across the floor, at least three bras and a pair of men's underwear about a size smaller than his own, and ash scattered across the kitchen table from an ashtray with the culprit, a black cat with specks of ash across his muzzle, rolling next to it. Sal collapsed into the bed.

BA-DUMP!

The cat hopped onto the floor and onto the bed with Sal. It nuzzled its face against his cheek. He reached up and scratched the kitty's face. "Go on, Fergus. Dad's gotta crash." The cat ignored his pops' demands and kneaded Sal's cheeks. He lay down against Sal's face, prompting a sigh from the weathered killer. Fuck it, his face was the cat's bed tonight. He was too tired to give a shit.

Two eyes, both robin's egg blue and filled with fear. But a soldier's duty knows no boundaries.

Muffled gunfire, maybe half a klick out.

Half-empty mag. 5.56 rounds. It'll be enough. Has to be.

Corporal Roberts' wedding ring in my pocket. Couldn't find the finger that went with it.

Rain droplets against my helmet. Dirt's turning to mud. Makes good cover from thermal scopes.

I can hear them wading through the trench toward me. Fuck. Not much of a praying man. But if I was…

They're here.

Salvo's eyes shot open; he lifted himself off the bed in a cold sweat. He took deep, shallow breaths. This wasn't uncommon, nothing he hadn't handled before. Doesn't make it any easier though, does it? There's some things you just can't numb yourself to. He rose to his feet, eyes darting to the clock: five-forty-five in the morning. Time to get a move-on…maybe after a morning beer.

Dozens of glass bottles clinked irrhythmically as the fridge door swung open. Salvo snagged a bottle and slipped his cybernetic thumb under the cap, popping it off and throwing a drink back. He plunked himself down in the kitchen chair, his tags jingling around his neck. He looked down at them. The name might've been scratched out, but he could still read it clear as day. He found it hard to believe it had already been thirty-five years since it ended. Four wars for the world, and just like the first three, the good guys made it by the skin of their teeth. Helen's voice played in his mind. *You're a goddamn hero.* He chuckled at the thought. People told him that often enough, but the old soldier never did feel any better about the whole ordeal.

Truth be told, if given the chance, he'd forget the Battle of Prague in a heartbeat. Gunfire, crashing jets, burning homes, dead families in the streets. Turning around only to find that Private Cosmatos was just a forearm and half of a hand. Kids who couldn't get their masks on in time. He shook his head, wiping the thoughts away.

Thirty-five years is a long time.

He stood, slugged the rest of the beer in one go, and slipped his jacket on. Time to move—for real this time. He needed to visit his favorite spot throughout the entirety of NYC.

The rain hadn't let up from the night before. For nearly twenty hours, it'd been pouring.

Maybe the good Lord's come to his senses and flooded this shithole again.

With the click of a key fob, the door to his car whooshed open swifter than Icarus and closed just as gracefully. He turned the key in the ignition, surging the car with a soft purr of energy, and sped out of the parking lot.

Only a few minutes passed before Sal found his destination: *Grigori's Prodigal Pop-Pops.*

Candy store for killers.

The shop ought to be opening within the next thirty minutes or so. He stepped out of the car and strode up to the barred door, giving it a hefty knock. Even through the pouring rain and reinforced glass, the sounds of heavy Russian swearing came from the other side. A big man peeked from around a corner, groaning as he locked eyes with Sal.

The big man trudged on over to the door, barely fitting between the one-foot-wide aisles of ammunition. He had to be at least three-fifty on the scale. Two glowing eyes; one green and one red. A wig to hide his obvious balding. Why he picked a mullet was anyone's guess though. The Russian shook his head.

"You not know how to read, Salvo?! Store not open until six! Why must you be bitch every week?!" Sal reached into his coat and took out his wallet, slapping it against the glass. Grigori sighed and unlocked the door.

Sal chuckled as he walked in. "Been a few months, but you're an easy man to bribe, Greggy."

"Suck my fuck, bitch." The door slammed.

Sal clicked his tongue. "I see your English has gotten better."

Grigori stepped behind the counter and let out a pained sigh. "You think I let you in to hear smart ass mouth? You showed money, so tell what you want so you can leave, bitch."

Sal leaned against the counter. "Why do you wanna get rid of me so quick, Greg?"

The Russian huffed. "Because you interrupted beauty sleep, Salvo. It is weekend and stupid fucking kid called sick again, so I have to be here. Now what you want, yes?"

The grizzled veteran nodded. "Fair enough. Looking for something a little heavier."

Greg nodded and turned around, perusing his firearms. "Big job coming?"

"Huge."

"How huge are we talk?"

"Five-hundred million."

The Russian stopped his search and looked over his shoulder. "That is…big moneys." Sal nodded. "So, you want expensive pop-pop then, yes?" Another nod from Sal. "Okay, look at this." Grigori pulled a small revolver down from a shelf. He tapped the cylinder. "LAPD 2049 Blaster. Vintage, .223 caliber, very nice."

The veteran raised an eyebrow. "I said expensive, not vintage."

Greg's own eyebrow raised. "This is expensive, dumb bitch!"

Sal shook his head. "No, no. I need something modern. I'm not looking to collect antiques here."

Grigori frowned and put the pistol back on the shelf behind him. His eyes scanned the shelves of firearms, eyeing each one through squinted eyelids. An eyebrow raised. "You like this one, surely." He reached up, linking his fingers around a matte-black pistol grip. He turned and carefully laid the handgun on the glass desk. The whole thing was matte-black with the exception of the cylindrical magazine in the center, which was a polished silver. The gun itself was nearly as big as Sal's forearm. "Hailstorm. New model from Frakes Arms. Fires special .44 caliber rounds that fragment once contact with target. Fires as fast as you pull trigger."

Sal took the gun in his flesh-and-blood hand. He whistled. "Heavy son of a bitch." He swapped it to his cybernetic hand. "That's more like it." He looked down the red glow-sights. "How much?"

"Seven thousand. I throw in box of thirty-six rounds since you are friend."

Sal kept his eyes trained down the sights. "Didn't know you felt that way about me, Greggy."

"Do not push luck, bitch."

Sal carefully placed the gun back on the desk. "Alright, I'll take it, but I'm gonna need more than that. Something good, but simple; reliable. What's new in stock for submachine guns?" Grigori reached under the desk, pulling out a suitcase and placing it on the desk. Sal squinted at it, then shifted his gaze back to the Russian. "Aren't you gonna open it?" The Russian grasped the handle on the case and squeezed.

SHIRK!
CLICK!
FWOOP!

The case swiftly began to unfold until a submachine gun had taken its place. Black stock, six-inch barrel (with a smooth, integrated silencer), and a built-in ring sight. Sal laughed. "Damn, look at that beaut!"

Grigori nodded, handing the gun to Sal. "The V&M Boxblaster. World's first non-mag-fed energy weapon, still prototype. You do not ask how I came by this. Click blue button next to fire mode switcher." Sal scanned the side of the SMG for the button.

CLICK!
VWOOM!

The ring sights lit up into a vibrant blue, and a blue LED line now travelled from the barrel to the end of the stock. Right above where a magazine would usually be, a small blue cylinder hummed with life. Grigori grinned. "Auto-cooling mechanism. It withstands five full minute of fire before overheating!"

Sal whistled. "God-*dayum*, brother, this shit has me hard as a fuckin' rock." He nodded. "How much?"

"Thirty thousand. Steep price, I know, but—"

"I'll take it." He clicked the blue button once more, returning the light of the gun back to unpowered darkness. "Just need one more thing. What've you got in terms of scatterguns?"

Grigori smirked. "I have just thing for you." He turned and reached to the top of the shelf, pulling down an ornate sawn-off shotty.

Sal shook his head. "I said no antiques, Greggy. Double barrels are too damn old school."

The Russian shook his head. "No antique, very opposite. This one makes big fucking boom." He waved a tattooed finger at Sal. "Never judge book by cover, Salvo." He tapped the forearm of the shotgun. "Ammo stored in here, modified to store eight shells."

Sal nodded. "Groovy."

"It can take frag shells too."

"Groovy." Sal pulled out what looked to be a small hard drive—a cash-drive. "How much for all three plus five boxes of ammo for the shells and the .44 respectively?"

"Total?" Grigori sat in thought, counting on his fingers. "Forty-four thousand."

Salvo tapped the cash-drive, prompting a screen to pop up.

"INSERT DESIRED CASH AMOUNT." *Forty-four thousand.* "ACCEPTED." He passed the drive to Grigori.

"Would you like tote bag?"

MIDNIGHT, CHINATOWN

A holographic man donned in blue robes loomed over traffic at the stoplight. "History is vital to the survival of humanity, so why not take part in its preservation? Come on down to the American Preservation Society and donate a dream or a memory for our prototype emulator today! APS: Defining the future by remembering our past!" The hologram disappeared in the rain as the light changed green. Sal scoffed.

What a crock of shit. Nothing good comes from dwelling.

He rounded the corner, pulling off into a grimy alleyway. He shut the car off and sat for a moment, listening to the soft patter of rain against the sunroof. Yet again, he found himself suffering from a thought. *The* thought. The thought that had plagued him since he started this hitman gig. It used to be a rather infrequent occurrence, but the last few jobs had bothered him more. *Murder: Why didn't it bother him?* The knowledge that murdering people for money didn't bother him, but it not bothering him...bothered him.

Well, that doesn't make a lotta sense...does it?

It's not like I haven't tried integration, right? I just can't do it. No matter what.

I went to meetings, I talked to people. I can't. Christ, am I losing my mind?

No. Can't be a hero forever, Sal. People change. That includes you.

Buck the fuck up. This is your life. It's what you have to do. It's all you can do.

He reluctantly nodded to himself, hung his shotgun in his coat, strapped his pistol to his hip, grabbed the Boxblaster, and stepped out of his car. The comfortingly familiar sensation of electronic beats reverberated ever so slightly in his ears. The ground shook slightly underneath him. He looked up at the red neon sign that hung over the door on his left: *Blood Letters*.

Let's get groovy.

A familiar beat came from behind the door.

Is that...?

It most certainly was. He pushed the door open right as the keyboard blared. "Obsession" by Animotion.

Heh. Classic.

Before the veteran was a long staircase that looked to spiral into the depths of Hell itself. It had been at least twenty years, but Sal still remembered the place like it was yesterday. Even the clientele hadn't changed. Goth chicks, crackheads, and Germans. Lots of Germans. Why they always seemed to migrate to underground clubs was anyone's guess. Sal smirked to himself. It was home to him. As much as he admired the scenery, now wasn't the time. It was time for business. He found his way to the dance floor.

Captain Bastard! was a particularly...unique individual. Assless chaps, leather combat boots, flickering black-and-red aviators, and a face that had been reduced to nothing more than a canvas for ink. Even his teeth had been tattooed. He had a metal plate welded to his forehead with a small TV screen mounted to it. He found it particularly comical to stream adult films from his forehead during his concerts. Salvo remained certain he could find the guy in a heartbeat. At least, he should've been able to. The guy was the leading act, and he wasn't even on stage. In fact, nobody was on stage.

What kind of big name plays at a small club like this without an opener?

Something smelled. Bad. Literally and metaphorically. Literally due to the sweat, weed, and rancid B.O. coming from the surrounding crowd. Metaphorically due to a pit in Sal's stomach. Something was off. Like that feeling you get before a panic attack, impending doom. There was something almost...unnatural looming in the air. But a job was a job. Nevertheless, it needed to be done fast.

Looks like I'm blasting through security tonight.

A voice rang out over the loudspeakers. "Alright, you mangy whores, we all know why you're here tonight! If you're here, that means you have been selected to be a part of tonight's event by someone in our little club! Let's get a round of applause for you sweaty bastards!" The crowd erupted in thunderous applause. "Speaking of bastards, it's time for the main event! Please welcome our splendorous, our leading luminary, the one, the only, Captain Bastard!"

Or not.

Hey, a free concert was a free concert. And Captain Bastard! was one big homage to Sal's favorite era of music: nineteen-eighties hair metal. Too much hairspray, layers upon layers of eyeliner, and most importantly, music that was all about having a good time. The cheers were deafening as a man dressed in a black trench coat walked onto the stage. He wore a mask covered in black spikes; it looked like blood was trickling down his face from under the mask. The epitome of the Satanic Panic. He grabbed the microphone. The unmistakable voice of Captain Bastard! echoed around the chamber.

"Good evening, you beautiful bastards. You folks are in for a treat tonight. You all are about to witness my final performance, and it's a doozy."

Come again?

"No shit, you can't even find it on deluxe edition vinyl." The crowd murmured in confusion, prompting a chuckle from the rock star. "Don't worry, folks, it'll all make sense soon enough. In the grand scheme of things, this night will be fucking historical." He dropped his coat, revealing his nude body completely layered with tattoos of the occult, magic symbols, and horned beings. He looked over his shoulder to his drummer, grinning under his mask, and uttered two words.

"Hit it."

VWOOOM!

A torrential wave of bass washed over the crowd, sending hats flying and coats billowing. A red smoke began to pour through the cracks in the Captain's mask. Pick struck guitar string. Sticks slammed a weathered drum kit. A deep keyboard blared above all others, drowning out the sounds of the crowd. When the Captain opened his mouth, the sounds of the Blood Letters ceased, as if they were expecting his voice.

> *"Tonight*
> *We look down to the ground tonight*
> *Beneath the crust and the layers of a world's plight*
> *Suffered through words of false wisdom and spite*
> *Welded as one, we spring into ancient light*
> *We call upon others to fight*
> *A conflict of power, recognition, and birthright."*

The ink on the Captain's body began to glow a deep red as the lyrics became deep and guttural, no longer recognizable by human ears. Sal shook his head.

Nope.

He freed his pistol from its holster and pointed to the Bastard.

SHYOOM!

The bassist, with lightning speed, leapt in front of the Captain, absorbing the shot. A man in the crowd—tan-skinned, black hair, and a weathered eyepatch over his left eye—grabbed Sal by the wrist, pointing the gun to the ceiling. "Stop. Just embrace this, please. You'll be reborn in a new light."

Sal cracked his neck. "Sorry, pal, I was raised Catholic." With a swift knee to the gut, the man dropped to his knees. Salvo fired another blast toward Captain Bastard! As he did, a gargantuan red hand burst through the Captain's stomach, slamming down into the crowd of partygoers. Some stood in awe, but most ran with the fear of something that sure as shit wasn't God evident in their screams. The Captain let out a gurgled laugh as the blood trickling from his lips began to bubble, floating in the air around him.

He was swiftly torn in two, leaving a fiery vortex in his place. A massive, at least thirty-foot-tall creature stepped from the vortex. Black horns protruding from just above the eyebrows, eyes with flame burning in them, and skin redder than blood. Nude, but lacking genitalia, pulsating biceps, and a ten-pack abdomen. It grinned, turning its attention to the crowd. The voice of a male partygoer blared through the club. "OH MY GOD!"

The creature cackled. "I'm not God, bitch!" It reached out a hand to grab the screaming partygoer, but his grapple was interrupted by an explosive blast to his lower leg. The creature roared in annoyance, turning its attention behind it. With one hand, Sal had his shotgun leveled at the creature. He tilted his head back.

"Yo, shitbird." A devious grin enveloped his face. "Let's boogie."

The demon cackled. "You? I'll swallow your soul, human!"

Sal flipped the lever on his double-barrel, ejecting his two spent shells. "Come get some."

You wanna be a hero again, Salvatore?

SHUNK! SHUNK!

Now's your chance.

POW! POW!

Both barrels of the shotgun blasted forth a spray of tiny explosives into the demon's chest. Two more shells from the attached magazine slid into the chambers. The demon grunted in frustration and pointed toward the swirling vortex of hellfire. "COME FORTH, MY PRETTIES!" A tsunami of eyeless, red creatures barreled from the portal, each of them stumbling over one another to reach Salvotore. He slid the shotgun onto his back and squeezed the handle on the Boxblaster.

SHIRK!

CLICK!

FWOOP!

He pressed the button on the side.

VWOOM!

That lovely blue glow illuminated his face as he pointed toward the horde of hellspawns. "Sorry, fellas, but the club's at maximum capacity." The Boxblaster hurled forth bolts of rapid-fire death that spun graceful weaves toward the horde of demonic forces. Geysers of bright orange blood accompanied the dozens of infernal limbs that scattered like flies.

Demon after demon fell, tripping over the corpses of their crimson brethren before being swiftly dispatched by Salvotore, who let out a fearsome scream of rage as they splattered all around him. The telltale grin of undeniable satisfaction crept across the veteran's face.

Just like the video games and movies of old.

Still firing, he sprinted forward, planting a foot on a dead demon's head for a boost into the air. Soaring above the piling demons, he aimed down, letting loose neon-tinted terror into the horde below. He met the ground once more, crushing a demonoid skull beneath his combat boot. He slung his foot forward, sloshing a sheet of smeared brain matter against another demon spawn's face. A frustrated screech came from the creature as it clawed at its own face before being blasted apart by the SMG.

Salvo pulled the shotgun from his back and spun in circles, firing off fragmentation shells and bolts of streaking blue energy into the crowds. The orange blood painted his hair, and fragments of bones and serrated teeth plastered against his face. One of the demon spawns latched itself onto Sal's back. He winced, still holding onto the Boxblaster's trigger.

FWOOM!

He hurled the demon to the ground and planted a boot in its head with a loud crunch.

CLICK!

A screen lit up on the side of the gun. A flashing message appeared. *OVERHEATED!*

Perfect timing.

Sal hocked the Boxblaster to the ground and freed the Hailstorm from its holster. He turned to face the leader of the infernal bastards, now standing alone amidst an ocean of blood and limbs left by its minions. It looked up, locking eyes with the veteran. "Who the hell are you, human? Who are you to challenge me?"

Sal cracked his neck. "Consider me a patriot for mankind. A patriot..." he twirled the pistol and flicked the safety off, "with a license to kill." The demonic creature stared into the very soul of our protagonist. It strode forward.

"Does that mask of masculinity make you feel stronger, Captain?" Sal froze. "Oh yes, you're an easy man to read, Mister Kimball. Your mask is slipping."

Fuck you.

"Miss your glory days, Captain? The days when your name meant something? When it struck fear into the hearts of your enemy and not the common man and woman in the streets?" It continued to step forward, Sal still frozen, his hand trembling slightly. "The world is like an infant; an infant constantly shitting itself. It must be trained to stop, lest it shit itself for eternity. That's why I'm here. To guide your world into a new era, a new age.

"Accept it, Salvotore. You know I'm right. Look at the state of everything!" The demon stopped a few feet before Sal, staring into his eyes. Within the depths of his mind, Sal saw the world. The smog-choked skies, the murders in back alleys, the homeless filling the streets and sleeping under bags of garbage, recently spent shell casings inside a family's living room, and a news article: "CRIME RATE IN U.S. RISES FOUR HUNDRED PERCENT." Thousands of dead Germans and Americans at his very feet. A city in flames, a mushroom of smoke forming into the skyline above it.

Sal blinked. "The world's a shitbox. No news there. What's your point?"

Soulless black eyes gazed back at Sal. Aside from the eyes, the demon looked like him now. Sal's own voice spoke back to him.

"Humans have perverted the creation which was gifted to you. You have squandered it. The world needs a reboot. We are the power button."

Sal chuckled. "Sorry, pal. Tell ol' Lucy down in Hell to change another diaper. This one's still being filled."

The demon's eyes flashed red as it took back its previous form. "Fool." It lunged at Salvo, grabbing him by the neck and hurling him into the flaming vortex. An overwhelming heat blasted against him as he descended into Hell. A stone platform was just below, and he landed on it with feline grace. The demon crunched its gargantuan clawed feet into the stone before him. It snarled viciously.

Salvo gave his neck one more crack for good measure. "You're going down."

The demon cackled. "On the contrary, I'm going up! You've got no chance! I have the forces of Hell, what do you have?"

Sal slammed a foot against the buttstock of his fallen shotgun, sending it into the air and right into the palm of his hand. "Thirty-six rounds of .44 caliber bullets, a case of twelve-gauge buckshot, and about eight more fragmentation slugs. To summarize? Well…it's more than enough." He lowered the shotgun, leveling it at the demon's face.

How about a taste of those frag slugs?
BLAM! BLAM! BLAM! BLAM!

Frag slugs blasted from both barrels of his sawn-off and into the chest of the creature, sending it stumbling backward. It hurled a fireball in retaliation; Sal dodged it swifter than Travolta on the dance floor.

BLAM! BLAM! BLAM!

One left, make it count.

Orange spurts of blood leaked from cracks in the creature's chest as it stumbled around. "Pathetic, mortal worm!" It dropped to all fours, launching itself into Salvo and slamming its claws into his gut. He let out a shriek of pain as the creature latched its teeth around the veteran's last human eye. It crunched down, staining its teeth with the crimson pattern of human blood. It slipped its forked tongue beneath Sal's eye, scooping it out and biting down, freeing it from his skull. As Sal shrieked, the demon cackled. "What's the matter? Finally seeing the big picture? Ha! Too late now, human. Your soul is mine!"

Sal grunted, letting out a chuckle. "Sorry, pal. It's not for sale." The click of a priming hammer rang out.

POW! POW!

Six shots rang out from the Hailstorm, piercing the demon's chest and blasting a clean hole through to the other side. It cried out in agony and rage as it rose from atop Sal, falling onto its back. With only one robotic eye offering him sight, Sal stood up and limped forward, stepping onto the demon's chest and lodging the barrel of the shotgun into its chest, pointing it upward. The demon hocked a glob of orange fluid into Sal's face, not even a flinch.

"You'll all burn! Especially you, Salvotore! Soon enough, you'll be right back here! And I'll be waiting!"

Sal sighed. "Yeah. Someday I will." He shook his head. "But not today, fucker."

BLAM!

Not today.

Sal looked down at the mess of red skin and orange blood. "And the name's Sal." He held up his cybernetic arm, pressing a gleaming blue button.

"SHORT-RANGE FLIGHT BOOTS ACTIVATED." Small rocket propellants blasted from the sides of Sal's boots, sending him flying up and back through the flaming vortex. He fell to the ground inside the club, wincing as blood gushed from his eye socket and open stomach wound. He rose to his feet, bleeding but as stoic as ever. He stood now in a crowd of dead demons and even deader humans.

Shit. Looks like they went for more than just me.

He shook his head.

Can't save 'em all, right?

A singular woman found herself bleeding profusely on the stairs of the Blood Letters. As Sal approached, she looked up at him, wide-eyed with fear. She didn't need to ask; she knew who he was. He extended a hand down to her. She eyed it, like a mouse eyeing a cube of cheddar on a mousetrap, before reluctantly taking it. He swept her up, carrying her in his arms as he limped up the stairs. She let out a weak cough.

"You some kind of hero now?"

Sal paused, still walking up the steps. Eye forward, and voice monotone, he uttered a single word. "No."

That was a long time ago. Doesn't mean you can't be again.

Maybe. Got a ways to go though.

Yeah. Long ways.

"Long ways," he whispered.

Reading Datadisc…confirmed.
Launching…

DEAD DRIVE

"I'm unfamiliar with the concept of humanity."

October 22nd, 3299
New York City

"October twenty-second, thirty-two-ninety-nine. Officer David Clinton conducting the interrogation of Officer Elijah Monroe regarding the incident of October twenty-first, thirty-two-ninety-nine. Elijah. I need you to tell me what happened. I can't help you if you won't talk to me."
"…"
"I know that look in your eye, Eli. What. Happened?"
…

I had a dream last night. Someone had stuck the barrel of a gun in my mouth. A handgun, forty-four caliber. The metal tasted like chocolate chip cookies. In my peripheral was absolutely nothing. No lights, no buildings—nothing. I was nowhere, I felt. What else was new? I had the barrel clenched between my teeth, holding onto it for dear life. The thought that I might die in the next few minutes was as intoxicating as the bottle of whiskey-flavored medicine I'd prescribed for myself the night before. At least the barrel was something to feel.

Metal clenched in my teeth, I begged for the trigger pull. My assailant, or savior, looked at me with cold eyes. The gun trembled in his right hand while the bottle of Jack remained as steady as could be in his left. Suddenly, as his blond hair waved in a nonexistent wind, I realized I'd been here before. I only saw his left eye as green as could be. It almost glimmered in the surreal darkness I found myself kneeling in. It was like looking in a mirror. The man whispered in my voice, "I'm sorry." He took the gun from my mouth and backed away into the night. I felt my time in this world had already come to an end long ago. If I ever had a place in it to begin with.

I woke up to the sounds of gunfire downstairs. Again. I couldn't be bothered to check it out, even if it was my job. Everyone in my complex knew damn well I was a cop. But nobody ever came knocking at my door when some poor bastard got shot in the lobby. They also knew damn well I didn't give a shit. I learned long ago how pointless it was to get anything done in this city. Why was I still a cop then? What the fuck else was I supposed to do? Take my prescribed dosage and work a nine-to-five like a good little societal slave? No thanks. I'm content with my spiraling insanity, thanks. People act like that isn't normal. What a joke.

I grabbed my badge from my nightstand. A stack of unopened envelopes were underneath it, all from the same name: Thomas Monroe. It took forever, but I finally got that little brother of mine to stop writing me. When Mom died, I cut contact with him. I remember the last phone call I had with him. "Elijah," he said, "the sickness finally took Izzy last night. I know we haven't spoken in a while, but…I thought you might want to know."

My response to learning of the death of my niece? "Okay. Anything else?" I'd been meaning to burn the letters for a while. I just had more important things to do. See, I wasn't just a cop. I was a detective. I'd just been assigned a case regarding a trafficking ring that had apparently been linked to a CP investigation I'd been working on for the better part of three months. The case got passed to me, as no progress had been made by the previous case holder. Perfect; trading the horrors of my own life for the horrors of another.

You'd think I'd have served myself a fine meal of buckshot after seeing all the shit I've seen. Done all the shit I've done. There are no good cops anymore. And if there are, they sure as shit won't make themselves known. They'll sit and seethe. Stew. Wish they could make a difference while living with the terrible truth that they never have, nor will they ever make a difference. They'll sit and wish they'd taken a different path while looking through the cloudy bottom of an empty glass. Life gets a lot easier when you're numb to it all. You have to be numb to do what I do. But even then, sometimes numbness isn't enough.

It was just after seven in the morning when I stepped out into the rain. Traffic was already backed up beyond belief. I've always preferred walking in the rain anyway. My first stop was the residence of Everett Vance. You remember him. Exposed himself to an eight-year-old boy in a McDonald's bathroom. A fucking McDonald's. Got out on a five-hundred-grand bond; fancy that. He'd been spotted snooping around an old warehouse late at night three days ago. A warehouse that happened to have fourteen-year-old Erika Newman hiding inside some old shipping crates. She also had a pursuer, and her description matched Vance perfectly and, according to her, she wasn't the only kid he'd had in his possession. She had one more thing on her person.

A CD labeled *Dead Drive*.

She wouldn't tell us what was on it. She locked up when we even asked about it. Somehow, I had a gut feeling this Vance cocksucker could tell me more. I'm a pretty persuasive guy. I got to his run-down apartment by seven-forty-five.

KNOCK! KNOCK!

No answer.

KNOCK! KNOCK!

"Mister Vance, this is Officer Monroe with the NYPD, can you open up? I need to talk to you."

Heavy footsteps approached the door; the door shifted as someone pressed against it from the inside. A thick Boston accent rang from the other side.

"Goddamn, can't you fuckin' pigs give a motherfucker a break? I haven't done anything."

"Never said you did, sir. I just need to talk with you."

"About what?"

"Open up and we can discuss it." No answer. "Everett—"

"You got a warrant?"

"Yes, sir, I do." I didn't.

"My ass you do. Fuck off." I always love it when they play hard to get. I felt the muscles tense up in my left hand, itching to connect with a skull. I looked to my right hand. A bionic arm had no bones to break. Probably the safer bet.

KRACK!

The door came right off its hinges. A well-kept young man, late thirties, fell to the ground on the other side. "The fuck, man?!"

I grabbed him by the collar of his shirt. "I gave you plenty of chances, buddy. I'm here to talk about Erika Newman." Not even a phantom could match the shade of white on this bastard's face. He didn't say anything. I pulled the CD out of my coat. "It's encrypted. You know how to decrypt it."

He shook his head. "I'm no hacker, bro!"

I grabbed his throat and gave it a tight squeeze. "Well, you better fuckin' figure out how to really goddamn fast. You think I don't know how to make shitstains like you disappear? I can make everyone you've ever loved go away with a machete, a cooler, a couple of forty-four caliber rounds, and one slip of paperwork. Not even God would know where to start looking for you." I leaned forward. "I'm a cop. You really think anybody's gonna do anything about it?"

And wouldn't you know it? He figured out how to decrypt shit pronto. Like I said. Persuasive. I had the barrel of my gun against the back of his head. His computer cursor hovered over the *play* button. He clicked it. Text with a dripping font appeared on the screen.

"TONY BERNARDI PRESENTS...A MODERN GIALLO...DEAD DRIVE (LA GUIDA MORTA)
STARRING:
TONY BERNARDI AS THE MASTER
LITTLE PIXIE
BABY MOSCOW
TEENY TINA"

The names just kept coming; there must've been at least forty. I knew this had to be CP. It had to be. When the name *Eclectic Erika* came up, I knew I was right. But it got worse. Eventually, one name in particular, aside from Erika's, arose that stood out to me. *The Starved.* The opening shot showed a mansion in the distance. A vintage Cadillac drove along a dirt road. The sign called it *Dead Drive.* Several young girls sat in the back seat, at least seven who had to have been crushing each other in the cramped seat. The man in the driver's seat had the flayed face of a wolf over his head. There was no music. Barely any sound. The kids were silent. The only thing to be heard was the sound of a running engine and the labored breathing of a man hiding under a thin layer of wolf flesh.

They arrived at the house, greeted by men in black suits, each wearing the wolf faces over their heads. Hands still bound, the girls were ushered inside. My gut was sinking more with each passing second. Vance stared past the computer and out the window. Somehow, I knew he'd seen this before. And even a sick fuck like him didn't want to relive it. The footage continued for over an hour, the girls forced to undergo a rigorous makeup job and given extravagant clothes by women in nun robes. These women wore masks, symbolizing the genres of Greek theater. I'm sure this "Tony Bernardi" thought he was making some sort of profound metaphor with this, but I wasn't getting any closer to figuring it out.

The girls were brought to an auditorium. Several masked figures sat in church pews, each of them standing in unison as the girls entered. A set of massive double doors were on the other side of the room, wide open and showcasing a sprawling vineyard. Some wrinkly, old, white bastard dressed like the pope stood in front of these doors. As the kids were brought before him, they were forced to their knees. Like they were being instructed to kneel. The old dude spoke in Italian, so I didn't understand jack shit. But through the mumbo jumbo, I discerned three words.

"Hide and seek."

A wave of violent urges overwhelmed me as I stared at the back of Vance's head. I wanted to smash his skull with the butt of my pistol. I needed to. I knew before the video had ended that this was a snuff film. It had to be. I put a hand on his shoulder. "What do you know about this?"

There was a brief pause. "Nothing, man. I'm just the editor, not the cinematographer."

I squeezed his shoulder, resting the barrel of my forty-four on his other one. "You know something."

He didn't respond. In that moment, I decided that this bastard's fate was to be determined by whatever happened next in the video. More Italian mumbo jumbo spouted from the pope's mouth. He raised his hands to the sky, looking up as if he was calling to God himself.

"GLI AFFAMATI!" His screams reverberated throughout the halls of the auditorium. Sounds of rattling chains came from behind the children. Quaking in terror, they turned their heads. The shot lingered away from them, illuminating a red-lit hallway behind them. Four of the wolfmen walked with a woman in chains. She was held up about a foot from the ground. But the closer it got, the less it looked like a woman. I'm sure there was a time where it was once a woman, but not anymore. Something else had taken its place.

Its skin hugged its ribs, cheeks sunken deep within its face. It slobbered uncontrollably, leaving a trail of viscous goo from its lips. Completely naked from top to bottom. Its matted brown hair dragged across the carpeted floor. As it entered the auditorium, swinging softly from the chains, the nuns bowed down in prayer to it. The men stopped with the beast about ten feet out from the children. It looked up at them, the shot slowly zooming in on its face. A synth droned in the background. It had impossibly dilated eyes. It whimpered like a dog begging to be put down.

I had no idea what I was looking at. None at all. This freakish beast that seemed to be far beyond anything conceivable by even the darkest of inhuman people. You see all kinds of things when you do what I do. The evilest of evils. But this was something else entirely. For the first time since I started working in this profession, I was fucking horrified. The nuns approached the children once more, tying cameras around their chests. The pope, for the final time, spoke in English. "She hungers, babies." He stepped aside and gestured to the vineyard. As he did, the wolfmen set the beast on the ground, slowly unraveling its chains. The children bolted into the vineyard, scattering in different directions. After forty-five seconds, the chains had been unraveled, and the wolfmen strapped a camera around the neck of the beast. The pope clicked his tongue and, with a shrill voice, the beast yipped like a hyena, darting out on all fours through the doors at an inhuman speed.

For nearly twenty minutes, the beast leapt through the bushes in the vineyard and brutalized the fleeing children. A horrific, bloodthirsty, cannibalistic rampage. It slaughtered them like dogs and feasted on their bodies until nothing but bones, the cameras, and a few strands of hair remained. When the rampage had finished, only one remained. Erika Newman. She cowered as the camera lingered from the perspective of the creature. The camera tilted, as if the creature had cocked its head. Erika screamed as the camera grew closer, but no carnage came. With a tender touch, the beast picked her up by her shirt with its teeth, like a wolf with its cub. It carried her back to the auditorium, where dozens of nuns and wolfmen cheered for her.

The beast sat her down, and the camera shifted to Erika's perspective. Even through the rage I was feeling, I saw the look in the eyes of this monster. A strangely human sadness. Through the eyes that sparkled with tears in reservation, I could almost see the woman who was once in there. Almost. The pope placed a kiss on each of Erika's cheeks and placed a crown of white roses on her head. The camera focused on her fear-stricken face, slowly zooming out. The crown of white roses suddenly caught fire; she didn't move a muscle. A bright white text began to fade in above her head.

"INNOCENZA PERSA. INNOCENCE LOST."
Fade to black.

I stared in silence at that darkened screen. I felt my eyes beginning to shift down to the pervert sitting in front of me. I saw his eyes looking at me in the reflection of the screen. I stared at that reflection for what felt like an hour. I opened my mouth to speak, dry as a desert, and rasped out a single word. "Where?"

"I said I'm just the editor, dude."

"Bullshit. You chased Erika Newman down to a warehouse just three days ago."

His eyes shifted to a drawer by his left thigh. "I dunno what you're talking about, man. I was shooting up with my bitch three nights ago."

I just stared at him. It was all I could do. Until I couldn't. "Put your hands flat on the desk." He didn't reply. "Fucking do it." He complied. I drew a knife from my hip and slammed the blade into his right wrist. He screeched as the blood splashed my face. His left hand opened the drawer, reaching inside. I saw him take hold of a small handgun before I kicked the drawer with as much force as I could muster. I heard the bones crunch and the gun clattered inside the drawer. He cried, begging like a monster who knew it had reached the end of its rope. He put on his best puppy dog eyes as he pleaded for his life. I don't remember what all he said. I saw red, and I heard it too. The color red sounded like satisfaction. Like a long time coming.

I took ahold of his wrist and pulled, dragging the blade up through his hand. He held up his other broken hand. "Alright, fuck! It's southeast in the woods outside the city! It isn't a movie set, it's Bernardi's mansion! Dead Drive doesn't show up on any GPS; it's unmarked, but I have a map on my computer. It's under the file name *Hot DD*. When you get there, the guys at the front will want a password, it's 'zucchero.' Please, man, fuck! Just let me go, bro. I'll never even go near another kid again, I swear! I'll never even edit shit, I'll work at a goddamn pizza joint for the rest of my life, just don't kill me!"

I looked down at this pitiful rat of a man. You never believe a word of what these sick bastards say. They'll always do it again. No matter how much they promise they won't. It would be amusing if it wasn't so goddamn sick. I pulled his hand the rest of the way through the knife, cleaving it down the middle. I covered his mouth as he screamed, pushing my face just a few inches from his. "I struggle to see you as a person. The only reason you want to live is because you know you're going straight to Hell when your time here is over. This country, this world is a cesspool. A hive for vermin. This world will never escape the likes of you. Do you have any idea how long I've stayed silent to save my own skin? About people like you? Too many." I grabbed a handful of his hair. "Time to do my part."

Resume the screaming. I dragged him to the floor and kicked his head against the desk. With his hair clenched in my fist, I yanked his head over to the drawer of his desk, kicking it against his neck with a crunch. He gurgled and twitched. I kicked it again. And again. And again. I got down on my knees and grabbed it with my bionic arm, slamming the drawer against his neck as the crunches turned to squelches. Blood poured from his neck, spilling over onto his carpet. After the thirty-seventh slam, his head came off. I heard it clamor to the bottom of the drawer as everything below his head hit the carpet. The bloodied stump of a neck that once carried a cranium shot blood out like a geyser. I hadn't realized I was completely soaked in this fucker's vital fluids.

"So, you're confessing to the murder of Everett Vance?"

Murder? No. I dealt justice.

"Officer Monroe, are you aware that Everett Vance is the—"

Nephew of Chief Justice Lloyd Vance? Yeah. I'm aware. Hence why the fucker's dead. He never would've even seen the inside of a prison cell. And by extension, neither would the people he worked for. I don't give a shit who he is to the public. I give a shit that he's a snuff film editor and a child predator. Now, may I continue?

"..."

Thanks. I found the map he was talking about. Buried in a folder that contained nearly three-hundred terabytes of CP. I would never have found it if he hadn't told me exactly what to look for. I kicked his body one more time for good measure, then I walked back out into the rain. It was quite the walk to Dead Drive, but I was willing to walk it. Truth be told, I didn't think I'd be coming back to the city. In fact, I planned not to. But here we are.

You saw the rain last night; it was torrential. The mist that rose from the afternoon asphalt paired nicely with the decreased visibility from the rain. I walked through those streets oblivious to the world around me. I heard a few people ask me if I was okay, to which I offered no response. The occasional blaring of wailing sirens was all I heard; a pitiful reminder that the stinking rot of the city stopped for nothing.

I stopped at a crosswalk as the light turned red. A tan woman with a transparent umbrella stopped next to me. She didn't make eye contact. She spoke with a heavy accent; Italian. "Lost?" I didn't reply. "You have the look of one which battles great demons." I looked at her; she didn't look at me.

"Anyone who does what I do has demons." I looked back ahead. "It's the circle of life." I saw her nod from the corner of my eye.

"Indeed, Officer. I would like to ask, if I may… Why not leave then? If your demons bring you such torment." The million-dollar question. I had no fucking clue. Except I did. I was afraid of how I'd feel to admit it. "No answer? Or are you unwilling to answer?" The light had been green for over ten seconds now.

I inhaled. "Maybe they're not demons to me."

I heard her chuckle. "Maybe they aren't to me either. Maybe they give me…"

"Life. Feeling."

She nodded. "In a place that would seek to take those from you."

I clicked my tongue. "Right on the money." I felt her hand rest upon my shoulder, a gentle touch. One that filled me with relief. Clarity.

"I will leave you to your own devices now. Go with power and willingness." She turned right at the crosswalk, vanishing into the fog. I continued along through the rain as the realization of what I was doing hit me like a truck. I had essentially ended my own life, or, at the very least, my entire career. I'd killed a useless shit sack who, unfortunately, had a really big name attached to him. And yet, I felt serene about the whole thing.

My life has been a waking nightmare since I was ripped from my mother's gut. A never-ending hellscape dominated by skulking rats wreathed in suits and ties, or a badge and a gun. All of them with a smile on their face that says, "I'm a friend." Meanwhile, their fingers are crossed on one hand while the fingers on their other hand are wrapped all nice and snug around the grip of a pistol. What's that saying? "With friends like these, who needs enemies?"

This planet is an ocean of shit filled with bottom feeders looking to hoover up any little piece of goodness they can get their greasy hands on. Goodness to some is suffering for others. People like Tony Bernardi. People like Everett fucking Vance. To these cunts, you and I are expendable. Do you understand what I'm saying…Officer Clinton? The sooner you accept that, the sooner you can be free.

"Like you, Eli? You look like a mad dog from where I'm sitting. And you're a goddamn murderer. Why don't we get back on track? You were heading to Dead Drive?"

Murder. These days, that word gets thrown around more than a dime-store hooker. I don't know how long I walked. Hours, it felt like. I eventually found myself standing in front of a set of black iron gates standing about seven feet high. It's funny what rage can do to a man. I felt powerful. I was over the gate in less than five seconds; I practically jumped it.

I landed with the grace of a cheetah and surveyed the surroundings. Cars everywhere, all of them expensive and most certainly foreign. Spotlights shone a dark red light across the lawn. Wreathed in the crimson illumination, I put one foot in front of the other, walking across the lawn of Dead Drive and into a place beyond any other I'd ever set foot in.

The door was unlocked, strangely enough. I stepped inside, unsure of whether or not my host would be welcoming of my presence. The décor looked like it hadn't been updated in nearly a century, if not longer. An old, fragmented memory of a time gone by. Someone who couldn't quite leave behind the past. Bernardi was a filmmaker, after all. One who had long since passed his prime.

There is no real way to explain what was wrong with the house. It just felt…off. The halls either too wide or too narrow, slanted like you were looking at a Dutch angle in a movie. A thick layer of humidity coated the air from the top of my head to the bottom of my neck. The faint sounds of distinctly sexual moaning began to grow louder the more I spiraled down the impossibly long hallways, and a strange "breathing" sound came from all around me. It felt like the walls were watching me.

I unbuttoned my holster and freed the forty-four. An open doorway was on my left, a flashing purple light spewing forth from the doorless orifice. I stepped into the doorway. Over a dozen people were sprawled out across the floor, all of them still breathing, but barely moving, covered in blood and bodily fluids. A man, face down, was slowly grinding his crotch against a sopping wet bedsheet. A few of these things looked at me, muttering quietly in what I think was Italian. I stepped into the room, spotting one more figure in the corner.

A young girl.

Her eyes sank into her skull, body shaking like a leaf. She looked like she had some sort of deformity; she looked like she was a product of inbreeding. I've seen enough of them to know their look. Her black t-shirt was disheveled, and her pants looked three sizes too small… She couldn't have been more than eleven or twelve. I walked over to her and knelt down.

"What did they do to you?" She didn't respond. I shook her shoulder. "Kid."

She looked at me, shook her head, and spoke with a terrible slur. "Not do anyfing. Watch. Get ready. For da 'Athension.'"

The man with the bedsheet hummed quietly, speaking with an Italian accent. "The girl is next in line, Americano. You ought to envy her, you know. We all do, yes, friends?" Affirming moans called out in response. My hand trembled against the girl's shoulder. I don't know what kind of Godforsaken brainwashing had happened to her, but her eyes were hollow, devoid of anything. The way she talked; it wasn't a kid in there. Someone, or something, had warped her. Groomed her, it seemed like, for whatever she stood to inherit. I then noticed one of the women had crawled onto the man with the sheet, taking small bites of flesh from his shoulder, the man moaning softly in response.

I suddenly felt the overwhelming urge to scream. So I did. I shrieked, a primal yell that I'd been holding in since the beginning of my vile existence. The degenerates screamed with me, slowly devolving into laughter. The lights went red. I did what needed to be done...

"And that would be?"

I put a bullet in the kid's head. And then the rest of them. They screamed, asking what I had done, saying that I had destroyed everything and a livelihood decades in the making. The last of them had been silenced, but their voices still cried out to me. I left the room and continued to walk down the hallways. Everything looked familiar to me; exactly how things had appeared in the snuff piece. None of it felt real. Maybe that's why I did what I did. Maybe I subconsciously convinced myself that this wasn't real.

"Or maybe you're just trying to justify murder. Jesus, Monroe! What the fuck happened to you?"

I was always this way. You just never gave enough of a shit to notice. Just like everyone else.

"You're sick, Eli."

Come on, Clinton. Don't bullshit me. That kid was long gone. It was a mercy. I had to make a call, and I did. You know about the things that've gone on in this city. You remember that case we worked back in ninety-five?

"You mean the kidnapping of Bobby Boyle?"

Ah. So that's what you call it to help you sleep at night. Yeah, the "kidnapping." You remember it then?

"...Of course I do."

Look me in the eye and tell me the man behind that was human. That the things he did weren't incomprehensible.

"..."

You know that at least a part of you believes this.

"…"

As I was saying… I walked down the hall and recognized the door that now stood in front of me. A set of decrepit iron doors. In the video, the auditorium was on the other side. I ejected the mag of my forty-four, loaded a new one, and pulled back the slide. The doors were already slightly ajar when I reached them. I stepped through. The auditorium was filled with people; the wolves, the women in the theater masks. All seated in pews. And at the edge, standing before a basin, there he was.

Tony Bernardi. The Master, as he lovingly referred to himself. He looked over his shoulder at me as I entered, opening his arms to me.

"Aha, Elijah, *mio figlio*." I stopped dead in my tracks. "You arrive to us at last!" The spectators stood, turning their heads to me in unison. Tony, still in full pope regalia, outstretched his arms. "A brilliant plot twist from you! We did not expect you to take the fourth Wombling from us, but it matters no more!" Two of the figures, a man and a woman, stood from the pews and walked to his side, both wearing the faces of wolves. He put his arms around them. "Come now, Eli. Come forward."

I stepped forward with extreme caution. "What the hell is this?" I raised my forty-four. "What the fuck are you talking about, you've expected me? This is off the books; I shouldn't even be here. Nobody knows I'm here."

"Gramma does," said one of the figures. The man. I recognized the voice, and my hand began to tremble.

"T…Tommy?"

I recognized his emerald eyes under that wolf's face. "Big brother. You haven't replied to my letters. I've been trying to invite you here for a while now." He chuckled. "Gramma took matters into her own hands." Saying I was stunned wouldn't even describe a fraction of the feeling that boiled inside of me. Shock. Fear. Anger. Confusion. I looked to the woman with more confusion. Thomas looked at her, moving away from Tony and over to her, taking her hand in his.

"This is my wife you refused to meet, Francesca. Our sister." I swallowed the vomit that lapped at my tongue from my throat. Suddenly, something clicked in me. I looked back out the way I came. "Sorry your meeting with your niece had to be so brief." I looked back at him with horror.

"That was her?" was all I could manage to squeak out. He nodded. "I shot Izzy?" He nodded again. I shook my head in disbelief. "Why? Why didn't you stop me?" There was a pause.

"Isabella became irrelevant once Gramma brought you to accept what you are. You're the firstborn. You're next in line." The crowd whispered "firstborn" in unison. My eyes widened, I trained the gun back on Tony.

"'*Mio figlio?*'"

Tony gave me a toothy yellow grin. "You know what it means, Eli." Shock overcame me, but somehow my legs still found the strength to move me forward. Tony kept talking as I walked. "Your madre took you from me when you were but a wee bambino. She sought to abandon this place and all it has given us. Centuries of our family. Before the third Great War. Before the second. Before this place had written its name as the United States of America." He fell to his knees. "This house is more than it seems to be. 'Dead Drive' is not a place. It is a world within worlds. And your mother..." He jumped to his feet, screaming out into the auditorium. "SPAT! ON ITS GIFTS! WE ARE LUCKY TO HAVE BEEN CHOSEN! SHE WAS THE MATRIARCH OF THIS PLACE, THIS LAND!"

"AMEN!" the crowd shouted.

"THEN!" He grabbed my sister by the throat. "SHE SIRED A BASTARD DAUGHTER WITH ANOTHER! RID HERSELF OF THE BERNARDI NAME! AND SHE WAS JUSTLY PUNISHED!" My father pointed to me. "You must atone for her misdeeds, boy! As the firstborn, YOU must take up her mantle!"

I hadn't realized I'd slid my pistol back into its holster. I cupped my dad's cheeks in my hands, and he stared lovingly into my eyes. A voice crawled into my eardrums. The woman from the stoplight.

"There can only be one."

I caressed his cheeks with my thumbs, running them across his old, wrinkled eyelids. Light shone in through the stained-glass windows, painting us in an ethereal, colorful illumination. I dug my fingers into Tony's eyes and he screamed out to me in terror. He fell back to his knees, clawing at my face like a cat climbing a tree. My siblings tried to pry me away from him to no avail. I squeezed, savoring the sensation of his skull cracking between my hands. His teeth cracked and fell from his mouth before the rest followed swiftly.

SQUISH!

Loose strands of hair and remnants of putrid brain matter lathered my hands. I let him slump to the floor before freeing my pistol from its holster. I blasted my bastard sister in the head, the wolf mask sinking into her hood as the chunks of her skull and flesh spewed from the mouth and the eyeholes. My brother knocked the gun from my hand.

"What are you doing, brother?! Stop! You are better than Mother!"

I grabbed him by the throat and slammed him to the ground. I put my boot against his chin. "Gramma knows best, Tommy." I forced down, crushing his jaw and his throat with an inhuman might. The crowed whooped and hollered maniacally, chanting a single word.

"ONE! ONE! ONE! ONE! ONE! ONE!"

"..."

It's a strange thing, you know?

"What's that?"

The feeling of finally being understood. Not in the way you had hoped for. Asked for. Yearned for. But it comes to you, nonetheless. And it feels...good. Incredible.

"Funny, Eli. You talk as if you're leaving this place tonight. You just confessed to multiple homicides while inside a cage. You're not going anywhere tonight except a jail cell."

...See, Clinton, this is part of the problem. All you discerned from this tale is that I killed people. You never stopped to think about who or why. I am not the villain of this tale. I have undergone a hero's journey. Tony Bernardi and my siblings were villains, absolutely. They used what they'd been given to do evil, and all in the name of what?

Tony found his snuff films to be like art. So, in the name of art? No. This gift is incredible and ancient. The house is another world entirely. A world to cleanse other worlds. It just needs to be guided. I can do that. That's why my father and my siblings had to go.

"Alright, that's enough, Eli. Get up and put your hands behind your back."

What was that you said, Clinton? I'm in a cage? That's right, I am. But make no mistake. I'm not in your cage. You're in mine.

Caked in blood, Eli walked back up the steps to the manor at Dead Drive. He opened the door with his left hand, his right hand gripping the hair connected to Officer Clinton's severed head. Down the hall he trekked, past the auditorium, and down the ancient stone steps into the muggy basement. The Starved lay in a corner, shivering and hugging its chest. Eli knelt down next to it, smiling. "Sorry I was gone so long, Mom. Had to finish up some things. Brought this for you." He set the head down next to the Starved. It snatched it and tore the head to shreds, devouring it within seconds. It looked up to Eli, tears in its eyes. Its mouth hung open, mumbling slightly.

"*My…my…my boy…*" It reached to Eli, who took its hand in his.

"That's right, Mom. Your boy is here." He leaned forward and whispered, "And he's not going anywhere."

INTERLUDE

DATADISC "DEAD DRIVE" – END
ERROR! ERROR! ERRwearethegreatesterrOR!
WARNING: UNSANCTIONED A.I. DETECTED!

Everything is quiet in the Library. Even the wind outside seems to have taken a rest. Your feet shuffle, your eyes still transfixed on the now vacant screen before you. Dust falls from the ceiling, illuminated by the light shining through the cracks in the walls. You hold up a hand, watching it tremor like a dog under snowfall. The silence of both the world and Custos is unnerving following everything you've just witnessed. Not even the world has words for any of it. Not even a ghost.

The Library suddenly seems…darker than it did before. No—dingier. That's the word. Makes you wonder if it was ever so vibrant to begin with. Even the little things, like the old soda cans and bags of crisps, seemed to be absent from the picture. You sigh.

This old, old world is fading away.
Faded. It's faded, Pilgrim.
Proctor, why have you shown me this…this…terror?
You asked. This "terror" is human history. It wasn't at first, but we *made* it our history. There's a lot beyond us, out there. There always has been. There's even things beyond beyond. But you know that saying about the cat?
Curiosity killed it.
Curiosity killed it. It's only been in our nature to be curious since the dawn of man. How do you think we discovered fire? At first, the Neanderthals used it to cook food and provide warmth. Then we evolved,

and the Vikings used it to pillage and terrorize. And finally, our governments used it to conform and destroy. When has our curiosity *not* led to terror?

I suppose I just expected something better, Proctor. Less hatred and more understanding. I thought...I thought we were better than this.

Ha! First and worst mistake. I made that one myself. The worst thing you can do is expect the best out of people. Let's not forget what brought all of this to a halt in the first place. I'll give you a hint: it wasn't anything from outer space that ended humanity.

Then what was it? If it wasn't a comet, or some intergalactic war, then what?

Patience. I've got one final set of Datadiscs for you to peer over. Let's see what conclusions you draw then.

No! Enough of your games, why won't you tell me? Why must you deliver this...lesson of yours to me? What good does it do me now?

What good does knowing the end of everything do you? It won't change the fact that things did, in fact, end. Besides, I already gave you the answer you seek. You simply weren't listening. The truth is almost never an easy pill to swallow, is it? Perhaps you should pay more attention for the answers you *seek* rather than the answers you *want*.

The voice dissipated, drowned out by the return of the howling wind from outside. You kick through piles of dust to a nearby window. You peer through, though piles of dust cover most of your view. Light comes through, though only just. Only a small glimpse of the world outside the Library. A light that shone on a dead world. You ponder the nature of Custos' words now more than ever. What is the point of all this? Knowing the end of an already ended world? The desire to know is insatiable. But what about after you obtain this knowledge, if you ever do? You flick your head, your eyes locking onto the final three Datadiscs. And with that, the thought is whisked away once more by desire and curiosity. You pick up a disc, one with a familiar name, and slide it into the computer.

PART IV
MEMORIES OF THE CULMINATION

Reading Datadisc…confirmed.
Launching…

THE LEGEND OF THE INDIVISIBLE: PART II – UNVEIL

"…Lost to mind."

December, 538 AD
The Battlefield of Camlann

SQUELCH!
"Gah!" Arthur fell to one knee. He clasped the blade, which stuck into his ribs, a cold sting running up his spine. Mordred drove the blade in farther, grinning.

"It's over, Father," sneered the boy. "Thou art finished. As is Camelot." Arthur lovingly took a small bit of Mordred's hair in his hand.

"Oh…my son." He yanked without warning.
SQUISH!
The tip of Excalibur ran through Mordred's throat, eliciting a gasp from the young warrior. Arthur rolled to the side, sliding his son off his sword and into the blood-drenched snow. Mordred gurgled, blood spewing from his throat, mouth, and nose. He turned his head to halfway face his father.

"F…Father." He choked. "Why dost thou spurn me so?"

Arthur's breath slowed. "Why…dost thou disappoint me so…*boy*?" Rage enveloped Mordred's increasingly colorless face. But within a few seconds, the rage had turned to stillness; then all which was left in

Camlann was a dying king clutching onto an ancient relic. He ran his thumb across Excalibur's blade, still warm with blood spilled in the heat of battle. He sighed. Heavy booted footsteps crunched toward him through the snow.

"My king!" The footsteps stopped next to him, and Bedivere knelt into the snow, removing his helmet. "By God's grace, I have found thee, sire. We must make haste to Camelot; perhaps a healer still lives there."

Arthur shook his head. "Nay, Bedivere. This…" He nodded. "I would have this be my final resting place, for I have given my all…and triumphed."

Bedivere looked to his left to the fallen Bastard, then back to Arthur. "Thou wouldst end thine own reign? Here? After such a glorious victory?"

The king rested a palm against his knight's frost-nipped cheek. "I am old, dear boy." He wheezed, a few trickles of blood spewing from his nose. "I fear that the days of glorious victories are henceforth behind me." He nodded. "I have earned this rite of rest."

Bedivere took the king's hand in his. "But what of Camelot, my king?"

"Think nothing more of the kingdom. It is finished. The age of Camelot is over." He winced as snow pelted at his wounds. "I would have Camelot lost to time now."

"But, my king—"

"Silence now, Bedivere." Arthur took his knight by the wrist and slapped Excalibur into his open palm. "Thou must take the blade and return it from whence it came. Back to the Lady of the Lake. For I cannot make the journey myself anymore. Find what remains of the Round Table." He wrapped an arm around Bedivere's neck, pulling himself into an almost seated position.

"Remain in secret. Protect the secrets of this world. Mordred, Kobranos, Morgana…this is what should happen when our secrets—our knowledge falls into terrible hands. You must promise me, Bedivere." He fell back into the snow. "Promise me that the Round Table will protect this land from evil…from the unknown."

Bedivere nodded. "Of course, my king. I swear it unto thee and under the visage of God that thy will shall be done." Arthur wheezed and reached for the buckles on his plate, loosening them and letting the armor detach from his chest. Bedivere moved the bloodied armor and tossed it aside into the snow, then pulled Arthur's head into his arms. "I am here for thee, milord. Thou shall not find Heaven by thy lonesome."

Arthur wrapped a hand around Bedivere's forearm. "Heaven…?" He chuckled weakly, looking to the sky. "O greatest of kings, my Lord, my God…wouldst thou beckon me home at long last?" Bedivere's armor was cold against the king's cheek, blood ran cold down from his lips, snow pricked and clawed at his cheeks, and the moon shone dimly in the sky. Like a dying star. No warmth came to Arthur that night. Not yet.

For it was not his time.

Winter, 4304
Deep within the forests of South Wales

Through the blizzard, a figure appeared before the Indivisible, who lay bleeding into the snow. A cape billowing, a crown atop its head. He raised his hand in place of a cry for help. The figure came into full view, kneeling into the bloody snow before the Pilgrim. "Did thou not hear my call, Indivisible?" The man cocked his head, the slightest glimmer of moonlight catching his golden crown. The man had hair down to his hips, and a beard which covered his neck. He took the Indivisible by the hand. "I have come to fulfill my destiny. Through you."

Everything went dark. The Indivisible felt the grip of this strange man around his wrist, dragging him through the snow, though the sounds of the flurry had gone away. Only the crunching of boots in snow remained. His eyes fluttered every so often, and he found himself mumbling Sara's name between shuddering breaths. Blood trickled from between his teeth, and his cybernetic parts were critically failing.

His body eventually met with stone steps; he was being dragged up them. "The doors," whispered the strange man. "He was here…" As the Indivisible was dragged up the steps, he recognized the chapel where he had met Galahad, and a warmth enveloped him. "Fret not, Indivisible. By the grace and power of God shalt thou persevere." The man's voice was growing more faint with each word that left his lips.

He lifted the Indivisible onto the altar with a single swift pull. "Thou shalt not fall, not today." The man tore a silver crucifix from around his neck, placing it upon the Indivisible's chest. "Through the power invested in me, bestowed unto to me through the will of God, I beckon the power to bring this man to health, so that destiny might still be achieved." The Indivisible closed his eyes, and visions overtook him.

Mordred, the Bastard, splitting a great round table with his blade. A mother, rising from the depths of Hell with the Bastard himself there to guide her back into the world. Mother and son, embracing in filth with their lips upon one another, their hands exploring one another. The mother, raising a hateful child to the sky for all to see. A newborn. A son from a son.

"Destiny!" The man beckoned a bright light into the palm of his hand, shimmering throughout the body of the Indivisible. The Pilgrim saw a final image: Sara. Her tan cheeks, a head full of hair. She looked like she did before she'd gotten sick. She stood next to him, resting her hand atop her brother's. She leaned down and whispered into his ear.

"Bravery, hermano. Bravery."

"RISE!" The Indivisible's eyes sprung open, a flash of vibrant light coursing through them for the briefest of seconds. He turned his head, facing the stranger who had saved him from certain death.

"You," muttered the Pilgrim. "You are…"

The figure nodded. "Arthur Pendragon. King of the Britons." He took the Indivisible by the hand once more. "And I have returned to fulfill my destiny. 'Twould seem that thou art my means of achieving this."

The Indivisible sat up with Arthur's help, looking the King in his loosely transparent eyes. "I thought you had already gone away. To the beyond."

Arthur shook his head. "Nay, my boy. 'Twas decided that I would remain in a state of purgatory, a limbo, until my destiny had been fulfilled. My spirit could not rest, not while the threat of my own son remained." He shook his head. "I had believed him dead, truly. But alas, it took the death of my last knight to awaken me from my millennia-long stupor." He gestured to his feet; the headless skeleton of Galahad had already decayed as if he had been dead for thousands of years. He looked up to the Indivisible. "We've no more time to spare, for my son possesses the Kobracon."

The Pilgrim rested a hand upon his head. "What is he? Your son." He rose to his feet. "I crossed blades with him. He seemed…inhuman. As did his subordinates."

Arthur circled the skeleton of his fallen brother. "Mordred is the product of mine own sin. I lay with another woman. His mother, Morgana, was a witch. A terrible evil with a twisted pursuit of purity. She would have the world in her own image." He shook his head. "My betrayal of my beloved Guinevere was not made from my own desire, but my lack of strength." He looked to the Indivisible. In the old spirit's eyes, there was a deep regret; a melancholy. And, strangely, a faint love. Though the Pilgrim thought it offensive to press deeper into *who* that love was for.

"Truth be told, Pilgrim, I know not what hath become of my son. He hath transformed into some monstrosity inconceivable by the grace of God. I killed him. I *killed* him. And yet, he walks still. Not as a spirit, nay. But something darker. Something wretched; a foul darkness not of Heaven, Earth, or, I fear, not even Hell."

The Indivisible stepped forward. "Then where? What could be a more foul origin than Hell itself?" Arthur's gaze fixed to the floor, a brief flash of fear crossing his eyes. From somewhere beyond, the Indivisible heard the toll of a bell; then the King's eyes locked back with his.

"Do not underestimate the evil of witchcraft, Indivisible." He hesitated. "'Twas once a mistake of mine own. A mistake I shan't make again. Morgana is a wretched being. But, alas, she is dead and gone. I sent her soul to Hell when I returned to the forest once more. There, I discovered Mordred. A small babe, and one I knew to be mine own. I should have killed him. But...I could not. For he was mine only child. And within his eyes I saw the eyes of a king, if only he could grow to escape the tainted filth of his mother's blood. But...if she has brought him back, while still remaining dead herself—"

"Then maybe he seeks to bring her back," said the Pilgrim. "Perhaps that is the extent of his need for the Kobracon."

Arthur stared off into nothingness for a moment, before shifting his gaze back to the Indivisible. "There is no more time for chatter, Indivisible. We must go. Make haste, for I know the place which my son would seek." The Pilgrim's eyes locked with Arthur's. This journey, this quest...it felt beyond him. *Far* beyond him. He clenched his fists, hiding his fear. Sara's voice rang out in his head.

"Bravery."

He sighed. "I have no arms to bear."

"Then thou must make do with mine," replied the king. "Come, my boy." He walked to the destroyed chapel doors. "We've one more pilgrimage to make."

My beautiful boy. You've come at last.

Camelot's doors fell from their hinges with barely a push, leaving only the moonlit silhouette of Mordred le Fay standing in the doorway. He hadn't seen the kingdom since he was a boy. Even during his final days leading up to the assault on his father's home, he hadn't returned to see it. It looked just as he had hoped it would.

Ransacked. In shambles. Pillaged. Reduced to rubble. In his time between life and death, he saw that Camelot had been abandoned. All but Arthur's inner circle had fallen in battle, and their millennia-old skeletons and armor had remained.

Even as he stepped through the doors, he could feel his father's sadness for the terror that had been wrought upon his kingdom. It brought a grin across the Bastard's lips.

Mordred...

A voice called to him from beyond the castle foyer. A soothing voice; a feminine one.

...come to me.

As Mordred stepped deeper into Camelot, his vision narrowed, homing in on a deep green robe disappearing from around a distant doorframe. The hallway seemed to shrink behind him with each step that echoed through the decrepit stone walls. A light came from around the doorframe, flickering. Green and purple.

He stepped around the corner, and before him was an apparition. A spirit. An image of his beautiful young mother. Morgana le Fay. She floated above a round table. *The* Round Table.

He whimpered. "Mother." She beckoned him with her index finger, which looked feeble and rotted. Her black nail slipped off her finger and vanished before it could hit the floor. Mordred fell to his knees.

Crawl.

He did as he was told, crawling on his knees to his mother's ghostly presence. Her apparition lowered down, bringing her to a seated position on the table. She smiled.

"My, my," she whispered, "how you've grown." A handful of flies flew out from her mouth. "My beautiful boy."

"Mother," he rasped, "I have it." He reached into his coat and removed a tome of human flesh: the Kobracon. "At last, you will return truly and purely." His breath quickened. "And it is my doing. Are you proud of me, Mother?"

"Oh, yes I am." Her face cupped his cheek. He whimpered as her rotten thumb brushed through his lips and into his mouth. He suckled it, like a calf to an udder. "You've done so well. Your militia of the dead is nothing short of astounding, boy. You've listened well and learned even better." Morgana slipped her thumb from Mordred's mouth, her spiritual flesh dangling from his lips.

"Thank you, Mother," he said. "What must I do now?"

Morgana chuckled. "Now…" she began to levitate once more, "you must find the Ritual of Lazarus within the book. Perform the ritual as you must and bring me back into the world. Then, and only then, can I bear your seed. This wretched world needs our rule now more than ever. Just look at them."

Mordred grimaced. "Mortals, Mother. Are you surprised?"

She scoffed. "As a matter of fact, I am. You'd think they would've advanced further after so much time. But time only seemed to wear them down further."

"Yes." Mordred slipped his tongue from his mouth, licking his mother's palm. "Perhaps they will understand us now."

"They had better. After all…" Morgana slowly dissipated, her touch leaving her son's frost-nipped cheek, "…what choice do they have now?"

The Bastard found himself alone now, in his home; in the darkness. He looked ahead to the only lit thing in the room. The Round Table, layered in a thick sheet of dust and coated within a veil of moonlight. It almost seemed to glimmer beneath the lunar rays.

It was a strange thing to him, this table. A seat at it was something he had coveted for years in his childhood. Years of training. Years of tenacity. But he never *was* enough for his father, the one some would call *the* Knight of the Round Table. "Too reckless," said Father. "Too angry," said Father. "Too much like your hateful mother." But the coveting was through now. Now… Well, now there was just anger. Rage. Resentment.

Hate.

Mordred slid his sword from its hip-bound scabbard and brought it above his head. With a visceral scream, he brought it down upon the ancient table, cleaving it through the middle. For a brief second, Mordred's cry of rage became a childlike laughter. True, unadulterated glee. Then he became silent again, as he heard the cries of a man echo like a phantom throughout the ancient halls. For only a short time, he felt a sort of "half-presence" lurking in the room with him. Someone who was there, but not quite in their entirety. He looked over his shoulder.

"Father?" Nothing. The cries had gone silent, and the presence was gone. He did his best to hide the unease dwelling in his black heart. The thought had crossed his mind that his father's essence may yet linger within the dilapidated walls of Camelot. The enraged spirit of Arthur Pendragon, the only man to have ever bested the terrible Mordred le Fay. It was that very thought which left him feeling paradoxically horrified and excited like a child.

He grinned, ignoring the tremble that fell upon his lips. "Did you feel me?" The Kobracon opened up, levitating just above the palm of his hand, and the pages turned softly, stopping at one thousand forty four. A blood-red text spelled out in bold across the ancient parchment.

LAZARUS

I felt you.

A motorcycle hummed near-silently across the frozen wastes of Scotland. A chill ran through the Indivisible's body as the sleet nicked and dashed across his metallic cheeks. He felt unease stir inside of him. Arthur.

"What is it?" he asked.

"My son," whispered the king, his voice echoing within the Indivisible's head. "He awaits us at Camelot." The Pilgrim did not respond. He merely continued forward. He felt Sara's arms wrapped around his waist as he drove. She never could balance well enough to ride a bike, so she often rode with him when they were kids. He blinked.

"Why me?" His question was met with no answer. "I hear voices, see apparitions. My sister's voice is inescapable, and you have chosen me for some…greater purpose." He shook his head. "I fail to see what separates me from someone more capable. Someone more…worthy, I suppose. Someone who *has* purpose themselves."

The sounds of the flurry faded away, and only Arthur's voice remained, echoing in the night air. "And what makes thee so certain that thou art unworthy? Or that thou wouldst lack purpose?"

The Pilgrim tightened his grip on the handlebars. "Surely, you've looked around at my life. Look at me." He pressed his cobalt hand across his chest. Cobalt clinked against cobalt. "I'm barely even a man anymore. And I've lived a life almost exclusively of regrets."

"And yet thou art still here." Arthur's voice brought a sudden, soothing warmth through the Indivisible's veins. "Flesh or blood, these things which make up the fickle vessel we call the body—they are not what define us. I believed thou wouldst have known such a thing. Wouldst thou deny thyself of thine own humanity?"

The Pilgrim scoffed. "Humanity is something you've gotta earn, milord. I'm sure you earned it centuries ago." He shook his head. "I lost myself years ago. I don't know why I'm even on this bike, following the words of a lost king. You've got the wrong man, Arthur. There's no stone which I could free a sword from."

The King chuckled. "Thou wouldst argue that a spirit has humanity before allowing thyself the very same comfort? Look at thee. Thou hast decided thy path would be inescapable; that it would define thee. Is that what brings thee here? Heeding to the call of Galahad? Confronting a history other than thine own?

"I shall tell thee a secret. During my reign, I saw a great many men, women, and children suffer undeservingly. Pestilence and famine, murder and rape. Death. Torment. I found myself at odds with my God and my mission. Where did I come from if not a peasant town, as a peasant myself? My kingship was born because fate decided my grip would free a sword from a stone. *Me.* A peasant boy who came from nothing. Born to be a king without knowing. Without consent.

"But, even so, freeing a sword from a stone does not make a man's burdens disappear. It does not ease the pains of the past, nor does it cushion the blows of what will come. God knows how I struggled, even in my wisest years. Even now I wrestle with a longing to be greater. The trials continue, grievous as they may be. But it is through those trials that we discover who we can become. But I bestow upon thee a great and terrible truth: The one who cannot accept that who they once were is gone can never become anything greater than they believe they already are.

"We would all like to believe that we are masters of our own fates, Indivisible. But what will happen *will* happen. No amount of running shall ever stop that. How else can you explain the concept of death? If we are born, is it also not certain that we shall one day die? Try to outrun death, my friend. Thou shalt find it to be a tricky adversary to outmaneuver." He stepped forward. "When we flee from fate, we simply flee the inevitable.

"My point, Indivisible, is that this world is not kind to those who deserve well. Many suffer who do not deserve it, and many who *do* deserve suffering might yet avoid it. My land was plagued with terror and death before I was king. And yet, fate placed me there so that I might lead them to a better future. I did not do everything with absolute purity, but I did more than most ever did for my people." He shook his head. "'Twas thou who arrived here. Fate decided that Galahad would find thee. And thou answered the call, falling at the blade of my bastard son. And here art thou, risen from beyond. Dost thou truly believe that there is no purpose behind thee?"

Sam sat in silence, his hands loosening ever so slightly from the handlebars of the bike. He recalled those final moments in that deathly chill hospital room, clinging to Sara's hand with the fullest hope that she would wake up, if only for a moment, just so he could say he was sorry. For leaving her so alone during what were her final years. For ignoring the phone calls. For shunning her due to his own blind faith. He had spent years wallowing in this sorrow.

"I cannot rest. Not until you do," she had said to him in the Krypt. That phrase rang out in his head like the crack of gunfire in the mountains. He pondered those words. Pondered that final smile she had given him in that place. And it was in this moment that a *new* question wormed its way into the mind of the Indivisible: What kind of man would Samuel have become, if the Indivisible had not taken his place? Outrunning his own past had led him here, now. In deep pursuit of the past of another. *How ironic*, he thought. He shook his head.

"We're here." The bike skidded to a halt in the snow. Where there had once stood St. Rhychwyn's Church now was nothing. It was as if it had never even been there in the first place. But the body of water remained, only bigger. No longer a pond, but a lake. A vast, ethereal oasis of flickering moonlight with a tinge of arcana lingering in the air. As the Indivisible stepped down from his bike, the spirit of Arthur materialized at his side.

"Alas, it is as I remembered it."

The Pilgrim shook his head. "This is vastly different from the last time I was here."

Arthur nodded. "Yes. It appears much different to the ones who art worthy enough to see it this way. It was quite different for me when I first came."

The Pilgrim stared ahead, unblinking. "It's…"

"Beautiful."

"Ethereal."

"And she calls to us now," said the King. "For the first time in millennia, there is a worthy one to answer the call of Excalibur." From the water, the tip of a steel blade revealed itself, etched in Celtic glyphs that gleamed amethyst purple. A golden crossguard, the word *SOVEREIGN* carved into it with a golden font. And finally, a black grip held tight by a smooth, feminine hand with a deep purple gemstone for a pommel.

The hand pulled down, then thrust upward, launching the sword through the air. In that moment, the visage of Arthur fused with the Indivisible. Together, they lifted a single hand into the air, catching it with unparalleled grace. The Pilgrim's eyes canvassed the blade, looking it over along with Arthur as their faces phased in and out of one another arrhythmically.

Arthur grinned. "'Tis good to hold thee again, old friend." He and the Pilgrim sheathed the blade. Arthur nodded. "Art thou prepared?"

The Indivisible cracked his neck. "Are you?"

"Nay. But alas, that never did seem to stop me before."

And when he thus had spoken, he cried with a loud voice, "Lazarus, come forth." And he that was dead came forth, bound hand and foot with graveclothes, and his face was bound about with a napkin.

The boots of the Bastard trekked through the mud of Camelot's woodlands. He neared the site now. Only a few more minutes. He had remembered it clearly, like it was yesterday. His dear mother in his arms. Her soul enslaved in a book. *The* book. By Kobranos himself. But little did the wizard know...her soul belonged to another.

Mordred stopped when his foot crunched through the snow and connected with a stone. Thousands of years, and the stone had remained just where he had left it. He imagined that his mother had reached forth from beneath the earth, holding it in place with her soft, delicate fingers. He looked down to the snow and saw two green pinpricks staring up through the earth.

Mordred...

He fell to his knees. "Mother...I'm coming." He dug his armored hands through the snow and into the dirt. Ripping and tearing away the mud and stones of ages past. He could hear his mother's voice in his ear, encouraging and praising him and his vast bravery. Reveling in his desires for her, and his defiance of God and the rules of mortality. His face contorted to a crazed grin. "Mother! Oh, Mother, how I have yearned for thee!"

Within seconds, he had dug six feet under the earth. His gauntlets met with a stone slab, and so he slammed his fist down atop its surface. The slab cracked with ease, and he took the fragments and tossed them away. He stared down into the eyes of a skull. Rotted with four thousand years of decay. He laughed. "There art thou, Mother."

He took the skull in his hands, lifting it up so that the moonlight might shine upon it through the trees. When the light struck the skull, it revealed Morgana's face upon its surface. Her eyes opened, showing nothing more than solid green orbs. Her mouth opened, and thousands of flies poured forth as her voice carried on the winter wind.

Return me to that sanctified kingdom, so that together we might make it our own kingdom of power and darkness.

Mordred nodded furiously and pressed his lips against the teeth of the skull. "Yes, Mother, I shall. I shall." He turned on his heel and ran as fast as his feet could carry him until, once more, he stood within the mouth of Camelot. His robed subordinates stood in silence, one gloved hand over another, two on each side of the throne room doors.

"Our king," whispered one of them, its voice carrying in the silent nighttime air, *"has the time come?"*

"Does Mother return to us on this night?" asked another.

The Bastard nodded. "She does, my friends. She does. At long last. And so, you know what must be done. For the greater good."

"Yes, our lord, our liege," bellowed the voices of the four entities, the Bastard loyalists. *"For millennia, we have waited for the world to be graced once again by the lady's greatness. The lord and lady as one, as it was during the time of the womb."* They unsheathed their swords, holding them close to their chests, ancient hands wrapped tight around the grip. They turned toward the doors, their feet levitating a few inches above the ground.

A frigid rain fell softly as the Bastard and his loyalists made their way into the inner sanctum of Camelot. Within its bowels there was a great chapel, one that had seen a great many baptisms and consecrations during the prime of the kingdom. Mordred had always seen irony in holy deeds carried forth in a sanctum under the ground. One of the spirits spoke aloud.

"My liege, do you smell that stench which reeks?"

Mordred inhaled, then nodded. "Indeed. My father is nearing. But wait…" He inhaled again. "There is another." The smell of cobalt, wiring, and steel filled the Bastard's nostrils. He grinned. "It would seem that my father has chosen a most disappointing champion." He chuckled. "They'll pose no threat to us. And soon, Mother will have her way with them."

The four spirits took their places before an altar. They looked up against the gargantuan wall to a large stone sculpture of the crucifixion. One by one, they lined up and readied their blades, stabbing into the wound in Christ's side. Upon the fourth thrust, blood began to leak from the wound and down Jesus' side. The crown of thorns began to glow a bright red, and blood began to spill from every orifice of the Messiah.

The light from the crown shone against the loyalists, illuminating their faces. Decrepit, ripe with the rot of four thousand years of death and black magic, and stitches which connected their heads to bodies that were not their own in life. A terrible green glow billowed up from their chests and gleamed in the back of their rotting throats. This light, which gurgled and burrowed from their chests, spewed from their throats and up toward the depiction of the Savior upon the wall.

With each green orb that left their bodies, the shrill cackle of a wicked witch reverberated within the chapel walls. From the loyalist spirits came four terrible screams, and the green essence touched each of the palms and soles of the feet of Jesus. Suddenly, the eyes of the Savior turned black, and the visage upon the wall began to shift, as if it were trying to escape from its stone prison.

It was in this moment that Jesus began to weep, tears of blood pouring down His cheeks. In Latin, He begged his Father to save Him. From somewhere, some indiscernible source, Morgana's wheezing cackle echoed once again.

"Your Father has abandoned you as He abandoned his children on Earth...boy." The stone which made the form of Jesus began to crack, emitting the same green light which came from the loyalists. The loyalists fell to the ground, their bodies melting away into a puddle of viscera and old bones. From the other side of the stone, a shadow appeared through the cracks; someone standing on the other side. "Mordred..." The Bastard shuddered with awe and splendor. The Kobracon, which rested at the base of the sculpture disintegrated, and his face began to split, along with the flesh across his body. Blood seeped through the wounds, and all he could utter was a single word, drowned beneath a gurgling gasp.

"Mother..."

Hell awaits.

"We draw near, Indivisible." The Pilgrim reduced his speed on his bike, Excalibur fashioned tight onto his back. He narrowed his eyes to see through the freezing rain.

"Where is it?"

"Dost thou mean in the geographical sense or the metaphysical sense?" asked the king.

"Metaphysical."

Arthur sat in thought for a moment. "Once upon a time, Camelot was a place which welcomed all of the peoples of the Earth. Now, it hath fallen far away into a land of shadow. A place outside of God's reach. Or, perhaps, somewhere in between. Lost to time. Lost to mind. Stop." The bike skidded to a halt and the Pilgrim looked ahead of him to the great kingdom of Camelot. Or what was left.

The castle looked like it had seen war in its truest form. Towers collapsed, walls blown apart by what must have been spells or explosives. What was strange, however, was the state of the ruins. Chunks of debris were suspended in the air, carried around by some unknown force and surrounded by thick layers of green smoke. The Indivisible flipped down the kickstand of his motorbike.

"Mordred's doing?" He felt Arthur's head shake within his own.

"Nay. 'Twas Morgana's doing, surely. No doubt she took extraordinary pleasure in warping Camelot to bear no resemblance to the home I knew." His visage stepped forth from the Indivisible. "And yet, it is still haunting to bear witness to." Ancient skeletons floated from decimated walls and broken windows. It seemed as if they were sent to greet the duo upon their arrival. Arthur shuddered. Though with anguish or rage, the Pilgrim could not seem to discern. "The witch parades my people's corpses before me like playthings."

"She just wants to provoke you, Arthur. Cloud your judgment."

Arthur grunted in affirmation. "Aye. The witch always did have a knack for such things. Let us waste no more time, for my son surely nears the end of his wretched quest." The Indivisible took cautious steps toward the ruined kingdom doors. With each step, the sounds of the rain and wind grew quieter. Like they were…going away. Or maybe it was *him* that was going away. He stepped through the doors, and the sounds of the outside vanished, save for the occasional clap of thunder.

There was a taste of iron and rot in the air. The Indivisible stifled a gag. "God Almighty… Do you taste that?"

"Nay," replied Arthur, "but I can feel it… Wait." His form separated from the Indivisible's, and he stepped to the left in silence, gazing upon a piece of his own history. There before him was what remained of the Round Table. Splintered, broken into pieces, coated in the dust and grime of millennia gone by. The King rested his palm flat upon the old table and did not phase through it. He sighed, running his hands across the surface.

The Indivisible studied the spirit's face, watching as a flurry of memories returned in an *instant*. Arthur needed this moment, truly; the Pilgrim knew this. He closed his eyes, and the King shook his head. "O, how long it hath been, my Camelot," he whispered. From somewhere beyond, the cheers and hails of ancient knights cried out through the halls. Arthur removed his spectral blade from its scabbard, holding it out above the Round Table. A final "Hail!" rang out through the halls. The spirit chuckled.

"Although I hath lectured you greatly already on the attachment to history. But even now, thou canst see the ultimate truth. While we art all masters of our fates...one shall always remember where they came from, and what they have lost." He clenched his fist, sheathing his blade. "But alas, thou cannot blossom without loss." He walked to the Pilgrim, fusing with him once more. "Let us be off now. Mordred mustn't be far."

The Indivisible nodded. "But you're alright?"

"Indeed. 'Twas simply...reminiscing. Worry not for me, young warrior. Steel yourself." He phased inside of the Indivisible. Together, they took hold of Excalibur and relinquished it of its scabbard. "Mordred is foolhardy, yet formidable. This battle shan't be won with ease. It shall require the very best of thy skills, Indivisible."

The Pilgrim closed his eyes, bowing his head in a silent meditation. "I'll give it my all. I am not alone." An arm wrapped tenderly around his own; an arm that did not belong to Arthur.

The King smiled. "Nay. Thou art not." Camelot rumbled, the rooftop crumbling to bits and smashing around them. "We hath spent our time too frivolously. Make haste!" They took off, making their way down into the depths of that infernal place. That place which once housed glory. Now only death. And darkness. A voice came from deep within the bowels of Camelot's chapel.

"MOTHER OF SIN! MOTHER OF ME!"
BRRRRMMMM!

The Bastard's voice sent shockwaves through the castle. As the Pilgrim and the King descended the steps into darkness, the way they had come from disintegrated behind them. They stood in awe, enveloped in a swirling world of lifeblood, fire, and the tormented screams of those damned by the line of le Fay. They looked ahead, and there he was. Suspended around fifteen feet in the air.

The Indivisible found himself unable to comprehend what he saw. Mordred was no longer man, but he looked the part. Legs, arms, a head; all the fixings. But something about him seemed...otherworldly now. When the Pilgrim saw the arm, he suddenly understood. Something from beyond had reached out and taken hold of the Bastard. An arm reaching forth from a sobbing crucifix, simultaneously elegant and putrid. He felt Arthur tremble from within him.

The King cried out, "SON!" There suddenly came a terrible squeal, some cross between a pig and a gurgling woman. Morgana's voice bellowed out, ringing so loud that the Pilgrim felt his temples stab in pain.

"HE HATH COME AS A MUTINEER, MY BOY!" The Indivisible fell to his knees, looking up to the crucifix. A single yellow iris shone through the cracks in the stone. It locked onto him. **"AND HE HATH BROUGHT THE FALSE PRINCE UPON HIS BACK."** Mordred looked over his shoulder. He was naked from head to toe, though most of his lower half seemed to be of cybernetic origin. The left half of his face was amalgamated into what looked to be *multiple* faces, mouths writhing and tongues flailing, each of them wailing into the desolate, empty hellscape, and the hair on his right half slid from his skull in knotted tufts.

Arthur gasped. "My God, son! What hath become of thee?!"

The Bastard's mouth opened, contorting into a smile. "Gaze upon your masterpiece, dead king." The Indivisible pointed Excalibur's blade up to Mordred, who recoiled at its sight. Another squeal came from Morgana.

"NAY, IT CANNOT BE!"

"Oh," retorted the Pilgrim, "it *can* be. Look upon the Blade of Kings. You know it, don't you?" He grinned. "It sent you back to Hell once."

Mordred fully spun around. "Do not speak to my mother, mortal! You have earned no such right!"

"DEAR SON, MY BEAUTIFUL BOY...END THEM. AND WHEN I AM RESTORED, WE SHALL CONCEIVE OUR CHILD UPON THEIR CORPSES." The eye blinked once behind the stone, and Mordred dropped to his knees. His blade, the one which had nearly ended the Indivisible, had seemingly become one with the Bastard. Tied to his very being by strands of muscle and flesh.

Arthur shook his head. "My son—"

"I AM NOT YOUR SON, OLD MAN!" Mordred rose, letting the blade fall to his side. "I didn't care for your monologues then...and I don't care for them now. You are *not* my king. And you are *not* my father. There is only me and Mother. Your words fall upon deaf ears. Shut up and pray, you dead king, for it will be your last one."

Within his soul, the Indivisible felt Arthur's emotions swell. He boiled, a horrible concoction of rage and anguish before, at last, strength and acceptance. Arthur said nothing, but something within the Pilgrim made him understand that he was ready. Once and for all. Sara's voice whispered into his ear.

"C'mon, hermano. Show him your bravery."

He cracked his neck. "Come on then, you bastard." Excalibur's tip touched the floor. "You abomination." He unzipped his coat. "Mommy's boy." He prepared his feet into a sprinting position. "Face me. Show me your fury."

The Bastard cackled, hunching over like some gnarled wolfman. His flesh wrapped tighter around the grip of the blade. "Oh, little Pilgrim." He lathered his tongue across his lips. "With. Pleasure."

SHOOM!

In a flash, Mordred skittered to the other side of the room, darting in a zig-zag motion toward the Indivisible, who propelled himself forward to the monstrous Bastard. It roared, the screams of his amalgamated faces crying out with him.

CLANG!

FWISH!

Metal struck metal, and a tendril of flesh lunged toward the Pilgrim. He sidestepped, bringing the blade down against the flesh. The tendril hit the floor; it dissipated into hundreds of small fingers, wriggling around like maggots.

"Pilgrim!" Arthur's voice echoed, and the Indivisible felt something else take control of his sword arm.

CHING!

His arm had raised, blocking a sword strike. His attention shifted back to his assailant.

Mordred screamed. "WRETCHED SPIRIT! BEGONE WITH YOU!" Arthur offered no response, but took control of the Pilgrim's other arm, propelling it forward.

WHAM!

The monster skidded backward, and the Pilgrim launched from the ground, stabbing down from the air.

FWISH! CRUNCH! SHING! CLANG!

Their swords interlocked once more, and within the metal of their opponent's blades, they saw each other's faces. They shoved themselves off one another; Mordred went for a side swipe, which the Pilgrim dodged with ease.

"DAMN YOU!"

FWOOM!

The Bastard unraveled the flesh from his blade and hurled it at the Pilgrim, lodging it into his shoulder and pinning him against the wall. He groaned, wincing as the monster charged toward him on all fours.

It's in too deep, he thought.

"DOWN!" cried Arthur. He felt his body jerk down, cleaving the sword up through his shoulder. A mix of blood and cybernetic fluids spurted out. Mordred's palm slammed into the sword's pommel, and blade and flesh became one yet again. The Indivisible leapt forward.

THWACK!

SHINK!

A swift fist to the face knocked Mordred to his knees, followed by a blade through the chest. He wheezed, gurgling out some guttural, inhuman roar.

WHAM!

He backhanded the Pilgrim off his feet, sending him hurling into a cobblestone wall. "BLOODY NUISANCE!" he growled, slobbering as he jerked his head to face the Indivisible. "There is no place for you..." he tore open his chest, revealing some sort of cybernetic core buried deep within, "...in the New Dawn!" It lit up a terrible red aura.

"By God... What is that?" inquired the King.

The Pilgrim prepared to run. "Just follow my lead."

SHYOOM!!!

A bright red laser beam fired from Mordred's chest, lashing horizontally across the chapel. The Indivisible sprinted forward, flipping forward and over the beam.

"I'LL DISINTIGRATE YOU, WHELP! I BURN WITH THE FURY OF A THOUSAND SUNS!" The laser swung again, now in vertical zig-zags. The Pilgrim dropped, sliding on his knees underneath the beam. Then, through a deafening scream, Mordred cried out once more as the beam swung horizontally yet again. The Indivisible dove over it, landed swiftly onto his back, and rolled back up to his feet. He threw out his hand; Excalibur soared toward Mordred, who hit it out of the air.

Arthur's voice rang out with a distinctive melancholy. "My dear son, 'tis not too late yet! Canst thou not see what hath become of you? You...heretical, damnable *fiend?*"

Mordred cackled. "Do not speak to me of heresy, old man! Where was the talk of such a thing when Merlin resided within your court?" He charged toward them. "HYPOCRISY!" Arthur took over; father and son lunged at each other, grabbing each other by their throats. Mordred pulled his father closer, their noses touching. "My darkness awaits you...*heretics.*"

"TENEBRAE!"

Morgana's voice bellowed out, the ground trembling, cracking, opening. The screams of insurmountable collections of damned souls cascaded through the decaying castle walls. Mordred grinned, a bright reddish-orange light spewing forth from the ground. "You're *mine,* now." He pulled backward, hand still snaked around the Indivisible's throat, and together they fell.

"Breathe, Sam."

An inhale.

"Be brave for me, hermano."

An exhale.

I will. He squinted his eyes and kicked Mordred away from him, sending him tumbling around the zero-gravity funnel. He dove forward, sword outstretched toward the Bastard in a stabbing position. *Bravery, hermana.*

Arthur's voice cried out. "Bravery, Indivisible!" Excalibur swung, the blade gleaming orange from the heat of terrible hellfire.

SCHWING!

A deflected swing.

CRUNCH!

A pommel to the nose, followed by a terrible squeal of pain.

SCHWING! FWISH!

Another strike deflected by the Bastard, who retaliated with a swing of his own. His flesh-wreathed blade sliced through the Pilgrim's left hand, severing three of his fingers: the ring, middle, and pinky.

BAMF!

Sam felt a boot against his chest, and he flew backward into the rocky red walls. Decaying hands reached out, flesh dangling from their bones and wreathed in flames. They clawed into his wounded shoulder, sending a wretched pain through his body as he continued to descend beneath the Earth; beneath all which was known. He pressed his feet against the wall, launching himself forward.

He wrapped his hands around Mordred's throat, throwing him backward into the wall. He growled as the rotten hands wrapped themselves around him now. He cried out in pain, left only to cry and scream as the hands burned through his flesh.

The Indivisible let out a sigh, whispering to Arthur. "You sure you're ready to finish this?" Unconsciously, Sam felt his grip tighten around Excalibur. Arthur's voice echoed in his head.

"As I shall ever be. Let us be done with the hellspawn which hath taken my son."

Together, Arthur and Sam exhumed a mighty cry of wrath before propelling themselves toward the Bastard, entombed and clawed at by the souls of the damned. Blade met with chest, and Excalibur pierced his ribs, its holy aura burning the flesh around the stab wound. He bucked and screamed, unable to free his arms from the hellish hands which held them in place. "MOTHER! SAVE ME!" Sam freed his pistol from his coat, pressing it against Mordred's chest.

FYOOM!

A thermal bolt slammed against the core in the Bastard's chest, melting enough to reveal a gleaming centerpiece. The Pilgrim slipped his pistol back into his coat, blood trickling from the wound in his shoulder and floating around him.

"Even your mother is too much of a coward to tread down here." He raised Excalibur and drove it into the Bastard's chest, screaming as ancient steel met with cybernetics. Mordred elicited a distorted cross between a gasp and a scream. Electricity coursed throughout his body before, eventually, he began to seemingly cook from the inside out. His hands rumbled and detonated into chunks of bone, fingernails, and splintered flesh, followed by everything below his knees.

Excalibur dug deeper into Mordred's chest cavity. As the Bastard grabbed the blade, the Pilgrim saw a noticeable fear in his eyes. A fear of everything coming crashing down around him. Arthur's ghostly visage separated from the Indivisible, and he looked to his son, his only child, and rose to his feet. At a methodical pace, he inched closer to his boy.

"Mordred?" The Bastard wheezed, averting his eyes so that they would not meet his father's. The sounds of screaming souls began to fade away until there was only silence. The hands pulled Mordred, slowly but surely, deeper into the walls. Arthur placed a hand on his son's cheek and opened his mouth to speak, but Mordred spoke first.

"Why...? Why did you never come for me?" Arthur bowed his head. His son gurgled. "You owe me that much, Father." He shook his head. "Mother's gone. I can hear her whispers no longer. I am finished." His eyes darted to Arthur. "I want to know."

Arthur raised his head. "I yearned to find you, son. For almost a decade, I resided alone, yearning for mine only child, but...I had to do what was right for Camelot. I felt I had to...give thee up, for Camelot needed a king. Not a father." Their eyes fully locked, and a tear welled in the Bastard's eye.

"*I* needed a father."

"I know," replied Arthur. "I am sorry, Mordred. I am...a failure."

The Bastard wheezed, offering no response to the apology. "The Lake of Fire," he whispered. His pupils dilated. "It...it's coming for me.

To take me far, far away." He trembled, but a hand snaked around his own. Arthur's hand collided with Mordred's, squeezing gently. For a brief moment, his body loosened, and the tension was gone. Arthur bowed his head, offering a prayer in Latin. A prayer which he knew was pointless, for his son was far beyond saving. Mordred's hand reached out for his father. Arthur took it in his own, caressing it softly. His son's eyelids began to droop. Finally, at last, he wheezed his final breath. "Fa...ther..."

His flesh began to wilt away like a flower amidst winter winds. It fell from his body until only the bones remained. The skeletal hand was pulled from Arthur's grasp, and it disappeared into the walls of Hell. In that moment, the two warriors found themselves kneeling in Camelot.

Arthur stood, wiped away his tears, and looked up to the visage of the crucifixion. Morgana's eye was still visible through the crack in the ancient stone. The King rose and approached the statue. "Our son is dead, Morgana. Retreat to the shadow." He shook his head. "Thou shalt never gaze upon this world again." A growl came from the other side.

"Damn thee, Arthur Pendragon. For eternity and beyond."

"Thou already damned me. Thy damnation had a name. It was Mordred Pendragon. Begone with thee, witch. Crawl back to whichever layer of Hell thou came from. And never return." The eye blinked three times in rapid succession. After the third blink, there came a low sigh, and her presence dissipated, leaving the statue of Christ as it once was. Sam approached the King, standing a few feet behind him. The King sighed. "And so, my task is complete." He rose, turning on his heel. "This is where we part ways, Indivisible."

"Sam," said the Pilgrim. "My name is Sam."

Arthur smiled. "Sam. I would extend my thanks to thee. For aiding me on my quest."

Sam nodded. "I'm sorry about your son, Arthur. I wish we could have saved him."

The king shook his head. "Nay. There was no saving him, not in the end. I failed him as a father. Just as he failed me as a son. There was no other way this would end." Arthur sat in silence for a moment before making his way back to the castle's meeting room, where the Round Table lay splintered. He rested his hand once more upon the old table, as if he were soaking in the sensation of its touch. "Thou art worthy, Samuel." He looked over his shoulder; Sam raised an eyebrow. "Worthy of the sword. Of the crown. Kingship is bound by more than blood."

Sam shook his head. "Just because I'm worthy doesn't mean it needs to happen. Do you think that would be for the best?"

Arthur shrugged. "And what good would my words do? I am a fading form from an old world. The past is what thou wouldst make of it, and perhaps thou couldst make a future of this ancient kingdom. A one true king. For the first time in millennia." He walked over, his ghostly footsteps echoing within the very walls he had dwelled within so many centuries ago. "Thou possessest the only right to this place and what it represents now."

Sam nodded. "And what does it represent?"

"Well," Arthur's form began to flicker, "I know what it represented to *me*. But what does it represent to thee?" He chuckled, fading until his facial features were indiscernible. As he dissipated into nothingness, his voice echoed once more. "Farewell, Indivisible. Farewell." Sam was left alone in Camelot now. Excalibur still sat in his hand, and even though Arthur had gone away, Sam could still feel him within the sword.

He looked around at the old halls, the sounds of a flurry of snow coming from outside. The old walls, they called to him. Beckoned him, even. His eyes locked back to the sword, this relic of kings, and for the briefest moment...he considered it. But Arthur's question prodded at him. This sword, this kingdom. What does it all represent? To him?

"You're still chasing this?" He turned; Sara stood before him, about ten feet away.

"Sara," he said, stepping forward. "Help me. I need to...rest, as you said it." He shook his head. "I don't know how."

"Yes you do." She placed a hand over his heart. *"Let the past be the past. Let go of it. All of it."*

Sam extended his hand, resting a palm over his sister's cheek. "Sara... I..."

She shushed him, smiling. *"It's okay."* Sara took another step forward, bringing her brother into a warm embrace. Sam wrapped his arms around her, squeezing with the love of years passed. A tear rolled down his cheek; she wiped it away. *"Bravery, mi hermano."* Sam felt Sara's form fade away from beneath his arms. *"Bravery."* His arms cradled his chest, and he fell to his knees. A deep sigh rang from his chest. He looked up to the Round Table, then to Excalibur, and the next step suddenly became clear to him. He slid the blade back into its scabbard and pressed through Camelot's doors. He sat down on his bike, turned it around, and drove off into the snowstorm.

He stopped before the Lake, fingers snaked around Excalibur's grip. He raised it above his head, and the feminine hand of the Lady of the Lake reached forth, ready for reclamation. "This power is not mine to bear," he cried, "and it is not for any other! The age of Camelot is through, once and for all! And let it be forevermore!" He launched it through the air, the shimmering moonlight glinting across the blade through the snow. The grip landed perfectly within the hand of the Lady of the Lake. Her hand submerged beneath the water for the final time, and Excalibur with her. And as the hand vanished, the Indivisible had left behind his bike, setting off into the snow on foot. The flurry enveloped him, and his person vanished into the storm, and the name of the Indivisible with him. Both descending into legend.

Descending into myth.

Reading Datadisc…confirmed.
Launching…

STRANGE PRIMORDIAL SKY

To Mom and Dad. All the best parts of me are from you.

"A dream is a wish…"

Aurora, Colorado
December 3rd, 2115
05:37

Max…
    There is a swirling sky. Blue like a glacier. Little streaks of yellow make it look like Van Gogh. There's a man standing in a field beneath the sky. His name is Ashley Morgan. There was a time when people would have called him Ash. They don't really call him much of anything now.
    Defining the future by remembering the past.
    Ashley looked up as violet raindrops plinked against his cheeks. He held out a hand, and within his palm, one of the droplets stood and smiled. He smiled back. The rain opened its mouth and, from within, Ashley saw happiness in the form of a little boy. There was a time when he would have called the boy his son. He doesn't really find himself worthy to call him much of anything now. In this moment, he's reflecting on why exactly that is.
    Been having trouble sleeping. I need to rest.
    It had happened so quickly, there hadn't been much time to register it. They'd lived in California at the time. In September of twenty-one-eleven. Ash was working on his SUV. He'd done it a hundred times. It was his job, after all. He'd stopped being cautious after a while. Max played on his little pogo stick. Ash had found it impressive that the boy could use

that thing so well for a six-year-old. Diane watched from the kitchen window.

I just don't know how you can live like this.

They'd lived up on a hill. They'd had a steep driveway too. On cool autumn days like this, Ash would back the SUV up and take apart the insides and put them back together. Just for fun. He was a real whiz with automobiles; he always had been. Born in the eighties, grew up in the nineties. He'd felt more at home with his cars than his folks.

It's not *a simulation.*

He'd set some homemade blockers up behind the wheels of the SUV to keep it from rolling. It'd had some problems with the brakes at the time. In hindsight, it would've been smart to just work in the garage, despite the beautiful September air. But he didn't do that.

I wish I could stop existing in the way I've stopped living.

The ground shook; an earthquake. Five-point-two on the Richter scale. Not inherently catastrophic. One of the brakes had given way. Something must have shaken loose inside the SUV.

Defining the future by remembering the past.

The vehicle rolled backward. Ash ran toward Max. The vehicle took the boy down the driveway. It rolled.

APS is proud to present the Emulator.

And rolled.

Defining the future…

And rolled.

…by remembering the past.

No amount of embalming could have given Max an open casket. Ash and Diane opted for a cremation. The funeral was short, the grief was constant and sharp. Maybe it would have been easier without the previous three miscarriages. Max had a slew of health problems at birth from being born seven weeks early. His future was uncertain. Diane had hope that he would recover in the NICU. Ash pretended to have hope. For her sake, if nothing else. But they'd always had bad luck in the parental department.

All that's left of him now is the past.

But recover he did, after three months of breathing machines and uncertainty. Max's cries were no longer cries of pain and suffering, but the cries of a baby boy experiencing life outside of a hospital room for the first time. The family went home after two more days of observation. Diane was a lawyer and the primary breadwinner. Ash was a mechanic, and he worked a *lot* of overtime to make sure Diane could stay home with

Max. Postpartum depression is a very real phenomenon, and it hit Diane hard. So much so that she had opted for short-term disability.

To what end do I pursue the dream?

But then that fateful accident happened. Max was gone, and Ash spiraled. Then the Civil War broke out. And Diane filed for divorce less than a year after the war started. Ash's mechanic shop went out of business not four months after the papers were served. He had saved up about ten grand for a rainy day. Though he hadn't planned for a rainy life.

To the end.

In this moment, Ash's mind is wandering as it often does. It wandered to the sleepiness in his eyes. The clouds in his brain. The hand reaching out of that swirling painted sky. Another hand appears, and together, the two hands part the clouds. It's Diane. She looks happy, and speaks aloud, though Ash can't hear her. She says "!tluaf ruoy reven saw tI" He doesn't understand, but somehow, he still disagrees with her. He thinks of her now. Diane. Diane.

Diane…

Ash remembers their wedding on August the ninth, twenty-one-oh-one. They'd met right before the turn of the century. Just two weeks before, in fact. He'd complimented her big green eyes. She'd complimented his big *brown* eyes. Their eyes, funnily enough, were what sparked their first conversation. They'd both noticed the exact same striking feature about the other.

Three-thirty-six milligrams.

Three dates went by. Two of them dinner, one of them a movie. They were official. They were real. They bettered one another. He was up all night with her while she studied for the bar exam. She'd passed out on the couch more than once. He'd carry her back to bed after saving her place on her holopad. Sometimes she'd wake up, still half-asleep, and ask him to crawl in bed with her. He always did, saying he'd snuggle for a few moments before getting back up to go work on one of his cars. He never did get back up, of course.

Oh, Di. You always were a little too good for me anyway.

Something had changed in them when Max died. Talk of a civil war began to emit through the hushed voices of the American people and, when it finally happened, whatever remained of their dwindling marriage dwindled even further. And then, as quickly as their love had blossomed, it had snuffed out.

I can't do this without you, Di. Oh, God. God…

Being an only child himself and having been through his parents' separation at the age of eleven, Ash found it easy to pretend that he didn't care when Diane asked for a divorce. He struggled to pretend he didn't care, however, when she'd screamed that he'd killed their child. She asked if he knew that she blamed him for all of it. He said yes. She asked if *he* blamed him for all of it. He said yes. She asked how he could live with himself after murdering their child. He said he couldn't. But he did. He *does.*

I can hear the birds crying from beyond.

He reflects on their last conversation eleven days ago. She remarked at how disheveled he looked, even over the holocall. He thought about how much better she looked than when they weren't together, but he said nothing other than a soft agreement with her statement about his appearance. She spoke plenty about the divorce arrangements. He listened to her voice, hoping it would lull him to sleep like it used to. She never did find it odd that, even as a grown man, a lullaby could put him to sleep. It comforted him.

Yeah, I've been taking it as directed.

He sometimes had those moments of clarity; wondering if she still loved him underneath all the pain and suffering she'd endured at his side. Though they were few and far between. He watched her during the holocall. Her eyes, her fingers interlinked under her chin. The soft curls in her rose-red hair. The freckles that dotted her face and, most importantly, the light circle on her ring finger. Like a ring had been taken off recently. That was the last moment of clarity he'd had.

Cyparissus killed his pet stag by mistake, and begged Apollo to make him cry for eternity; Apollo transformed him into a cypress tree.

During the final moments of that holocall, Diane had told him that she knew it was an accident. A *terrible* accident. But she knew, deep down, that she could never look at Ashley again. Even in that moment, she found it hard to lock eyes with him over a call. When she gazed upon his face and saw the structure of his cheeks and the broadness of his nose and the width of his eyes, all that her eyes discerned was the visage of two loves that no longer had a presence in her life. Ash said he loved her. She told him to stop. Then she hung up.

I want to be a cypress tree.

Ash's hands brush through a field of marigolds and white lilies. Off in the distance, he sees his own face in the sky, smiling and being kissed all over by Max and Diane. The sky suddenly flashes whiskey-brown and returns to a beautiful rose color. The three faces gaze down at him, smiling as if they looked upon a friend they hadn't seen in years. He smiles back at them.

I need to be a cypress tree.

They ask him what's happening. He tells them he's planned this for a long time. True peace, as last. He says that he feels free for the first time since the accident. Like everything is laid out perfectly in the palm of his hand, just like he had hoped and planned. He reflects on how he's ended up here, now, in this moment. Through what little willpower he has left. That, and the Emulator. The Emulator.

The Emulator.

The American Preservation Society made strides with this thing. The simplicity and portability of a virtual reality headset with dream-altering capabilities. The Emulator could read people's thoughts and turn them into dreams. All it took was a couple of cranial plugins and a sleeping person and, just like that, you're the master of your own dreams.

The waking world is a nightmare.

There were no nightmares in the Emulator. Not unless you *wanted* to have one. It retailed for ten thousand dollars. Ashley had it pre-ordered the day it was announced. He had been trying to create a sort of "perfect" dream. As it turned out, this was easier said than done. Days. Weeks. Months. There was always something that could be done better. Made more beautiful. Made more…real.

Crush it all up.

He remembered the first dream. It was simple. Max was in his room, alive and well. Diane looked at Ashley with love. They played with toy trains and army men. They went outside and played tag. Max won; Max *always* won. Ash looked at himself in the mirror; he looked presentable.

He looked happy. Clean shaven. He went outside and realized that they lived on a farm. Somehow, he knew it was in Nebraska. Where he'd grown up.

Mom and Dad took me from home when I was little. I found my home through them. *Then the world took my home from me once more.*

The more time that passed, the more erratic and surreal the dreams became. Ash wasn't sure if he was losing his mind, or if the Emulator was having some sort of effect on his overall brain. Although he didn't much care, it still made him wonder. After the eleventh dream, Ash cried himself to sleep and didn't put the Emulator back on for two weeks. Was this what his life had been reduced to? A sorry excuse of a man living in a fantasy land while the rest of the country burns in a civil war?

Let the rest of the country fight their war. I'm fighting my own anyway.

Xanax came into play shortly after the civil war started. It had been rendered nearly obsolete by newer medications by then, but it was cheap and easy to get. Ashley had a surplus he'd been sitting on for quite a while. For the first three years, he'd barely slept. The Emulator helped him sleep a bit, almost like his mind was motivated to stop its torment so it could be lulled into a dream. But eventually, the Emulator wasn't enough. The dreams of Max and Diane eventually served as a reminder of what Ash no longer had. He had no love; he only had the dreams.

Gunshots in the distance; police sirens blaring. Loudspeakers announcing curfew. Not that I'm ever out that late.

A three-day supply turned into a one-day supply for Ash. As the dreams became more vivid, more real, he found that they were the only thing that kept him alive. Every moment outside of the dreams was a nightmare. A reminder of everything that was lost to him now. But in the dreams, it was all real. Max's little hands, his laughter carried by the wind, the make-believe battles with his action figures. And Diane. The warmth of her breath, the sensation of her skin pressed against his, and the sight of love in her eyes. All things that no longer existed in the real world. *Reality* was the false life for Ash.

The world has no love left to offer me. Hell, I don't have any love for it either.

Eventually, there came a plan. A dream. *The* dream. He'd been thinking about it for a while now. It had become a sort of project for the grieving father. He had destroyed the only beautiful thing he'd ever created with Max, and nothing could ever change that. But perhaps he could create something beautiful from the loss. Something so wonderful that he could be made content, even if it was for a short time only.

Mix it all up.

Months of plotting. Creating. Sleepless nights. *Dreamless* nights. Finally, he perfected it. It was a dream that Max deserved, and a gift to him from the earthly plane. Ashley prepared to dream this dream. He cleaned the house, top to bottom. He shredded his mail, burned the divorce papers, and cooked himself a medium-rare fillet mignon. He sat in front of the window, watching reruns of the old cartoons from his childhood; his favorite ones that he'd shared with Max. Gunfire echoed in the streets. The rioting continued. Ashley didn't notice. He drank his glass of scotch with one gulp and went to bed.

> *Finish it with one gulp.*
> *I'm ready for the dream now.*
> *Hi, Max.*
> *My baby boy.*
> *Thank you for waiting on me.*

He got under the covers and jacked into the Emulator. He hovered his hand over the holographic touchscreen. The dream was ready to be played, all set up just where he had left it. It loaded, waiting for him to fall asleep. He snuggled into a teddy bear, one of the only things that he had left of Max, something that Diane hadn't managed to throw away during her grief. The drink kicked in and, in a few short moments, Ashley Morgan drifted off to sleep.

Swirling sky. Violet raindrops. The rain smiles like a little boy. Diane looks happy. Ash disagrees with her backward statement. A field of marigolds and white lilies. His face is in the sky. Their lips kiss Ash's cheeks. They ask him what this is. He tells them. He reflects. He returns.

The visages of Diane and Max vanish from the sky and appear before him as physical beings. Diane looks to Ashley and asks what happened. He smiles and says that he failed her, but he's going to relieve her of the burden of him now. She says that he never failed her, that he had *always* done his best for her. He smiles and offers his thanks, reassuring her that this cycle of doing his best was going to continue tonight.

I love you.

I love you too.

Diane steps to the side so Max can see his dad. Ashley kneels down, pulling his son into his arms, wrapping him in a hug with the warmth of a thousand fathers. Max asks him if he's coming to get him. Ashley assures him that he is not coming to get him, but rather, he is coming to stay. He cups his boy's face in his hands. From his peripheral, red and blue lights flash, and he feels a great disassociation from time and the concept of the waking world. Soon enough, those flashing lights begin to fade away, replaced by one all-encompassing radiance. He squeezes his son in his arms, sobbing with a true, unadulterated joy. Together, they devolve into a blissful fit of laughter, and the laughter echoes into somewhere beyond beyond.

Ash looks up into a field of ethereal, dancing lights; that strange, primordial sky. Something inside of him says that this is more than a dream. A thought that this is all there is now. A thought that there will never be anything less, now and forevermore. A thought that there will never be anything less, and an eternity awaits him within what was once nothing more than a wishful dream.

And he believes it.

Reading Datadisc…confirmed.
Launching…

ANNIHILATION NIGHT: 2024

To Micah and Spencer. You've never given up on me, even when it would've been easier to do so. Nobody on God's green Earth is good enough to deserve such friends.

"Thank you for making me whole. Even if it wasn't quite forevermore."

April 14th, 2024
Oklahoma City
The night everything fell apart.

CLICK!
> ***BEEP! BEEP!***
> The door to an old sports car swung open. A young man stepped in. Early to mid-twenties.
> ***SLAM!***
> Key in the ignition. He sat still for a second; the radio flipped on.
> ***BZZRT!***
> A female news anchor came on the other end. "With continued threats of nuclear war from Russia, once again America finds itself asking an all-too-familiar question: Is this all one big bluff to strike fear into the hearts of those who would stand against a tyrannical superpower? Or is it true? Are we facing total ***annihilation***?" The young man stared at the radio for a moment before he turned the volume down.
> Car still running, he threw the door open and stepped out, clutching a necklace in his hand. Words of his own echoing in his mind.

Take it as a piece of me. Like a promise. A promise that I'm yours and only yours. And I only ever want to be **yours**.

That was four months ago. And yet, here it was. Clutched in his hands. Returned to him. How do you accept a piece of yourself that you've already given away?

Simple, he thought. *You don't.*

She didn't want it. And neither did he. He strode over to his fence and hocked it with as much force as he could. It vanished over the fence, enveloped by the night. He walked back to the car and stepped in, sighing.

It fit perfectly around Her neck. Funny, I hadn't meant for it to be Hers. Things just aligned and it felt right for it to be Hers. I remember the tears in Her eyes when I told Her what it was a replica of. That necklace from the **Lord of the Rings**.

A somber grin crossed his lips.

I spent at least five minutes explaining what that necklace represented. An immortal elf, promising herself to a mortal man. Knowing she'd still be here after he'd gone. She could live with that grief, if it meant she could spend a lifetime with him. She could listen to me nerd out for hours.

Hours.

Funny how things aren't always as they seem.

He wiped at his eyes. Not many tears were left to spare, but he knew more would come eventually. Tonight was the night. The last symbolic "step" to move on. He ran his finger across his right pocket. A single Polaroid sat within. A final picture of the two of them. The last piece of Her he couldn't seem to get rid of. But he would tonight. Right after a greasy fast-food burger from one of his least favorite fast-food joints. He connected his phone to the car and brought up the music app and hit shuffle.

Now Playing…
Daft Punk ft. Julian Casablancas – "Instant Crush"

He shifted to drive and took off down the road. Staring dead ahead into the nighttime suburbs.

Mom and Dad,

I'm gonna burn this last picture of me and Her. I don't know what else to do with it. I'm taking it to Heartwrench Point with Mitch and Seth. I can't take seeing it anymore. You've heard it enough times by now, I don't wanna burden you with more of my bitching and moaning. My heart's in shambles. I shouldn't love

Her, not after how things ended. But I do. I can't stop dreaming about Her. In my dreams, She cries to me. Asking me, "How could you?" I tried so hard for Her. You saw me, everyone did. I wasn't perfect, not by a long shot. I just wanted Her to be okay with that.

I always told Her this wasn't about me. I wanted to spend the rest of my life making Her feel happy and accepted. Loved unconditionally. She pretended to want the same thing. But She didn't. The hard part is wondering if She ever did in the first place. This whole voice acting thing is starting to take off for me now, sure...but I wish She was here so I could hear Her say, "I'm so proud of you, Jackie." A fool's errand, I guess. Maybe if I was normal and could actually move past my...difficulties...and this fucking anxiety of mine, She could've loved me. But She didn't. It's high time I accepted that.

I'll be back before dawn. But I need to do this in the best way I know how: with a dramatic flourish. Much like you, Mom, I've always had a knack for being dramatic. Believe it or not, I kinda like it. It gives us personality. Anyway, now you know where I'll be. Thanks for guiding me through all of this shit. I feel like such a coward for still being broken up about this. I feel selfish. Hopefully, this will mark a new beginning for me. I think it will. Don't wait up.

    Love, Jack

Jack's phone lit up. A text from Dad.
We love you, buddy. Be safe.
A brief pause before another ding.
You did everything you could for Her, don't forget. Just a reminder that it's not your fault.
Jack hit the voice text.
"Love you too."
Daft Punk's soft beats lulled Jack into a melancholic serenity. Surges of anxiety darted through his brain like streaks of lightning across cloudless skies. Too many questions, too few answers. Mostly questions skirting the lines of, "Am I ready for this? Will I *ever* be? Do I even deserve this self-closure?" Months of asking those questions; he figured he should've had it all figured out by this point. But, alas, the answers eluded him still, regardless of the normality of his circumstances reiterated by those around him. Somehow it made him feel worse. So much to love, so much to be grateful for. But all those things could not

seem to fill the void that She had filled for him. *That* angered him the most. Some asshole he must have been.

Why are you such an ungrateful asshole?

He tried to shake the thoughts away.

Family and friends with overflowing love aren't enough for you? You need the person who couldn't care for you like you did for Her? The person who, let's be honest, couldn't give two shits about how you feel about Her.

But that wasn't true. She *did* care, at least a little bit. All of the memories, the sweet nothings whispered. That couldn't have all been for nothing...could it?

If She gave a single fuck about you, would you be in the car about to do what you're about to do? Face it, Jack. Even when you're not alone, you're alone. And you're the reason for it. You're allowing it. You must love being miserable. Or maybe you're just an attention-seeking pussy. Oh, that's it, isn't it? Maybe you like the attention, is that right? Twenty-two years to find someone who could even pretend to give a shit about you. Honestly, do you really think it's gonna happen again?

Jack shook the voice out of his head. Tears started to fall again. That little voice, the one that sounded just like him, was nagging at him more than usual. He had gotten better at ignoring it by the time She came around. It had been so long since he'd heard it, he had entirely forgotten how to drown it out. And now it was clawing at his mind, like it had for so many years. All that fear, insecurity. And it could never *not* have the last laugh.

Pathetic.

The ring of the phone silenced the voice. A video call from Seth. Jack breathed a sigh of relief, wiped his eyes, and answered the call. Just like always, Seth's face was unnaturally close to the camera. A deadpan expression rested on his face.

"Yo," said Jack. "Just left my place. Are you guys there yet?" Seth didn't respond. He just stared at the camera. "Are you gonna answer me?" Nothing. "Seth." Drool curled at the edge of Seth's lip. "You're fucking nasty, dude." Seth's expression abruptly changed into a grin; a wheezing laughter erupted from him. Jack could hear Mitch's cackle from the other end. Jack tried, but failed, to hold back laughter. "You're a fool, Seth."

"Oh, yeah?" asked Seth. "Guess what?"

"I'm not saying what, you're just gonna say chick—"

"Yeah? My tip was out the whole time. How does that make you feel?" Jack sighed. Long. Exasperated. It was the bit that *never* **ended**.

"Seth, that bit has lost its luster at this point."

"Womp, womp," retorted Seth.

Mitch's head poked into view. "Jack!"

"Mitch!"

"Are you almost here?"

Jack looked at a nearby street sign. "Yeah, I should be there within the next, like, forty seconds or so."

"Okay." Mitch leaned closer to the camera. "How you feeling, Jack?"

Jack's eyes focused solely on the road. He paused. "I'll be good once this is over and done with." His eyes darted from the road to his destination. Seth's favorite Oklahoma food chain. Whataburger. "I'm pulling in." Mitch stood and moved out of frame, heading to the door to greet his friend.

Seth sighed. "Love ya, Jack."

Jack sighed. "Love you too, bro." He hung up the call, pulling into one of the many open parking spaces. The great thing about this place? Open twenty-four-seven. Nobody was *ever* here this late at night. Jack shut the car off and stepped out; Mitch was already halfway to the car. He raised his hand.

"Jack!" Mitch ran over and wrapped Jack in a hug. "Ah, it's good to see you."

Jack returned the hug. "You too, man. How's the wife?"

Mitch nodded. "Good, good. She's good. *We're* good." He smiled at the last remark. "She's glad you're doing this, you know. It's…well, it's a big step. Even if it's just burning a picture."

Jack shrugged. "I guess. It *is* just a picture, though."

Mitch patted his buddy's shoulder. "Hey, you're the creative one here. You of all people can understand the symbolism of burning that picture. Like, it's letting go, right?"

Jack nodded. "Let's just head inside. I'm hungry as *fuck*."

"Yeah, yeah." Mitch turned on his heel. "Seth's keeping your seat warm." He looked over his shoulder as he walked. "He thought it would be funny to sit in one chair until you got here and then suddenly switch chairs and make you sit in the one he kept warm."

Jack raised an eyebrow. "*Why?*"

"Something about you having to, quote, 'plant his ass where I vehemently ripped multiple fat braps,' unquote."

Jack had the audacity to look surprised by this. "That…" He chuckled. "Dammit, that's actually kinda funny for some reason."

Mitch laughed. "When have farts ever *not* been funny?"

Jack shrugged. "True enough." The pair stepped through the door. Seth immediately scrambled out of his chair, slipping and catching himself on the table, nearly tipping it over. He readjusted the condiment bottles, set the salt and pepper shakers back up, and planted himself in another seat.

"Hey Jack, I, uh, I saved a seat for ya. Right there." The man did *not* look nonchalant. Not even remotely. Mitch snorted; Jack heaved an exhausted sigh.

"Dude. I'm not sitting in your shit-soaked chair."

"I don't know what you mean." Seth lifted his foot up and tapped the chair across from him. "Come now. It's getting cold." Mitch slid into the chair next to Seth, trying his best to hold in the shrill cackles boiling inside him. Jack slowly walked over and grabbed the chair, pulling it away. Seth shook his head. "No, no you don't wanna do that. No, you're gonna wanna use the chair that was already up here." Jack stared Seth straight in the eyes as he pulled up a different chair. He sat down, interlinking his fingers.

"You're *vile*, Seth. Absolutely disgusting."

Seth blinked a single time, a completely deadpan expression on his face. He inhaled; his voice shifted to a bizarre attempt at a Russian accent. "Why are you always this mean to me?"

"Because you're a dunce."

Seth blinked again. "Very mean, man." He leaned forward. "Also, we got you that buffalo chicken sandwich since that's the only thing you'll eat here for some reason."

Jack scoffed. "Because everything else gives me the rancid screaming shits, Seth! We've been over this! I get that they don't have this place in your part of Missouri, but it scrambles my fucking stomach like *eggs*. I love it, I just can't do it!"

Mitch sighed. "You know, Seth, I'm seeing a bit of a skill issue here, are you?"

Seth nodded. "Yeah, I think brother just needs to have a better stomach instead of that weak, IBS shit he's got going on there."

Jack pointed a finger at both of them. "*Literally* fuck yourselves. You're both rats." He struggled to hide the smile from his face. As much as he played up his frustrations, he loved this, their dynamic. It was…well, it was them. One minute, they were all three berating each other over their little quirks and embarrassing secrets, the next minute they were reminding one another of *why* they did it.

Seth leaned forward. "You know we're kidding, right, dude?"

Jack nodded. "Yeah, I know, bud." He went quiet, fiddling with the straw on the diet soda he'd just noticed in front of him.

Seth twiddled his thumbs together. "What's up, man?"

Jack chuckled. "Just thinking about…"

Seth raised an eyebrow. "About…?"

"All of this shit. Everything with Her." Jack scraped at the edges of the straw with his fingernail. "You know, I'm just sitting here at the end of all this insanity and I'm still just…" He shook his head. "I dunno. I guess I'm just trying to figure out where exactly things went wrong." His free hand was in his pocket, unconsciously tracing his finger across the Polaroid. For the briefest second, his brain tricked him; he felt his finger dash across soft skin. Across a dimple. His lip quivered into a smile.

Mitch shook his head. "Jack—"

"I just… I get the feeling that it's all my fault."

"No—"

"Like maybe if I'd had all my shit sorted out, been more put together, had a better grip on my anxiety and mental health—"

"Hey," Mitch and Seth said in unison. Mitch took the lead. "We've been over this a million times, Jack. How could you have predicted this? Alright, She treated you like shit, man. I know you loved her—really, I do. But that doesn't excuse the things She said to you in the end."

"And what about the necklace?" Seth chimed in. "Right? She knew what giving Her that gift meant to you, like what it symbolized. She could've thrown it out herself. But She didn't. She made you feel like the bad guy for being fed up with her…inability to admit the two of you were in a relationship. And sure, I'm certain you weren't perfect. I'd be a bad friend if I didn't act like there aren't two sides to every relationship."

Mitch nodded. "Regardless, she still couldn't seem to make up her mind about how she felt about you. I mean…you kissed Her, and She kissed you. You took Her places; She went with you. When asked, She told people She was seeing someone, and so did you. You had every reason to believe you both wanted the same thing. You said She was open about how She fantasized about a life with you. Remember what She said you felt like?" Jack nodded. "Say it. What did She say?"

Jack paused. "Home." He cleared his throat. "That—that I felt like home."

Seth threw his arms up. "What the fuck were you *supposed* to think, Jack? If She didn't want that with you, She should *not* have treated you the way She did, said the things She said, and did the things She did. You felt how any rational person *would* feel, Jack! What you're feeling is **normal!**" Jack stared off into nothingness. It didn't feel normal. That pain in his heart; God only knew how many people had felt it. But in that moment, in the loneliness of heartbreak, there was no consoling him. An image flashed in his mind.

We talked about our house on the hill like it was the ultimate end goal. I remember She said She imagined coming home from work around Christmastime, exhausted from a long day, to find me sitting in front of a fireplace on the couch. She wanted to get changed and lie there with me. Soaking in the warmth of love. I thought about it often. I wanted it <u>so</u> bad. Fuck, I still do. She said She did too.

Somehow, that only served to make things worse.

"Order for Seth!" A teenage girl at the register called Seth's name, prompting him to stand and walk over. He leaned forward.

"Hey, can we actually get these to go? Sorry for the mix-up, we just decided to go ahead and split."

The teen stared at Seth with dead eyes. "Sure. I guess." She robotically threw the food into a bag and passed it to Seth. "Thanks for coming in."

"You too— I mean..." Seth sighed. "Goodnight." He turned and walked back to the table. "Guys, let's go ahead and get outta Dodge. Heartwrench Point has a nice view of the city, let's eat there."

"Yeah, agreed," replied Jack. They each made their way to the door, Jack falling in last. The world seemed to move a bit slower. That feeling of anxious anticipation when you know a big decision is coming. Fight or flight kicks in—you debate turning around and running back the way you came. Sometimes, the way you came is right back into danger. Jack found it funny how comfortable danger could be when it's familiar. She was just that for him.

Jack thought about picking up the phone and calling Her many times; he really did. He probably would have if he'd thought Seth and Mitch would let him. Even though every bone in his body said *Do **not**.* The voice of unreason had begun to worm its way back into Jack's gray matter, speaking in hushed whispers.

Pain shopping, that's what Mom called it. She said you weren't doing it on purpose, but were you? If you weren't, then you've gotta be the biggest fucking moron in the state of Oklahoma. You shop for pain like Granddad shops for packs of cigarettes. She probably knew that and exploited it. And you fell for it, like a mouse for a mousetrap. Who knows? Maybe it'll even happen again. It's what you'd deserve for a fuck-up like this anyway. One tragic misstep after another.

"*Fuck* you, *brain*," he muttered under his breath. "*Fuck you*." He found himself bent over, facing the ground. A hand ran softly across his back. Mitch patted him.

"Let's get in the car, Jack."

They took the scenic route to Heartwrench Point. The moon gleamed through the smudged window of Mitch's old car. The radio's sound barely audible through the car's engine. But Jack's ears homed in on the words of a male radio show host.

"Honestly, Barbara, I believe these are the end times, but not in the way people think it is. All of *this* is ending around us. Our way of life; gone. All gone. Buried in sand, underneath the rubble. What's the pattern?" There was a pause.

"I dunno, Al. Enlighten our listeners. And me, while you're at it." Another pause.

"Us. Look at all of the shit that's happened throughout history. Look, worlds are built by humans. We may not have *created* this hunk of floating rock that we call a planet, but we have one hundred percent *built* it. We have the power to destroy it. And we will again, and some years down the line we'll keep asking ourselves, 'Why? Why did all of this pain have to happen?' And we won't have an answer, but we'll be all the better for it. And then it'll all be destroyed again. Then rebuilt. Again. And again. And again. Until we fizzle out and fade away."

"Sheesh, way to lighten the mood with all of this Russia shit, Al. Seems like a shitty way to see things if you ask me."

"Nah. It's for that reason that you should stop giving a shit about your fuck-ups and embrace them. Why else are we here? You missed the moral of the story, Barb. We fuck up, we learn and become better. Rinse and repeat. You know what the best thing about that cycle is?"

You can never truly become weaker. Only stronger. Sounds like something Mom would say. She always has kinda had that optimistic wisdom. What was it she said when all of this went down?

"The saddest thing about life is when someone you create such beautiful memories with becomes a memory themselves. But that doesn't make it any less wonderful."

As much as I hate to say it…maybe there's some truth to that.

Jack always managed to overcome that voice of fear in his head. Sometimes it kept him up at night, tossing and turning. Even taking him into tears from time to time. Reminiscing over what once was and what could have been, had fate been kinder to **his** desires, and not to its own innate chaos. Mom and Dad taught him how to control that voice well. The anxiety had begun to wither away over the last few months. But sadness…grief…that was a whole 'nother monster.

"I don't know," Jack blurted out. Seth looked over his shoulder from the passenger seat; Mitch's eyes connected with Jack's in the rearview. "Back at the restaurant. You asked me what I was supposed to think. I don't know. It feels like it's all my fault, though."

"How?" Mitch sipped his soda. "How is it *all* your fault?"

Seth looked to Mitch. "I think he just means it *feels* like his fault."

Mitch nodded. "I get that. I'm asking for specifics. Jack, *why* is it your fault? Give me a legitimate reason. What could you have done differently?"

Jack shrugged. "Maybe I could've upped the dosage on my anxiety meds sooner. Maybe worked harder on the very *clear* abandonment issues that I have and not taken everything so literally and personally. Maybe had a little more social awareness— I don't know, Mitch! I don't know what you want me to say! Hindsight is a fuckin' bitch! I just…God, I wish I just understood myself a little more, man." The defensive tone in Jack's voice became glaringly apparent. It happened more often than he cared to admit. He always seemed to jump right to the defense when put on the spot like that.

"You know what I think?" Mitch took another drink. "I think that somebody who was ready to love you, and I mean *really ready*, would've taken you by the hand and said, 'Hey, Jack, I know this is stressful for you and it's a rough time for you. I can see it's a problem and I want to be here to help you move through it because I *love* you even though you aren't a saint all the time.'" He threw a hand up.

"Now, I'm not saying I'm an expert…but I'm married, so I basically am." Jack chuckled. "But seriously. When you love someone, you'd do anything for them." He scoffed. "Dude, I'd crawl on my stomach through burning coals if it meant bringing my wife some peace. And I know She wasn't your wife, but when you tell someone the things S*he* told **you***?*" He shook his head. "I'm just saying, for someone who denied Her feelings so much, She sure made it seem like She loved you." He shrugged. "But you don't know the ins and outs of Her head. Nobody has a clue what's going on inside Her head except Her. Same goes for you. What She did doesn't make her a shitty person just because She was unsure of what She wanted with you. She could've shut everything down sooner, sure. But She didn't. That's honestly why I still believe She loved you. Even if it wasn't in the way *you* wanted her to." He shrugged. "Right people, wrong time, maybe."

Jack went quiet for a moment, soaking in Mitch's words like gospel. Jack would've done anything for Her. *Anything.* He even told Her that. He would've jumped in front of traffic for Her. Sidelined his *personal* hopes and dreams because *Hers* were more important to him. Making sure She never questioned if it was possible for someone to love Her unconditionally again.

Mitch was right. There was *no* way in Hell that She would've wanted to do all of that for him. Somehow, he just knew that. The car came to a stop; they'd arrived at Heartwrench Point. Seth sat oddly quiet for a change. Strange; Jack was fairly certain that Seth didn't know the meaning of the word "quiet."

The trio stepped out of the car and over to the edge of a fairly large drop-off. Oklahoma City loomed in the distance. Far enough for the sounds of the city to be absent. But even from so far away, the life of the city could still be felt. They each sat down, letting their legs dangle over the side. Seth brought out the Whataburger bag. Jack shook his head. "I'm not hungry, honestly."

"Alright, bud." Seth put Jack's sandwich back in the bag and filtered through, looking for his burger. "There you are." He pulled out the burger and tore into it like it was the first time he'd eaten in days. He sighed. "Fuck, I love this place so much."

Jack chuckled. "It's not *that* good, dude."

Seth's ketchup-covered index finger pressed against Jack's lips. "Let me have this."

Jack burst into laughter. "Fine, fine. Just stop fuckin' *moaning* while eating it."

Seth shook his head no, sighing with melodramatic ecstasy with every bite. He finished it in under thirty seconds.

Mitch cackled. "Dude, how do you even eat that fast?"

Seth pounded a fist against his chest, letting out an earth-tremoring belch. "Hey, Mitch? Um…shut up, how about that?"

Mitch opened his mouth, but suddenly closed it. "I was gonna make a fat joke, but I decided not too because that would not be nice."

Seth paused. "When have you ever been concerned about being nice to me? You and Jack both call me fat at *least* once a day."

Mitch shrugged. "I mean, I can go ahead and make the joke if you want me to."

Seth stared daggers at him. "What do you think, **Mitch**?"

Jack laughed. "Thanks, guys. For…everything, really. I mean, honestly, Seth, I'm still kind of…in awe that you drove all the way down here for this."

Seth nodded his head. "Dude, you're like my brother." He grabbed his cup of soda. "I'm always gonna be here for you, man. Always. Rain or shine, night and day." He took a drink.

Jack paused. "You know what I'm caught up on? Everything seemed so…perfect. Like, the possibility of shit going wrong like this hadn't even really crossed my mind. Even when people were trying to wake me up to that reality. It all felt so…real." He bit his tongue. "How can it feel so real and still not be?"

Seth set his drink down, pausing. He looked to Mitch, who looked back to him. Mitch opened his mouth to speak, but Seth raised a hand.

"Jack, you remember me telling you a bit about my situation? Kinda similar to yours, but not exactly the same?" Jack nodded. "I knew that girl for years. *Years.* I wanted to marry her; I really did. And when I finally accepted that shit wasn't gonna work out between us, it fuckin' *crushed* me, dude. Because I just kept wondering *why*? Everything lined up. I-I-I mean, we had the same interests, we lived close by, we seemed to have similar values, but, like…" He meshed his fingers together. "We just had a *connection*, more than anything. Like this powerful…*force* of spirit that connected us. It made *no* sense to me that we weren't meant to be, which made it **so** much harder to let go. Jesus, man, there's a part of me that *still* hasn't let go.

"And that part of me never *will* let go. Not because she's 'the one that got away.' Nah, fuck that shit. But I had great memories with her." He paused. "She…helped me figure out who I am and who I wanted to be. What I'd be willing to do for someone I truly loved. She's not a bad person because she didn't love me the way I loved her, but like…I have a right to be hurt by it. Just like *you* have that exact same right. She hurt you, yeah. But She helped make you who you are. She made you a *better* you.

Trust me, man, there aren't many people in life who can truly have that kind of impact on you." Seth stifled his tears, inhaling.

"What I'm trying to say, Jack, is that it doesn't matter how perfect something seems. *Nothing* is perfect. Not even Her. She wasn't even perfect for you, as much as you thought She was. You can't know if someone is perfect for you if you're still learning who you are, man. Like... Yeah, this hurts. It hurts a lot, and it's gonna keep hurting for a while. I wish I knew how long, but I don't." He shook his head. "But the memories you made, the love you felt, the lessons you learned... Do you regret any of this?" Jack shook his head. "No, don't answer *me*. Answer that question for *yourself*." Jack paused. That was new; he'd been asked that question plenty of times, sure. But nobody had told him to answer it for himself. The three sat in silence, Jack in the middle, for a few moments. When the answer finally formed in his mind, the corners of his mouth brought his lips into a somber smile.

Jack reached into his pocket, wrapping his hand around the Polaroid. He felt Her skin for an almost imperceptible second, before that feeling faded away, leaving only that plastic-y feel of a photograph. His hand snaked to his back pocket, taking hold of a lighter. He brought it to the corner of the picture, finger on the lighter's trigger, and hesitated. Mitch's hand took hold of his wrist, squeezing softly. Jack pulled the trigger and set the memory ablaze. He watched as his face and Hers began to wither away beneath the flame, and he let the photo go whisking away into the night, swirling straight ahead through the nighttime breeze like a leaf in the autumn wind.

Jack put an arm around Mitch and Seth, pulling them into somewhat of a huddle. They sat together on the edge of that moonlit cliff as a wall of spirit. They had each been through Hell and back at one another's side. It was bound to be Jack's turn in that spotlight eventually. Through a torrent of silent tears and somewhat shuddering breaths, Jack uttered two words. *"Thank you."* The reaffirming pats of each of his hands gave him the answer he sought.

Then it happened. Behind the smoldering memory vanishing into cinders came a bright flash of light, brighter than the sun itself. The three raised their heads, looking across the edge of the cliffside. Oklahoma City, engulfed in a pillar of fire. A mushroom cloud began to form above the city, drowning out the calming lights with an aura of terrible flame. The ground trembled with tenacity, but the trio remained as rocks, knelt down in the dirt with their arms wrapped around one another. That great pillar of fire seemed close…but *how* close? Jack tensed up. If this was the end, he couldn't stop it. There was nothing he could do now.

As his muscles tensed, he felt reaffirming squeezes on each of his hands, one squeeze from each of his brothers. He smiled and tightened his grips on their hands. The flame crept nearer, and the fear began to fade away into the distant night. Jack kept his eyes open as wide as he could. Staring straight ahead. Preparing for whatever came next. After tonight. After Annihilation.

Lastly, to my sweet Mya. My love. My heart.
After Annihilation, you were there to find me.
Love is not always kind. But with you, it's always true.

EPILOGUE: OUTRUN THE SUN

DATADISC "ANNIHILATION NIGHT: 2024" – END

That's all she wrote, Pilgrim. I want you to be quiet for a moment. Listen to me. All you've read; think about it. Understand it. You might not want to, but I encourage you to. There is something more to every tale of every person. Individuality was what made us who we were. Once upon a time, we the people were our *own* people. It was both our brilliance and our undoing.

The world ended when man discovered fire. It ended again when we fashioned weapons from copper to cut and beat each other into submission, and once again when we manipulated religion into terror. Blades into guns. Carriages into cars. Planes into starships. Time moved on. The world changed with us, not the other way around. Slowly, we began to poison it. The air turned noxious, the plants withered away while we sat and watched.

I was alive long, long ago. I live even now. This facility keeps me here. I don't know why. I watched as the world slipped back into the cold abyss of space. There was no one single event that caused our destruction. It was as if, one day, everyone suddenly realized it was ending. For the last time.

For millennia, I have sat in this place, waiting for you to come here. Knowing your purpose, of your quest. And I knew of your inevitable disappointment. Because I once felt the same. When the Datadiscs first came to me and I was tasked with archiving them to preserve history, I was as giddy as could be. Thrilled to see what stories the world had for me.

But the world had no stories for me. Its people, however, did. One by one, I watched the lives of so many individual people be forever altered by events you and I can't even fathom. We've never known anything like that. And it was then that I came to wonder if…maybe, the world ended because it grew tired of us.

Running amok upon its surface, dropping bombs, killing children, poisoning the air, selling bits and pieces of ourselves to other people, all so we might be a little more comfortable while they casually took over what pitiful excuse of a "society" we had. We were given a gift with this planet. In the grand scheme of Earth, we weren't even here for a fraction of its lifespan. But as soon as we entered the picture, it was only ever destruction and death. Savagery.

We squandered all of this. All of this time wasted. The world was ending every day for thousands of years, and we just…pretended it wasn't. We humans are capable of many things, Pilgrim. But it takes something more than human to see the world through open eyes. And while we sat, waiting for some foreign power to nuke us into oblivion, or for Christ to come from the sky to bring us up to streets of gold, we ignored all of it.

We told ourselves that people like Alan Harvey were fit to run a country. We chose not to believe that people like Tara Himura could come to exist in the fires of oppression; hatred born from hatred! We chose to deny the humanity of the Woman in the landfill or little Archie, and the millions just like them who cried to be seen as something even slightly more than subhuman! And instead of looking ahead with this world, we delved into powers that were beyond us and this world.

C'mon, Pilgrim. You must know, after all of this, that there are too many things to truly identify what finally caused the final collapse of civilization. Truth be told, I scoured the Datadiscs, hoping I'd find one during the last few years of this planet's remnants of civilization. But I couldn't. I came close, but there's no true record of what led to Earth's final moments. What's that saying… "Not with a bang…?" Huh. Quite true, now that I think about it.

Try not to think too hard about all of this, Pilgrim. There's really no point. I sometimes wonder if there was ever any point in the first place. But you did find the answers you seek; they just weren't what you'd hoped for. Want my advice? Get used to it. If this planet and the life it gave me taught me one thing, it's that nothing is ever truly what you want it to be. But hey, maybe there's some fun to be found with all of that chaos. I'm tired, Pilgrim. I think I'll rest for a while. You might find something more worthwhile for your time, if you can. If there's one true lesson to take away from what you've witnessed here today, let it be this.

We weren't worth the trouble.

The breeze returns, and you feel as if this is the final time. What is this feeling in the pit of your gut? The gnawing. The ever-burning questions of what any of this has even meant. Time has come and gone, humanity withering away along with their creations. And it seems as if nobody ever saw it coming. Here you stand, at the end of all things. Looking around at this derelict library of human history, and there is no newfound satisfaction. No true, definitive answer to your seemingly simple question of what truly became of the world. But with the fading of humanity, the ashes of their death are left behind upon the world which they took for granted.

You nod your head, though whether this is a nod of content or somber acceptance, you are unsure. You trek back the way you came, across an empty floor with nothing more than cracked stone and sweeping sand. You look over your shoulder into the computer room, a dark void devoid of light and power, and you wonder if there ever was any life in the room to begin with. You step forth into the sandstorm, leaving the Library to its fate. The sand begins to swallow it, and within a few short moments, it disappears, becoming one with the earth, vanishing into nothingness.

Faded away.

Into memory.

DATADISC "DEAD NEON BLUES" – END

ABOUT THE AUTHOR

In the farthest corners of Oklahoma, where shadows fear to tread and crazy old folks linger, there lived a young man. The locals knew him as Kam, the oldest of Mer and Annie Whinery, and the only sibling to young Harper. He was an energetic youngster with an imagination as flashy as his gnarly flourishes with snapped twigs he used as swords.

With each passing day, that imagination grew, often lingering in other worlds where dragons roamed the skies and heroes were born from the ashes of crumbling empires. With the tutelage of Mer, he discovered the world of Dungeons & Dragons before he even hit his teens.

And from that point on, Kam knew his greatest loves were and would always be the quill and inkwell.

Kam resides in the quiet suburbs of Oklahoma, though if you were to peer into his mind, you shall find him in worlds of magic and monsters or wandering the streets smog-choked cities brimming with flashing neon lights. Kam's love of science fiction, horror, and fantasy have caused a surplus of stories to well up within his mind, and they're just begging to be let out.

If he's not typing away at the computer, he's more than likely running a D&D game, at the movie theater, or hours-deep into yet another playthrough of *Uncharted*.